Through the Tears

Sandy Cove Series Book Two

Rosemary Hines

Formatting by 40 Day Publishing
www.40daypublishing.com

Cover photography by Benjamin Hines

www.benjaminhines.com

Printed in the United States of America

To our children, Kristin and Benjamin

"I know the plans I have for you,"
declares the Lord.
"Plans for good and not for evil.
Plans to give you hope and a future."
Jeremiah 29:11

PROLOGUE

Michelle Baron sat on the edge of the couch, heart racing as she looked at the envelope in her trembling hand. *I guess this is it,* she thought. The return address seemed harmless enough. Fairfield Lab, Portland, Oregon. But this envelope contained information that could change her life forever.

Once Steve knew the results of the DNA test, he might change his thinking about their daughter, Madison. Her heart ached because of the distance between her husband and their new baby. Madison was a gift. A gift from God. And now she and Steve would know the truth.

The baby whimpered softly from her cradle. "It's okay, Maddie," Michelle cooed as she gently stroked her daughter's wispy hair.

Why couldn't Steve just accept Madison as their daughter? She gazed down at the three-month old child, who was now sleeping peacefully again. Her fair coloring and rosy cheeks reminded Michelle of the first time she met Steve in the university library. Glancing over at the wedding picture that stood on the end table, she smiled momentarily. "Guess opposites really do attract," she said as she reached toward the nape of her neck and began twisting a strand of her supple black hair.

Everywhere they went together as a family, people commented on the uncanny resemblance between baby Madison and Steve. "A real clone," was Steve's law partner's first remark. "Did you have any part in this?" he had asked jokingly, looking at Michelle.

Though the world had no problem assuming he was Madison's father, Steve remained insecure. It was obvious from Roger's comment that he had not confided in his trusted associate and friend. His withdrawal and detachment frustrated Michelle as much as it hurt her. This was a time they should be celebrating. But the tension between them was a thick fog that threatened to suffocate their love for each other and destroy the family they had begun.

"Oh Lord," Michelle sighed, gazing at the unopened envelope through the tears that filled her eyes. "Help me."

The presence of God wrapped around her like a warm blanket.

I know the plans I have for you, plans for good and not for evil. Plans to give you hope and a future.

Michelle took a deep breath. "Thank you, God." Her quivering hands placed the envelope on the coffee table.

CHAPTER ONE

Two years earlier in a hospital in Bridgeport, CA

John Ackerman slowly opened his eyes. Piercing, needle-like pain shot through his pupils filling his head as the fluorescent lighting bombarded his senses. A scream struggled to escape, but the only sound he heard was a soft moan.

Suddenly a face appeared to hover over him. It was blurry and distorted, but the voice was familiar. "Daddy?" it asked anxiously. He tried to reach up from the bed and touch the face, but his arm was like lead and his fingers barely flickered. Almost immediately, he felt a warm touch as his hand was squeezed gently.

"Daddy? Can you hear me?"

John struggled to speak. Nothing. He strained his eyes to focus on the face, but it remained a blur. Where was he? Why couldn't he move? Who was this face with the familiar voice? Confusion and panic gripped him.

"Someone come quick!" the voice called out. Another face joined the first one. It spoke loudly and clearly.

"Can you hear me, John?"

Beeping sounds next to his head contributed to his anxiety. He wanted to answer the face, but no words came. Again he moaned. His lips moved as he tried to speak, but only garbled sounds emerged. His eyes widened as fear consumed him.

The first voice spoke again. "It's Michelle, Dad. I'm right here. You're in the hospital."

Hospital. Michelle. John was desperately trying to make sense of what he heard. Icy fingers were pressing on his wrist. He felt chilled and began to shake.

"Let's get another blanket on him," the second voice said.

John felt his body being covered with something warm and soft. He closed his eyes momentarily.

"Daddy! Don't leave us. We need you," urged the familiar voice.

An image shot through John's mind. It was a dark-haired girl on a porch swing. She was smiling and laughing as she played with a kitten. Michelle. My little girl. She needs me. John forced his eyes to open again. He tried hard to focus. Though she was still a blur, he could tell this young lady was much older than the girl on the swing.

"I'm right here, Dad. I won't leave you."

A tear trickled down John's cheek. He wanted to respond, but was trapped in a body of lead.

"Please go find my mom," he heard her ask, as she dabbed his cheek with a soft tissue.

John felt his hand being caressed again by the warm touch. It helped to calm him. The voice continued to speak.

"You're going to be okay, Dad. Hang on. Don't give up. I know you can make it through this. We're all here. We'll help you, Dad. Just please don't leave us."

Another face appeared over him a minute later. He knew this face, even in its blurry state. His heart beat frantically as the face spoke.

"It's me, John, Sheila. You've been asleep for a long time," she said, gently placing her hand on his face. She began to quietly cry.

John wanted to reach out and embrace her. He

wanted to hold her in his arms and say he loved her. All he could do was moan.

"It's okay, honey. Don't worry. We're here for you. Don't try to talk right now. Just rest," she said between sniffles.

Mother and daughter collapsed into each other's arms. They were both crying, half from exhaustion and half from elation. "He's going to make it, Mom. I just know it," Michelle said, wiping her eyes.

"Go find your brother, Michelle."

Before leaving, Michelle squeezed her father's hand. "I love you, Daddy. I'll be right back."

Sheila took her daughter's place in the chair beside her husband's hospital bed. As she held John's hand, she thought about all that had taken place in the past few weeks. First his struggles with the court case, then his disappearance, and finally the discovery in the motel that he had shot himself.

"Dear God, help us," she prayed silently but fervently.

Joan was sleeping soundly on the motel bed across the street from the hospital when the phone startled her. Before she could rouse herself fully, her husband Phil was answering it. He sat on the edge of the bed and took her hand in his as he spoke to their daughter.

"Oh, Sheila -- that's wonderful!"

Joan swung her legs over the edge of the bed and sat up beside him, watching his expression as she tried to read the conversation from one side.

"Should we come over there?" Phil asked, glancing over and smiling at his sleepy-eyed wife. He nodded as he listened. "Okay. We'll see you around 5:00 then. I'm so glad you called, honey. This is great news."

A moment later Phil was replacing the phone on its receiver. He grabbed her in a joyous embrace. "John opened his eyes! He's beginning to respond!"

"Thank you, Jesus," was all Joan could manage as her eyes filled with tears.

After another hug, Phil explained to her that Sheila said they should go back to the hospital at 5:00 that afternoon. Dr. Jeffries would be making his rounds around 4:30, and they would have more information after he examined John.

Glancing over at the open Bible on the bed, Joan knew Phil had been reading his Bible and praying for their son-in-law while she slept. She watched as relief washed over her husband's tired body. He stretched and yawned, a peaceful smile radiating from his weathered face.

"You need a nap, Pastor," said Joan, smiling and patting him on the back. "Here, stretch out on the bed for a little while. We still have a couple of hours before we go back over there."

Phil nodded. "You're probably right," he replied with a weary smile.

He eased himself onto the bed and within a few minutes, he was snoring softly. Joan smiled and snuggled down beside him. "Thank you, Lord, for this wonderful man and for making me a part of his life," she whispered before drifting back to sleep.

Tim and Steve were silently staring off into space when Michelle found them sitting at a table in the lounge. "Dad opened his eyes!" she exclaimed excitedly.

"What?" Tim asked, standing in response. Steve quickly joined him on his feet.

"He just opened his eyes. He's trying to respond to us, but he can't talk. He just keeps moaning. Mom sent me to find you," she continued, her words tumbling out excitedly.

"Let's go," Tim replied.

The three of them hurried back to the ICU. Finally. A piece of hope. Michelle grabbed her husband's hand. She seemed so young and vulnerable with her tousled hair and sleepy eyes. He squeezed her hand and smiled, praying that God would somehow bring good out of this after all.

A voice of darkness penetrated John's consciousness. *You are mine, John Ackerman. You belong to me.*

"Dear God, help me," John prayed silently from his prison of flesh. From somewhere in the darkness, a force of peace enveloped him and calmed his racing heart. He could see his wife sitting beside his bed. She looked into his eyes intently. How could he tell her he loved her, and he never intended things to end up this way? He tried to speak, but the words were beyond his grasp. He struggled to reach up and touch her face, but his hand only flickered slightly by his side.

Sheila reached down and took his hand in hers. "I love you, John," she repeated, her voice trembling.

He closed his eyes for a moment. When he opened them again, a young man was sitting by the bed.

"It's me, Dad. Tim."

John tried to discern the features of the face next to him. Tim. Their baby. But this was not a baby. This was a grown man. He felt confused, exhausted, and overwhelmed by frustration. His strength was spent, and he closed his eyes as he escaped into a fuzzy darkness.

CHAPTER TWO

Steve couldn't get his mind off Michelle during his trip back to Sandy Cove. Her father's attempted suicide was like a surreal nightmare. If only he could have stayed at the hospital in Bridgeport. But Roger had already covered for him all week, and the law firm was getting backlogged with several new cases. Besides, he really wanted to try researching John's case to see if he could help clear him of the charges that had driven him to such desperation.

An eerie silence engulfed Steve as he went into the house. The place seemed cold and empty, darkened by the closed blinds and draperies in every room. He thought about how Michelle was always the one to open up the house each morning after he left for work, closing the window covers after dark, as if lovingly tucking in the house. The smell of dinner cooking and the sound of her voice usually greeted him at the end of each day.

Now Steve heard only his own footsteps echoing on the wood floor. Even the cat was gone, taken care of by Michelle's friend, Monica. *Sure am glad I'm not single*, Steve thought, wondering how guys felt coming home to this emptiness every day.

He flicked on several lights, picked up the pile of mail that had accumulated on the floor of the entryway beneath the mail slot, and plunked himself down on the couch. A framed wedding picture on the end table caught his eye. Picking it up, he touched Michelle's face with his finger.

His mind flashed back to their wedding. How beautiful she looked coming up the aisle on her father's arm. Then he remembered her drawn expression as she leaned over her father's hospital bed in Bridgeport. "Oh, babe," he sighed aloud, slumping forward on the couch and cradling his head in his hands.

Michelle's life was turned upside down by her father's attempted suicide. Steve knew that she would never be the same carefree girl he had married. A part of him grieved, yet he firmly believed God was going to bring good from this trial in her life.

Meanwhile, Steve had a lot of business, both personal and professional, to attend to. First, he decided to call Monica to have her bring the cat back home. Though Max could be a pain in the neck at times, he knew the little fellow would help fill the empty house.

Monica answered the phone on the first ring. "Hi, Monica. It's Steve."

"Hi, Steve. How's everything going?"

"Well, I guess you'd say it's going as well as can be expected," he replied. "Michelle's dad is holding his own, and he appears to be responding somewhat."

"That's great," she replied. "How about Michelle? How's she doing?"

"She's doing okay. Her family's very close. They're all there together."

"I'm glad. Tell her hi and that Beth is praying for her dad."

"Beth?"

"Yeah. My mother-in-law, Beth. She's staying with us for a while."

"Oh. Okay, I'll tell her. Thanks. Tell Beth we can use all the prayers we can get." Steve heard Max meowing in the background.

"I guess Max wants to say hi too," Monica

observed.

"Well, actually, that's what I'm calling about. I'm back home right now for a while, and I wondered if I could come over and pick him up. The house is really empty," he added, his voice dropping slightly.

"You sound tired, Steve. I've got to run over to the store in a few minutes anyway. I'll drop him off on the way."

"Thanks, Monica."

"No problem. See you in a flash." Steve surveyed the pile of mail again, but was too exhausted to tackle it. He wandered into the kitchen. "Dinner..." he mumbled to himself, pulling open the freezer. Nothing looked very promising. He tried the pantry. A can of chili caught his eye. That would work for tonight. He was just opening it when the doorbell rang.

He found Monica and Max waiting for him on the front porch. Max was struggling to free himself from her hold as he wailed mournfully. "He really hates the car, doesn't he?" she observed with a grin.

Steve nodded, retrieving the disgruntled animal from her arms, shaking his head as he patted Max. "Come on in."

"Let me get his stuff from the car," she replied. "Be right back."

Max leapt from Steve's arms and bolted inside. "Glad to be home, buddy?" he asked. Monica returned, carrying a basket bed filled with toys and cans of cat food. "Where did that come from?" Steve asked, eyeing the unfamiliar bed and play objects.

"I couldn't resist. He was so lonely for you guys," she explained almost apologetically.

"You're too much, Monica. What do I owe you for these items?" he asked, shaking his head and smiling.

"Nothing. They're my little gifts to Maxwell," she said, leaning over and stroking the cat. Max returned her gaze and continued to purr loudly.

Steve laughed. "You had quite a vacation, didn't you bud?" The cat just looked at him innocently, then stretched and scampered away. Time to inspect his castle and make sure everything was still in place.

"Want to sit down?" he gestured to the couch.

"Okay, but I can only stay for a minute. So tell me more about Michelle's dad," she asked.

"Well, he is coming out of the coma and seems to be recognizing people. He's responding a little, but it's still pretty early to tell how much recovery we can expect." He paused and then added, "Michelle seems really encouraged. That's what matters to me right now."

Monica nodded. "I can't imagine what she must be going through. How did her dad get so messed up to do something like this?"

"He's involved in a legal problem. It's too complicated to explain right now, but I guess he couldn't see any other way out."

"Wow."

"Yeah. Wow." Steve stared off into space, picturing John with all those monitors and IVs hooked up to him. He shook his head as if to shake the image out of his mind.

Monica stood. "I'd better get going."

Following her to the door, he said, "Thanks again for taking care of Max."

"Anytime. I'll miss the little fellow," she replied, smiling. "Tell Michelle she's in my thoughts. We all miss her at class."

He nodded as he reached for the doorknob and ushered her out. The cold night air woke him up a little and stirred his appetite. Coming back inside, he headed for the kitchen, remembering the can of chili he had opened. Max followed him and perched on a stool in the corner. He licked his paw and rubbed it over his face as

Steve poured the chili into a bowl and placed it in the microwave.

His cell phone rang as the chili was beginning to bubble. Michelle's face appeared on the screen and he quickly flipped it open. "Hi, babe."

"Hi," came Michelle's sweet voice.

He smiled and leaned back against the counter, closing his eyes to picture her face in his mind. "How's everything?"

"Okay, I guess. But I miss you already."

"Me too." Max rubbed up against Steve's leg as if to comfort him. He reached down and picked him up. Just as he was about to say something to Michelle, a loud bang sounded from the microwave, startling Max, who leapt from Steve's arms, scratching him in the process.

"Oh great," Steve muttered, rubbing his arm.

"What's up?" Michelle asked.

"My chili just exploded, and the stupid cat scratched me."

"Max is home?" she sounded surprised.

"Yeah. Monica dropped him off a few minutes ago."

"How does he seem?"

"He's fine. Spoiled actually. Monica bought him a bed and some toys."

"Sounds like something she would do," she said, her voice lifting somewhat.

Steve pulled open the microwave oven and groaned. "What a mess," he muttered under his breath.

"What's a mess?"

"The microwave. There's chili everywhere."

"Oh, no. Did you forget to cover it?"

"Cover what?"

"The chili."

"Oh. Yeah, I guess I did."

"Do you want me to call back later?" she asked.

"I don't know what I want, Michelle. I just want you here with me." He heard his voice crack. Brother, this is all she needs now. A whining husband.

Michelle was silent. "Listen, honey. I'm really sorry. I know you can't help it."

"No need to apologize. I miss you too," her voice was lower and trembling a little. "Do you think I should come home?"

"I think you'll know when it's okay to do that. God will show you."

"I'm not very good at all this, Steve. You know I'm just starting to figure out the whole God thing."

"I know. Just be patient. He'll show you."

"You sound like Kristin." Her voice brightened a little, and Steve knew she was thinking about her lifelong friend.

"I'll consider that a compliment," he replied.

"Good. You should. Well, I guess you'd better go clean up that mess in the microwave."

"What. You don't want me to leave it for you?"

"Funny, Steve."

"Okay. Just thought I'd ask."

"Yeah, right. Well, I'd better get off the phone. Mom will be back soon, and I told her I'd go over to the café with her for dinner."

They wrapped up their conversation and Steve set his phone down on the counter, heading over to survey the damages in the microwave. Most of the chili was still in the bowl, but it was hard to tell by looking at the walls and ceiling of the oven. Picking up a washcloth from the sink, he mopped it out and sat down to eat. Max was never allowed at the table, but Steve didn't say a word when he jumped up and sat in Michelle's chair.

A few minutes later, Steve rinsed out his bowl, and slinging Max over his shoulder, he headed up to bed. Completely exhausted, he could barely force himself to undress and brush his teeth before collapsing. Max curled up at his feet and slept undisturbed throughout the night, Steve never once moving from his original place and position.

CHAPTER THREE

A week had passed since John opened his eyes. Though progress was labored and the doctors were guarded in their prognosis, he continued to show gradual improvement. Now he could nod his head for "yes" and move it slowly from side to side for "no". His face still remained mostly expressionless, despite the myriad of emotions engulfing him.

A constant vigil was held at his bedside with Sheila, Michelle, Tim, Phil, and Joan taking rotating shifts. Their only diversion was the detours the women sometimes took to swing by the nursery and view the newborn babies. Michelle seemed particularly interested in stopping by on a regular basis to gaze into the window, watching the nurses care for their tiny charges. She also found herself frequenting the gift shop, admiring the adorable baby gifts and the gift cards that showed newborn infants cradled in flowers, loving hands, or pumpkins.

Up in Sandy Cove, Steve worked tirelessly to catch up on the caseload that was overwhelming Roger. In addition to the work he found at the office, he promised Michelle he would look for a way to resolve her father's embezzlement charges. As soon as he got settled back at home, Steve contacted a network of corporate lawyers, all friends of his uncle, faxing them copies of John's case and getting their input. While most agreed the circumstantial evidence weighed heavily against John, several had viable suggestions that could uncover the truth.

One attorney in particular, Clark Christianson, was confident the case could be won. He had a prior client with similar charges, and he had effectively routed out the actual perpetrator, winning a resounding victory. Although he was a high profile attorney in great demand, he agreed to give the matter some time and attention over the coming weeks.

These types of cases fascinated Clark, and after hearing this, Steve thanked him profusely, breathing a silent prayer of gratitude to God for opening that door. He was eager to call Michelle that evening and tell her about their conversation.

Tim was getting restless. All the waiting made him edgy, and he needed a break.

He was sitting with Sheila and Michelle one afternoon, eating a late lunch. "Mom," he began tentatively, "I'm thinking about going home for a few days. I could check on everything at your house and bring the mail back up here."

Sheila smiled at him. "Okay, honey. I know it's hard for you to sit around like this."

"I'll stay here, Tim," Michelle added reassuringly. "We'll call you every night and let you know the latest news about Dad."

Relief washed over him. He could almost smell the ocean air as he thought about home. Looking in on his parents' place and collecting the mail gave a sense of purpose to his temporary escape.

They were just finishing up when Phil and Joan arrived.

23

"Are you guys just now getting lunch?" Joan asked, looking concerned.

"It's easy to lose track of time in there," Sheila replied. "The nurse finally shooed us out and told us to go get something to eat."

"Well, I would have shooed you out long before this," Joan remarked.

Sheila smiled. She looked over at her father and saw him shrug his shoulders as if to say, "Once a mom, always a mom."

Tim explained to them his plan to return home for several days, thankful his grandparents seemed to understand. He decided to stop by the ICU for a few minutes before heading home. Sheila gave him a list of items to bring back from Seal Beach when he returned. They were short on basics, including changes of clothes, because of their emergency trek up to Bridgeport.

Sheila and Michelle were both fighting exhaustion, so they decided to return to the motel and rest for a few hours. As they entered the hospital elevator, they found themselves joining a young couple with a new infant in the mother's arms. Dad was loaded down with flowers and luggage and grinned sheepishly as he tried to squeeze against the elevator wall to make more room.

"Congratulations," Sheila said with a warm smile.

The baby's mother looked up. Her expression was aglow with love and joy. "Thanks," she replied.

"Does he have a name?" Michelle asked, noting the "It's a Boy" balloon the father was trying to hold in tow.

"Jacob," he replied as he looked down at his new son. "We'll be calling him Jake."

"What a cute name."

Sheila wrapped her arms around her daughter in a side hug. "Some day you'll be giving me an adorable grandbaby, right, Mimi?"

"Yeah, Mom," she replied, giving a patient smile.

Just then little Jake scrunched up his face. "They make the funniest expressions, don't they?" Sheila observed with a smile.

The nurse, who was holding the handles of the wheelchair for mother and baby, nodded as Jake's mother caressed his cheek gently with her fingertips.

"I can remember the little furrowed brows on your face when you would first wake up," she said to Michelle. "It was almost as if you were trying to figure out who I was and where you were."

Michelle turned and gave her an "enough, Mom" expression. After they got out of the elevator and watched the new family exit, she sighed. "Sure wish we were here for that reason."

Sheila nodded in agreement. "There's nothing more exciting than the day a baby is born, honey. You and Steve will remember those times forever. The moment the doctor places that tiny new member of your family in your arms is the moment your life changes in ways you could never imagine."

"Were you scared, Mom? I mean the first time you held me?"

"I think every new mom is a little scared. Suddenly you realize a tiny baby depends completely on you." She paused, reflecting on her first steps into motherhood. "You'll be a great, mom, Mimi. And I will love every second of being a grandma."

Michelle looked into her mother's tired eyes and could see the tears swell. But this time they were tears of anticipated joy. "I can hardly wait, Mom. The way things are going with my school options, who knows? I might end up waiting to start my career until after we have our family instead of the other way around."

"So you weren't able to get into the university for the fall?"

"Everything is so messed up with the economy and the cutbacks. Plus I was late getting my application in. I really didn't think there would be any problem since I'm a transfer student and my grades are pretty good. But they were absolutely adamant about no late applications, so I'm definitely excluded from the fall term. I'm too late to sign up for the regular fall session at the community college, but I was able to get an anthropology class that runs from October through January. That way I can get one of my general education classes completed while I wait for the spring term to start. It only meets twice a week, so that'll give me more flexibility. I can always drop it if you need me to help with Dad."

Sheila could see the frustration on her daughter's face. "Things will work out. At least you're getting started back with your classes."

"Yeah."

Though she knew it was hard on Michelle to be away from Steve, she was so thankful for the comfort of her daughter's presence. "I'm glad you're able to be here with me right now," she said as they exited the hospital and walked toward the motel.

"Me too, Mom," Michelle replied softly.

Everyday Phil prayed aloud over his son-in-law and read him short passages from the Bible. It seemed to relax John, and it gave an added sense of purpose to the time spent sitting by his bed.

Joan would sometimes close her eyes to listen to

her husband's voice. His steadfast diligence, yet gentle approach blessed her, and John's improved state encouraged them both. Today Phil had selected Psalm 103 to read. He and Joan settled into their chairs beside the bed, and Phil began to pray.

"Dear Lord, We are so thankful for all you have done here. Thank you for bringing John back to us. He is so loved and needed. Help him to understand that, Lord. Give him the willpower to fight until he is fully restored to complete health and wholeness. We ask, also, that you would use this time of waiting, resting, and healing to draw John close to you. Help him know you and understand your love for him. Help Sheila, Michelle, and Tim. Give them strength, hope, and faith. In Jesus' name, amen."

At the mention of Sheila and the kids, John had begun to moan softly. Phil and Joan simultaneously placed their hands on him in response.

"It's okay, John. Your family is strong. You will get better. God will get us all through," Joan said reassuringly.

The nurse interrupted them momentarily to begin John's feeding. The soft whir and click of the machine gave the room a heartbeat of its own as the creamy liquid was dispensed into the tube that led directly into John's stomach.

Once she had left the room and they were seated again, Phil began to read,

"Praise the Lord, O my soul; and all my innermost being, praise his holy name.

Praise the Lord, O my soul, and forget not all his benefits –

Who forgives all your sins and heals all your diseases,

Who redeems your life from the pit and crowns you with love and compassion,

Who satisfies your desires with good things so that your youth is renewed like the eagle's."

Phil paused for a moment as Joan nudged him. Looking over, he saw John's closed eyes, but his head was nodding slowly as if in agreement with the words. Smiling back at Joan, he continued,

"The Lord is compassionate and gracious, slow to anger, abounding in love.

He will not always accuse, nor will he harbor his anger forever;

He does not treat us as our sins deserve or repay us according to our iniquities.

For as high as the heavens are above the earth, so great is his love for those who fear him;

As far as the east is from the west, so far has he removed our transgressions from us.

As a father has compassion on his children, so the Lord has compassion on those who fear him;

For he knows how we are formed, he remembers that we are dust.

As for a man, his days are like grass, he flourishes like a flower of the field;

The wind blows over it, and it is gone, and its place remembers it no more.

But from everlasting to everlasting the Lord's love is with those who fear him."

As he spoke the last words, John drifted off into a peaceful sleep.

Hot water pounded on Michelle's neck and back, as she stood half- asleep in the shower. She felt so tired. She could barely manage the effort of shampooing her hair. As the water gradually changed from hot to cool, she

forced herself to get out and dry off. Slipping into her favorite robe, she was grateful for the parcel Steve had sent. Familiar items were such a comfort. It was hard to explain, really, but the coziness of her own robe lifted her spirits and gave her a brighter outlook.

Walking quietly back into the room, she saw her mother sleeping on the far side of the big bed. Sheila had not bothered to pull the covers back before collapsing, and Michelle could tell by her posture that she was probably a little cold. Carefully, so as not to disturb her, she covered her mom with an extra blanket. Sheila stirred slightly and murmured something indiscernible, then drifted back to sleep.

Michelle stretched out on the other side of the bed, pulling a portion of the blanket over her bare feet. As exhausted as she was, she couldn't fall asleep right away. Her mind was filled with thoughts about the conversation with her mother after they rode the elevator with tiny baby Jake and his parents.

What would it be like to have a newborn?

Michelle tried to imagine being at a hospital for such a joyous event. She could picture the excitement on Steve's face and how much fun it would be to plan for their child's arrival. The nursery, the tiny, adorable baby outfits, and the joy her mother and grandmother would feel. Should she shelve her schooling for now and turn her focus on starting a family? With the university delaying her application, it seemed like a step backwards to take classes at a community college. But at least she could get the anthropology class taken care of for now.

Visions of Trevor crept into her thoughts. Memories of him teaching the class on personal evolution and their discussion about New Age philosophies also drifted into her mind. These competed with scenes of her grandfather sharing his perspective on truth. She had so much to sort out.

Michelle couldn't deny her attraction to Trevor. Though she loved Steve and had no regrets about marrying him, Trevor had a certain magnetism that made her heart race and her face blush whenever he entered a room. She thought about the weekend seminar they had attended together and how close she had come to succumbing to his charms.

What would Trevor say to her when he found out about her change of direction in spiritual matters? Would he try to dissuade her from returning to the Christian faith of her grandparents? How could she make him understand all she had learned from her father's attempted suicide? Would they still be able to be friends? And wouldn't starting a family actually help cement her bond with Steve? Surely that would erase any lingering feelings for Trevor.

As Michelle wrestled with these questions, Trevor sat in his condo in deep meditation. He was using guided imagery to picture the destiny he hoped to attain. In his mental scenario, Michelle was hiking up a mountain path in front of him. She turned and smiled his way, offering her hand in a gesture of intimate friendship. As he touched her, she drew him close, into her arms.

Trevor nodded his head. Michelle really did need him. She was so innocent and vulnerable. And now she was far away -- in California with her family. He was concerned about her grandparents and the impact they might have on her in her current fragile state. He could imagine them using all kinds of tactics to manipulate Michelle's thinking with their antiquated Christian ideas and practices.

How could he rescue her from a regression to

those outdated beliefs? His calm state gave way to a restless pacing as his concern for her escalated.

What am I doing? I need to get focused. Trevor walked over to the kitchen, poured himself a glass of wine, and sat down to think.

CHAPTER FOUR

Someone was gently shaking Michelle's shoulder to awaken her. She opened her eyes and found herself on the motel bed beside her mother. Trevor was standing over her. He put his index finger to his lips and nodded toward her sleeping mother. Michelle returned his nod, acknowledging the importance of silence so as to avoid waking her mother. She slipped off the bed, careful not to make a sound.

Trevor beckoned her to follow him. Mesmerized, she softly padded across the carpeted room and out through the door he held open for her. Slowly, without a sound, they eased the door closed, leaving Sheila sound asleep within.

No words were needed between them. Michelle intuitively knew Trevor was taking her for a ride on his motorcycle. Holding her hand as she trailed closely behind him, she did not hesitate to go. Her heart was pounding with the anticipation of the thrill of a moonlit ride. Trevor looked over his shoulder at her and smiled. He gestured toward the gleaming motorcycle parked at the curb. She nodded and smiled back.

They climbed onto the bike, Michelle inching her body forward until her chest was pressed against his back. Wrapping her arms around his waist, she felt safe and secure as he pulled out into the street. The hum of the bike and the peaceful quiet of the late night sky hypnotized her. She completely lost track of time and space as they rode up a long, winding highway leading into the Sierras. Trevor skillfully guided his bike, giving grace to every movement of the powerful black beast. It felt like a dance as they glided around each bend in the road, working ever nearer to the summit.

Not a word was spoken between them. Nothing mattered except the feeling of oneness they experienced. Michelle's heightened senses were sharply attuned to her surroundings. The moon bathed the empty highway in an iridescent glow. Towering pines cradled the ribbon of roadway, their branches reaching out like arms extended in friendship toward the lone riders. The air felt cool and refreshing on her face as it streaked through her long, dark hair. Trevor's body warmed her torso beckoning her to lean even closer against him.

Finally reaching the summit of the mountain, he guided his motorcycle off the road and onto the paved viewpoint bordered by a low guardrail. He parked the bike and helped Michelle off the back. They stood side by side gazing out over the earth below them, the twinkling of streetlights down in the valley were sparkling like diamonds on velvet. Trevor turned Michelle's body toward his. Without speaking they embraced and his lips found hers. She responded without hesitation, melding her body against his.

"You are mine," he said without words. She nodded.

A bell rang harshly, breaking the reverie. Michelle tried to hold onto the dream, but it slipped away. She turned over on the bed, irritation coursing through her as she sought the source of the ringing noise.

Sheila was already up, flipping on the switch and picking up the receiver of the phone on the nightstand.

"Hello?" she said, her voice cracking as she forced herself awake. Michelle sat up and shook her head as if shaking off her dream. She pulled herself back to reality and watched her mother's face for signs of good news or bad.

"It's Steve," Sheila said, handing the phone to her daughter.

Michelle cleared her throat. "Hi Steve," she began, pushing Trevor from her mind. "How's everything at home?" She glanced at her cell phone and saw the voicemail icon. Apparently she'd left it on vibrate again.

"Fine. But Max and I miss you. How's your dad doing?" Steve asked, genuine concern evident in his voice.

"He's doing pretty well. He's responding more and more all the time. The doctors are blown away."

"I'm so glad, babe. Well, here's some more good news. I may have found a lawyer to take on your dad's case."

"Really? Tell me about him," she said, sitting upright on the edge of the bed. Covering the mouthpiece on the phone, she whispered to her mom, "Steve thinks he's found an attorney for Dad." Sheila's face lit up.

"His name is Clark Christianson. He has an office in Redondo Beach."

Michelle nodded, jotting down the information on a notepad, partly to refer to later and also to include her mom in the conversation. Sheila looked pleased about his location. Redondo Beach was less than an hour away from their hometown.

"He specializes in these kinds of corporate cases and recently had a very similar one to your father's," Steve explained. "The guy's a pretty high-powered attorney, but he seemed interested in your dad's case. I'll be talking to him on the phone tomorrow."

"Thanks, honey. I really appreciate you going to all this trouble. I know you're swamped at work. How's everything going there?"

"I'm beginning to see my desk again," Steve

quipped. "When I decided to become an attorney, I pictured myself in the drama of the courtroom, not in the chaos of an office piled high with paperwork."

"Hang in there. You'll get caught up," Michelle said, trying to sound encouraging.

"I miss you, hon."

"I miss you, too," she replied, a wave of guilt washing over her as she remembered her dream about Trevor.

"Maybe I'll fly back down for the weekend," Steve said tentatively.

"Whatever works out." She didn't want to make him feel unwelcome, but at the same time she knew he had a mountain of work he was trying to get through.

"I'll know more tomorrow," he told her.

"Okay. If you decide to come, give me a day's notice, so I can get us our own room," Michelle replied.

"Oh yeah. I almost forgot you're sharing a room with your mom. Did I wake her up when I called? She sounded kind of sleepy."

"Actually we were both asleep. We came back from the hospital around three, and both of us fell asleep."

"Sorry about that. I didn't mean to wake you guys up. In fact, I thought you might be out for dinner when you didn't answer right away."

"That's where we'll be headed next. Probably to the cafeteria at the hospital and then back up to sit with Dad," she replied.

"How's everything going at the hospital?"

"Dad's holding his own. I think we're all feeling more optimistic about his recovery."

"That's good."

"Steve?"

"Yeah?"

"My mom and I saw the cutest baby and his

parents as they were leaving the hospital."

"Oh, yeah?"

"He was so adorable and tiny. Mom started talking about me when I was a baby and then about how she wants to be a grandmother." Michelle glanced over at her mother and smiled.

"I'm sure she'll get her chance," Steve replied.

"Well, guess I'd better get off the phone and get ready for dinner," Michelle said reluctantly.

"Okay, I won't keep you any longer. Tell everyone hi for me."

"I will. Talk to you tomorrow," she promised.

"Love you, babe."

"Love you, too." She gently placed the phone on its cradle and turned to her mom. "Hungry?"

"A little. How about you?"

"Yeah. Let's go get dinner."

After freshening up, they left the motel room behind and headed out for another long night at the hospital. The sight of the full moon overhead brought Michelle's dream back to the surface. She wrestled within herself, part of her wanting to push it away and part wanting to hold it close.

Trevor sat on the balcony outside of his apartment and gazed up at the huge sphere in the sky. "Wish you were here with me tonight," he said to himself as he thought about Michelle and sipped on his glass of wine. He focused his mind, sending thoughts of oneness to this enchanting young lady with the dark, flowing hair.

He imagined them dancing together to the soft music playing in the background, the bouquet of the Chardonnay reminding him of the fragrance of her perfume. Trevor felt intoxicated by the images flooding his senses. He allowed his mind to explore a fantasy with Michelle. It was easy to imagine Michelle outgrowing her marriage with Steve. The shackles of tradition would fall away as she evolved into the free spirit she was meant to be.

"As I think, so shall it be. As I see us, so we shall be," he chanted softly into the night air.

He nodded. He believed it was true. One day he would have a chance for an intimate relationship with Michelle, and he thanked his inner guide for the confirmation.

Steve was milling over his conversation with his wife. Why didn't she seem eager for him to come back down for the weekend? Was he reading something into her response that wasn't there? Or did she really seem ambivalent about seeing him?

Max interrupted his thoughts with a reminder that it was his dinnertime.

"Okay boss. I'll get you some food," he said. He fed the cat then got his own lunch out of the fridge -- leftovers. Picking up his Bible, he settled into the breakfast nook and began to eat and read.

Having read through the book of Revelation with his old high school buddy, Ben Johnson, Steve was convinced of the need to establish his own personal relationship with God. Ben Johnson had helped him understand how to do that. Once the popular jock and party animal of their high school, Ben was now a born again Christian and pastor who was about to start a church up near where Steve and Michelle lived in Sandy Cove, Oregon.

Steve hadn't heard from Ben in about a week, so after he ate his dinner and read a couple of chapters in the gospel of John, he decided to give him a call. He needed someone to talk to about all that was happening with Michelle's dad.

Ben's wife, Kelly, picked up the phone on the second ring. "Hello?" Her voice was soft and gentle.

"Kelly? This is Steve."

"Oh hi, Steve. How's everything going with Michelle's dad?"

"He's getting stronger every day," Steve said happily.

"Thank God," she replied. "It's truly a miracle."

"Yeah. Even Michelle recognizes that. Did Ben tell you she's started praying again?"

"That's great, Steve." Kelly's enthusiasm was contagious.

Ben's voice could be heard in the background. "How's the packing coming along?" he called out to Kelly.

"Fine. I'm almost done with the kitchen cupboards. Steve's on the phone."

"Here's Ben, Steve," Kelly said cheerfully.

"Hey there. Are you calling from Bridgeport or Sandy Cove?" Ben's big voice boomed from the phone.

"Sandy Cove, unfortunately," Steve replied.

"Is something wrong?" Ben's tone changed to one of concern.

"No. I'm just missing Michelle."

"Well that's understandable. So I take it she's staying with her mom."

"Yep. They're sticking close to the hospital."

"How's Michelle's dad?"

"He's getting stronger and more responsive all the time." In spite of the good news, Steve knew his voice lacked its usual spark.

"That sounds good, but you sure don't. What's up? Why the heavy mood?"

"Actually, I'm concerned about Michelle," Steve began, feeling a little embarrassed to be bringing it up.

"What about her? Is she having a hard time dealing with all of this with her dad? The last time we talked, it sounded like she was turning back to God."

"This may sound crazy, but when I talked to her tonight on the phone, she didn't seem to care one way or the other whether or not I flew down there for the weekend. It really threw me off."

"I'm sure she didn't mean for it to sound that way, Steve. She's probably got a million things on her mind right now. Try not to take it personally."

"I know; you're right. Guess I'm just feeling sorry for myself."

"No, you're just missing your beautiful bride. I think you should fly down there and surprise her. You know, come to think of it, Kelly and I will be driving through northern California this weekend on our way up to Oregon. I told you we found a house to rent, didn't I?" Ben asked.

"No, I don't think you did. Where is it?"

"You'll never believe this, but we are actually going to be living about three miles from you in the outskirts of Sandy Cove. We found a great little fixer upper with a big living room/dining room combination that will be perfect for home Bible studies to help get our church started. You should drive by there and check it out. It's on the corner of Fir and Second Street. The gray house with white trim. 408 Fir is the address."

"I'll swing by and take a look tomorrow," Steve replied.

"And back to this weekend. If you think you'll be flying down to Bridgeport, maybe Kelly and I could stay one night there, and the four of us could go out to dinner or something," Ben suggested.

"Sounds good to me. I think you're right. I'll surprise her. She asked me to call a day in advance so she could get us our own room at the motel, but I think I'll just call the front desk and make the arrangements myself."

"Good idea. I know she'll be happy to see you, Steve."

"Hope you're right."

"Trust me, I am. So tell me exactly what's happening with John," Ben said.

"He's making eye contact now and is able to nod or shake his head slightly to answer yes and no questions."

"That's great."

"You should see the doctors. They just walk around with their mouths hanging open."

"God's got their attention."

"Yep," Steve replied.

"Well, why don't we plan on meeting up in Bridgeport Saturday afternoon? Kelly and I should be rolling into that area around 2:00. We could just go straight to the hospital and meet you guys there," he suggested.

"That would be great," Steve said. "I'll call the motel and book two rooms for Saturday night, one for you and Kelly and one for me and Michelle."

"Hey, thanks. Then we don't have to worry about where to stay. See you Saturday."

"Saturday. And thanks again, Ben."

He felt much better after he hung up the phone. Ben really knew how to put things into perspective, and he liked the idea of surprising Michelle. "I should have thought of that myself," he said, fumbling through the mail and miscellaneous paperwork as he searched for the motel's phone number.

It would be great to see Michelle and hold her in his arms again. And it would be fun to spend an evening with Ben and Kelly. He shot up a prayer asking God to nurture a friendship between Michelle and Kelly. Steve was concerned about how Michelle would manage back in Sandy Cove with all her New Age friends now that she was reaching back to her roots in Christianity. Kelly could be just the bridge she would need to get re-grounded in her faith.

CHAPTER FIVE

The week flew by quickly, and before Steve knew it, he was handing the cat over to Monica for another weekend of pet sitting. Max seemed delighted with the arrangements, and Monica was happy to have her adopted "baby" back for a couple of days.

Steve had been using Michelle's Bible ever since he started studying scriptures several months ago. Now that she was praying again and reaching out to God, he thought it would be a good idea to take it down to Bridgeport and leave it with her. It was time for him to have his own Bible anyway. He was continuously fighting the urge to write his own personal notes in the margins. Besides, this Bible had been a gift to Michelle from her grandparents. They would be happy to see her reading it during this drawn-out time at the hospital.

Because he wanted it to be special to Michelle, he had taken it to have her name embossed in gold on the cover and then had wrapped it in a gift box. Packing to leave for Bridgeport, he carefully sandwiched it between clothes. Then he picked up his new black leather study Bible, deciding not to pack it in his suitcase, but rather to carry it onto the plane to read during the flight.

Wandering through the house and closing all the blinds and draperies, he recalled the empty feeling he'd experienced coming home a week ago to a vacant, closed-up shell. He was already beginning to dread his return on Sunday night.

At least Ben and Kelly would also be arriving up in Sandy Cove. He'd driven by their rental house on the way home from work and was pleased it was so close to where he and Michelle lived. Maybe he could have a few dinners with them during the days ahead while Michelle was in Bridgeport. He could bring Chinese food over on Monday, so they wouldn't have to bother with fixing dinner on their first day of getting unpacked.

Steve also hoped he and Ben would get into a regular Bible study together. He really valued the weekend they'd spent digging into Revelation while Michelle was off at her New Age Conference. He had so much to learn about the scriptures, and Ben was an able guide.

Who knows? Maybe he could even get Roger to join them in a weekly study. Roger seemed like the kind of guy who would be open to that. He was basically a down-to-earth person with a sense of deep love and responsibility for his family. Contrary to the stereotypical image of attorneys as sharks, Roger set a good example for Steve as a person of integrity.

Steve picked up his bag and his Bible and headed out the door. He imagined Michelle's expression when he surprised her in Bridgeport. For a moment, a wave of hesitation washed over him as he remembered her seeming ambivalence on the phone. Shaking off his concern, he closed the door, locking the bolt securely behind him.

Michelle was sitting in her motel room by herself. Her mom was at the hospital with her dad, so she'd come back to send an email to her best friend, Kristin. She still couldn't get over the excitement of Kristin's announcement that she was getting married. What a surprise it had been to have her show up at the hospital chapel. It was almost as if God sent Kristin to show her He really did hear her cries and was responding to her pleas.

Kristin's fiancé, Mark, really impressed Michelle, and she was thrilled her friend had found such a great guy. It sure seemed weird though to be surrounded by all these pastor-type friends all of a sudden. First it was Steve's old high school buddy, Ben, showing up in Sandy Cove and preparing to plant a church there. Now it was Kristin marrying a youth pastor.

Michelle wondered if this might be some kind of conspiracy on God's part to corner her back into her childhood faith. Whatever it was, she was glad she had time in Bridgeport to sort through her beliefs. A part of her still clung to what she had been learning and experiencing in her New Age classes and studies, but a bigger part was feeling more at home with the faith of her grandparents.

Grandpa Phil was great. He knew how to make himself available without forcing any ideas or practices onto her. She loved to listen to him pray over her father and read the scriptures to him. His voice communicated a quiet confidence, and she could see how it seemed to relax and reassure her father.

Settling down at the little table by the window, Michelle flipped open her laptop and started typing an email to Kristin. She felt totally safe pouring out all her thoughts and fears with her childhood friend. Kristin knew Michelle inside out and loved her in spite of her faults. Unconditional love -- that's what Grandpa Phil called it. He said God loved Michelle with that kind of love too.

Well, right now, Kristin was more concretely accessible than God was. So Michelle would write to her friend and allow God to read it over her shoulder.

Hi Kristin,

I'm so glad you came to Bridgeport last week. Steve was right. I really needed you. I love the way it seems as if no time has passed between us each time we see each other again. You are such a great friend, and I hope we will be friends forever.

Dad is doing so much better. He can look at us now, and he nods his head for yes and no. Sometimes I can barely contain my excitement at his recovery, but other times I think about what Dr. Jeffries said about how Dad would feel if he had to live his life as an invalid, and I get really worried. You know how he is. Can you picture him allowing people to take care of him for the rest of his life?

Please pray for him and for all of us. He still has a long way to go. The doctors don't say much, but he can't move his left side at all, and he barely moves his right hand. He looks so vulnerable just lying there on the bed all day and all night. Sometimes he winces like he is in some kind of pain, and sometimes he just closes his eyes and won't open them for the whole day. Anyway, we need lots of prayers. I guess you know a lot about praying, being engaged to a pastor.

Can you believe it, Kristin? I'm so excited for you and Mark. After all that waiting, you are getting the best! So how are the wedding plans coming along? I'm eager to hear all the details. Wish I could be there with you to help with everything. I need to clone myself twice – once to be with Steve back at Sandy Cove and once more to be with you in Southern California.

Steve was thinking of coming down here for the weekend, but I guess he must be too swamped with work. Every time I bring it up in our conversations, he is very evasive and says he's not sure. Sometimes he seems kind of distant. I guess it must be hard for him to know what to say or do when he's here with us in Bridgeport. We're always talking to doctors, or sitting with Dad, or crashing on a couch or our motel beds from utter exhaustion. It really doesn't give Steve and I much time to be together or talk. I miss him, but I'm so busy and tired most of the time, that it seems almost better to be apart right now.

There's something else I need to talk to you about, but I don't want to write it in an email. Maybe I'll try to call you one evening this week. It's kind of personal, so I'll have to see if I can find a time when Mom is out of the room. I'd call right now, but I know you'd be at work.

Well, anyway, I guess that's all for now. I'm sure I'll be here for at least another week or two. Thankfully I've got my laptop now, so you can write whenever you get a chance.

Thanks again for coming last week. Best Friends Forever! Love, Michelle

Michelle yearned to see Kristin. She needed to work through her feelings about Trevor, and Kristin could help her do that. She'd really listen to her without passing judgment.

Michelle knew she belonged to Steve and it would be wrong to have any kind of relationship with Trevor other than strictly friendship. But her feelings wrestled within her as she fought the chemistry she couldn't deny. Kristin seemed like the only one who could help her figure all this out.

Trevor and Starla sat at the back of the New World Bookstore, sipping licorice tea and talking about Michelle. Starla felt a cosmic responsibility for Michelle, the young lady she had taken under her wing and guided gently into levels of expanded consciousness.

Now she and Trevor were pondering Michelle's vulnerability down in Bridgeport. Starla's rounded frame, engulfed in a floor length Indian print dress, sat forward in her wicker chair as she rubbed her open palms together, her waist length gray hair flowing down her back.

"If her grandparents weren't there, she'd probably

46

be fine," Trevor stated thoughtfully as he pyramided his fingertips. His piercing blue eyes narrowed under his furrowed brow.

"Yes. She could easily weaken to their influence. Especially under the circumstances," Starla continued, staring into the black tea. "Let's join together and send her guidance via the channels. Hopefully she will be responsive to their leading."

Both parties closed their eyes and sat upright. Other than the occasional sound of the wind moaning softly outside, the room was silent.

Several moments later a low hum resonated from deep within Starla. Soon Trevor's body responded with a hum of the same pitch. The sound crept into every niche of the locked bookstore. Starla and Trevor's faces remained expressionless as they emitted this continuous tone. Eventually they fell silent again.

Then Starla spoke. "Gods of the universe, Spirit Guides who lead us, send your wisdom to Michelle. Set her free from the bondage of her ancestors and their archaic beliefs. Elevate her to higher levels of consciousness. Use all that we have taught her to show her your better path to truth."

Trevor rocked back and forth in his chair, his eyes still closed. He began to chant a nondescript term over and over. Shadows enveloped them as Starla joined the chant. And the wind continued to howl outside the darkened bookstore.

An image of Trevor popped into Michelle's mind. She was remembering one of her classes on personal evolution she and her friend, Monica, had been taking at the bookstore. She pictured the class settling into their closing meditation, the one they performed at the end of each session. Sitting in a circle with their legs crossed and their eyes closed, they held hands and hummed a tone.

It started with Trevor and would work its way around the circle until they were all emanating this sound of resonance. The hum lasted for a few moments and then quietly receded into silence. Then Trevor would help them connect with their universal selves. "We are all one," he would affirm. "We are all one," they would chant in unison.

At first the meditation had troubled Michelle. It seemed so far out and mystical to her. But after several weeks, she came to look forward to those moments of oneness with the other class members and especially with Trevor, whose charisma had captivated her.

Sitting by herself in the motel room, she felt the hum starting up within her soul. Part of her wanted to yield to it, and part was alarmingly urging her to flee. She allowed a short, soft sound to escape; then she stood, closed the laptop, and walked out the door.

Steve set his Bible on the empty seat beside him, his mind filled with thoughts of Michelle. Silently he prayed for her, pouring out his heart to God and asking for strength and protection for his beautiful bride. He hoped his appearance at the hospital in a couple of hours would be a blessing to Michelle. His arms ached for her and his heart yearned to shelter her with his love. He prayed God would bridge whatever distance he perceived developing between them. Was it his imagination or was Michelle actually pulling away?

Steve was lost in his thoughts when the airline attendant gently tapped him on the shoulder and asked him to buckle his seat belt for take off. He quickly complied, retrieving his Bible and holding it firmly in his hands.

"Nervous about flying?" the attendant asked.

"No, just got lots on my mind," Steve replied.

"I hear you," she responded sympathetically. "Have a great flight, and let me know if you need anything."

Steve nodded and watched her walk to her seat and belt herself in. She looked up at him and smiled. He returned her smile, closed his eyes, and leaned back against the headrest as the plane surged into the air.

CHAPTER SIX

The clock on the wall displayed 9:00, but the weariness of a midnight hour pressed on Michelle's aching shoulders. Her mom and grandparents were across the street at the motel while she sat with her dad.

They usually tried to stay with him until eleven each night, taking turns resting and keeping him company. Each shared the unspoken fear that if left alone, John Ackerman would quietly slip back into his coma. It always took awhile to get him to respond in the morning, so by the end of the day they hesitated to leave him.

Michelle rolled her head from side to side to try to release some of the tension as she sat slouched in the chair by his pillow. Her eyelids were drooping, and she blinked to force them open. Sherrene, their favorite night nurse, approached her with a Styrofoam cup filled with steaming hot coffee.

"Thanks," Michelle said, retrieving the cup from her hand. "He's so quiet tonight."

"Yes, I've noticed he seems to close his eyes around 8:00 the past few evenings. Sometimes he perks up again, but other times he'll be out until morning."

"You don't think he's regressing, do you?" Michelle's voice was thick with concern.

"I think he just gets tired, Michelle. This is a daily battle for him. But he's trying to hold on," she added, reaching over and adjusting the covers draped over John's still form.

A gentle knock on the doorjamb distracted both Michelle and Sherrene. Standing there in the opening to the cubicle was Steve, holding a bouquet of wildflowers.

"Steve!" Michelle rose to her feet nearly spilling her coffee.

"Hi, babe," Steve grinned, opening his arms.

Handing her cup to Sherrene, Michelle and rushed into his arms.

She collapsed as she leaned heavily against him. At times like this, she realized how much of a burden she was trying to shoulder by herself. Just standing there in his embrace, she could feel the tension draining from her body.

"How did you get here?" she asked, pulling back to look into his eyes.

"I walked," he replied with a straight face.

"Very funny," Michelle retorted, grinning.

"Actually, I flew, but I would have walked if it was the only way to get to you," he added, leaning down and kissing her forehead.

"How romantic," Sherrene observed, winking.

"Don't get him going," Michelle warned. "It'll go straight to his head."

Steve drew her back into another embrace, while the nurse quietly slipped past them and out to the nurses' station.

"I'm glad you're here," Michelle murmured.

"Really? I'm glad you're glad," he replied with a grin.

"But you should have called me. Now we won't have our own room," she added with a sigh.

"I took care of that. I called and got us a reservation for tonight and tomorrow night."

Michelle looked up at him. His eyes were filled with love. They kissed each other tenderly as she soaked in his familiar embrace and kiss.

"I have another surprise for you, too," Steve added.

"What's that?"

"Ben and Kelly found a house to rent a few miles away from ours."

"Cool." She smiled as she thought about what a great friendship Steve and Ben had developed after all these years.

"That's just part of the surprise. They're driving up to Oregon in a rented truck with all their belongings, and they're stopping in Bridgeport overnight tomorrow. I got them a room at our motel."

"That's great," Michelle said, trying to sound enthusiastic.

He seemed to sense her hesitation. "They won't be here until at least the middle of the afternoon tomorrow," he explained, as if to reassure her they would have their own personal time together.

Sheila walked in the cubicle just as Michelle was nodding to Steve. "Steve! I didn't know you were coming down!" she exclaimed, turning to Michelle.

"I didn't know either," Michelle said, grinning. "He surprised me."

"What a wonderful surprise," Sheila observed, hugging him.

"Speaking of surprises, what are you doing back here?" Michelle asked her mother.

"I decided to come sit with you after I got your grandparents settled back in their room. You looked so tired when I left. I hated for you to be here by yourself."

"That was sweet of you, Mom, but I'm fine. Really."

"I can sit with her," Steve said. "You go back and get some sleep."

"Not on your life," Sheila replied. "You two

haven't seen each other all week. Go back over to the motel and spend some time together. I can stay here. Besides, I miss John while I'm over there."

"I know how you feel, Mom," Michelle said, stepping into the conversation. "But you need your rest. We won't be helping Dad if we get exhausted and end up getting sick. Steve called ahead and got an extra room, so you don't need to stay here on account of us."

Michelle watched her mother gaze down at her father and sigh. He looked as if he was sleeping peacefully, his chest slowly rising and falling with the gentle rhythm of his breathing. She could see her mom's eyes fill with tears. But something inside Michelle told her these were tears of joy that her father was still alive. And somewhere in those tears, she suspected her mother was wrestling with concern about whether or not he would ever fully recover.

"Are you okay, Mom?" she asked.

Her mother nodded. "Just a lot on my mind." She slowly tipped her head from side to side and rubbed the back of her neck.

"You look exhausted," Michelle said. "Let's walk back over to the motel together." Taking her mother's hand, she added, "He'll be fine for the night. He's resting comfortably."

Sheila sighed deeply. "Okay, sweetheart. I guess you're right." She leaned over and kissed her Michelle's father's forehead. "I love you, darling," she whispered to him. The only response was his steady breathing and the continuous beeps of the monitors.

Steve and Michelle escorted Sheila to her room, and Michelle gathered up her things. Then Steve led her to a room nearby. As they entered, Michelle noticed the identical layout and décor. She felt instantly at home. "It seems like we've taken over the whole resort."

Steve smiled in reply. This was definitely not a resort. But it was safe and comfortable. And now it gave him a place to reconnect with his wife.

They sat down side-by-side on the edge of the bed. Steve draped his arm over his wife's shoulders. "So how are you holding up?" he asked, compassion filling his gaze.

"I'm fine. But I'm worried about my mother. She is so exhausted, Steve. She doesn't realize what a toll this is taking on her. I'm really concerned she'll end up collapsing."

"I've been praying for her, and for all of you," he added, feeling a little vulnerable bringing up the subject of prayer.

"Thanks, honey. Keep praying." She hesitated then added, "Steve?"

"Yeah?"

"What would you think of starting a family before I finish school—like reversing the order and having kids first, then my career later?"

Steve looked her in the eye. "What brought this up?"

"I don't know. It's just that I'm frustrated about not getting into the university for fall. And then all this with my dad and the hospital. It would just be so great to have something positive for all of us to focus on now. Can we at least think about it?"

He could tell this wasn't the time for debate. "Okay. We can think about it."

Her eyes sparkled. "I'll still take the anthropology class this term."

"That's a good idea," he replied with a smile. He stood up and stretched, then went and grabbed his water bottle. "How are your grandparents doing?" he asked as he sat back down beside her.

"Grandpa Phil is a tower of strength, but you can see his age slowing him down some. Grandma is her usual optimistic self -- so calm and confident that Dad will recover. I'm sure they were sent here to help Mom make it through."

The way she said sent made him wonder if Michelle was recognizing God's hand in their situation with her dad. Then again, it could be another one of her New Age ideas surfacing. It was hard to tell. He simply nodded his head in agreement.

"Are you okay about Ben and Kelly staying here tomorrow night?" he asked.

"Yeah. I just wish you and I had more time together. I didn't realize how much I missed you until I saw you standing there tonight." She sighed. Her voice sounded strained, as if she might start to cry.

"I love you, babe," Steve whispered softly into her ear, inhaling the scent of her cologne.

"I love you, too," her voice cracking, as she began to cry.

Steve put his finger under her chin and turned her face toward his. He used his thumbs to brush away the tears then leaned forward and gently kissed her. As he began to sit back up, she wrapped her arms around his neck and pulled him close, her lips meeting his once again.

"I need you," she murmured between kisses. "I need you, too," he admitted in a throaty whisper.

Michelle turned lazily over in bed. She smiled as she gazed at her husband sleeping peacefully beside her.

He looked so handsome and strong. She snuggled back under the covers, pressing up against his warm body, realizing how much better she slept with him by her side.

She was glad he'd decided to come down for the weekend. It helped take her mind off Trevor. As she draped her arm over his chest, he stirred slightly and then opened his eyes. "Sorry, I didn't mean to wake you up," she said softly.

"It's okay. I don't want to miss a moment of our time together," he replied with a wink, drawing her into his arms.

"Morning breath," she warned as he bent to kiss her.

"As if that would stop me today," he chuckled pressing his warm lips to hers, and she wrinkled her nose at his rough chin.

"Good morning, porcupine." Steve had a heavy beard, and he usually shaved on his way to and from work every day. She wasn't used to this much stubble on his chin, even in the mornings.

"Okay, okay. I'll shave." He started to get out of bed.

"You're not going anywhere," she exclaimed dramatically, pulling him back into an embrace, purposely ignoring his beard, and kissing him with fervor.

They both burst out laughing. "I've got an idea." Michelle's face lit up. "I'll shave your face." She leapt out of bed and headed for the bathroom to get his electric razor.

"I don't think that's such a good idea," he said dubiously.

"Just relax. I've got this under control." She held the razor in her hand trying to figure out how to turn it on. She slid a ridged lever upward and jumped slightly as the razor hummed into action.

Steve laughed at her startled expression. "Give me

that thing!" he said, trying to sound serious.

"No way. I'm going to finish the job."

"That sounds ominous."

"Just relax. You won't feel a thing," she promised as she approached.

Steve pulled the covers up over his head.

"Come out of there, you coward!"

He peeked out and then pulled the covers quickly back in place.

Michelle decided to try another tactic. She lifted the covers from her side of the bed and climbed underneath with him.

"Ahhhh!" Steve yelled as he rolled out of bed, landing with a thump on the floor.

She crawled across the bed and threw herself down on the floor on top of him. They wrestled and rolled across the carpeted floor, the razor buzzing in her hand.

Eventually, Steve was able wrestle it free and made a mad dash for the bathroom. He locked himself inside and started shaving.

Meanwhile, Michelle sank down onto the bed laughing. It seemed like such a long time since she and Steve had wrestled like that. He really was a lot of fun when he wasn't consumed with work.

She walked over to the dresser and looked in the mirror. Her hair was a mess and her eyes had dark circles under them from yesterday's makeup that she had neglected to wash off the night before. Licking her finger, she rubbed off the black marks; then picked up her brush and ran it through her long dark hair. She spritzed on some cologne and climbed back into bed, sitting up against both pillows.

Steve emerged from the bathroom clean-shaven. His bare chest revealed his solid frame. She was amazed he still looked so athletic even though he didn't really have time to work out since he got his job at the law firm. She smiled as he approached her.

"Truce?" she asked tentatively.

"Truce," he agreed, falling onto the bed and kissing her. She could taste the mint from his toothpaste, and his face felt smooth against hers. After a moment, he popped up and said, "How about breakfast in bed?"

"Are you kidding?"

"Nope. I checked with the coffee shop when I got here yesterday. They deliver breakfast to the motel until noon."

"What time is it?" she asked, unable to see the clock from her position on the bed.

"It's nine-thirty."

"Nine-thirty? I should be over at the hospital by now." Steve's face dropped, and Michelle could see his look of disappointment. "I guess I could go around noon," she admitted. "Then Mom, Grandma and Grandpa could get a break for lunch."

"That sounds like a good idea. Then we'll be there when Ben and Kelly arrive."

"Okay. You win. Order the breakfast," she said with a smile.

Picking up the phone, Steve called the coffee shop. He ordered an omelet, a stack of pancakes with blueberry syrup, two coffees, and a large orange juice. Michelle's stomach started growling just listening to the order.

After he hung up, she beckoned him back into bed. He smiled and climbed under the covers beside her, enjoying the feel of her slender curves and the fragrance of her cologne. He rested his head on her chest, and she ran her fingers through his hair massaging his scalp. He loved having his head rubbed, and he hummed with appreciation.

They were both close to drifting back asleep when

a soft knock on the door indicated the arrival of breakfast. Michelle pulled the covers up to her neck, while Steve slipped into his jeans and strode over to answer the door.

After the delivery boy left, she reached for her robe, but Steve intercepted her, pulling the robe off the bed and tossing it onto the dresser. "We're not eating at the table, Madam. Remember, I said breakfast in bed."

She smiled and nodded. "Yes, sir."

Propping herself up with the pillows, she let the covers slide down again revealing her beautiful silk chemise. Steve was momentarily distracted from retrieving the breakfast. She could see the twinkle in his eye. "Hey, buddy, get the breakfast," she said with a laugh.

"Oh, yeah. Breakfast. Coming right up." Steve brought the cups over and placed them on the nightstand. Then he opened up the box and brought the plate with the omelet over to her.

"So I get the healthy breakfast, and you get the sweets?" she asked with a pout.

"Actually, I thought we'd share both of them. How about if we start with this omelet and work our way to the pancakes for dessert?"

"Works for me," she replied gleefully.

They snuggled together under the covers and shared a fork, taking turns feeding each other bites of omelet and sipping on the same large orange juice.

Finishing up, Steve carried the empty plate over to the table and returned with the pancakes and syrup. As he carefully balanced the plate on her lap, he attempted to feed her without dripping syrup all over the bedding. He was fairly successful with the exception of one large drip that landed on her chest.

Mimicking a ferocious animal, he made a dive for the drip, growling and shaking his head like a lion while he licked it off. Michelle laughed hysterically, almost knocking over the entire plate. Looking up into her sparkling eyes, Steve planted a wet blueberry kiss on her lips.

"I'm so glad you came for the weekend," Michelle said lovingly.

"Me, too. Max never shares his breakfast with me."

"It's a good thing we have Monica to take care of him while you're gone," she said, laughing.

"She seems to have grown very attached to him," he replied.

"Maybe she just needs a baby of her own," Michelle suggested with a smile.

"Maybe we do, too," he added with a sly grin.

"Oh, really?"

"Really. I'm willing to think about it, babe."

She was surprised but pleased. "I'm glad. I think about it a lot lately. Every time I go into the gift shop on my way to or from seeing Dad, I stop and look at the adorable baby outfits and blankets. Mom and I like to stop by the nursery too. Being in a hospital changes your perspective on everything. You see some people coming to die and some coming to welcome new life."

Steve gazed at her thoughtfully. "What about school? You really want to wait on that?"

"I know I need to finish, but my heart just isn't in it right now."

"I understand. Especially with everything going on with your dad."

She nodded, looking down at her hands resting on her knees. Suddenly her eyes pooled with emotion as she glanced back up at her husband. "Is it crazy to be thinking about babies at a time like this?" A tear slipped out and trickled down her cheek.

He wiped it away and kissed her forehead. "No,

babe. I think it's a good time to think about the future. We've always planned to have a family. I'm not sure there's ever a perfect time to do that. But I don't want to see you give up your dream of being a teacher, either."

"I know. Same here. This just feels right to me now."

"Let's pray about it, Michelle. Then we'll decide."

She nodded and smiled. "I love you, Steve."

"Feeling's mutual."

As they embraced, she glanced over his shoulder and noticed the clock. "We'd better get up and get moving. I've got to get over to the hospital."

"Race you to the shower," he grinned as he jumped up and bolted toward the bathroom.

CHAPTER SEVEN

Ben and Kelly Johnson were up before the sun peeked into their window, the alarm clock echoing raucously in their empty bedroom. Their furniture had been loaded into the rental truck the day before, and they were camping out in sleeping bags in the middle of the master bedroom floor.

Ben threw his pillow at the alarm clock, flipping it onto its back and pressing in the off button. "Nice job," Kelly murmured with a sleepy smile. Her eyes began to close again.

"Up and at 'em, Madam," he chided. "We're on the road in half an hour."

She groaned and pulled the sleeping bag up over her head. "Okay, okay," came her muffled reply.

Wiggling out of his bag, he began rolling it up. Just for good measure, he patted his wife on the shoulder through her heavily quilted covering. "I'm up, I'm up," she responded, unzipping the zipper and sitting upright.

"I'll roll up your bag while you start getting ready," he suggested.

"Okay. It won't take me long," she replied with a sigh, shuffling in the direction of the bathroom.

Thirty-five minutes later they were walking out of their tiny bungalow in the sleepy town of Sierra Madre for the last time. Kelly sighed as she remembered Ben carrying her over the threshold on their wedding day. It was a cute, if not incredibly small, cottage, and they would miss the quaintness of its simplicity as well as that of the town itself, nestled up against the foothills of the San Gabriel Valley.

"This has been a great little place," he commented as if reading Kelly's thoughts.

"Yep," she sighed. "But I'm excited about the move. God's going to do a great work in Sandy Cove."

"Let's hope so," he replied with a smile.

Although he wrestled with self-doubts, his wife steadfastly believed in him. It was her faith in him and in the God they served, that gave Ben the courage to step out and try this call on his life.

They closed the front door gently and climbed into the rental truck that was loaded with their worldly possessions. As Ben climbed into the driver's seat, Kelly took her place beside him. "Penny for your thoughts," she said with a yawn as they pulled out of the driveway.

He looked at her and smiled. "I think you should get some more sleep."

Kelly knew him well enough to know he was probably wondering if he would be up to the challenges ahead. He'd already expressed his concern about how they would find the first people for his opening Bible study. He wondered how they would adjust to life in the Northwest. She knew that most of all he worried about whether their savings account would hold out until one or both of them could get a regular paying job.

In spite of her husband's tendency toward self-doubts, Kelly was so proud of Ben and his willingness to be this responsive to a call by God. She hoped she could be a supportive pastor's wife and meet all the demands of that responsibility. Though it felt a bit overwhelming, she was certain this was God's will for her and for her husband. Even their parents had been amazingly supportive of their move. Surely the Lord was going to supply all their needs as they stepped out in faith to serve

Him in their new hometown.

Maneuvering the bulky vehicle toward the freeway, Ben cautiously merged into the number three lane. He would cruise there until he got a better feel for the monster he was navigating.

Kelly leaned against the window, using her pillow as a headrest. "I'll wake you up when we pull off for breakfast," he promised. "Thanks, Pastor," she said with a smile. Closing her eyes, she attempted to stop the continuous parade of thoughts marching through her mind. It would be her turn to drive in a few hours, and she knew she'd do better if she had a little more rest first.

As Kelly slept, Ben thought about their destination for that night. They would be with Steve and Michelle up in Bridgeport near the hospital where Michelle's dad was in intensive care. He sent up a silent prayer for them. It was hard to imagine how Michelle must be feeling during this aftershock from her father's attempted suicide.

Steve looked to him for spiritual guidance, since he was the one who had led Steve to a relationship with God, so Ben prayed for wisdom and the right words to minister to his friend. Although Ben trusted God, he lacked trust in himself. His secret fear was somehow disappointing God the way he felt he had disappointed his dad during his partying years. He hoped someday to make both his father and God proud of him and what he had become.

While he drove, he listened to a country western station strumming melancholy sounds about love gone sour. His dad was a country music fan, and Ben had gotten hooked while he was still a young boy riding in their old Chevy truck to the various construction sites where Ben would 'help' his father on Saturdays. Something about this music seemed to fit naturally with driving a truck. He smiled to himself as he tapped the steering wheel to the beat.

The freeway was wide open at this early hour. He glanced down at his watch. 6:10. He'd start looking for a fast food restaurant around 6:30. Coffee was sounding really good to him, and he wished they had kept the coffeemaker out for this morning. Oh well. He'd be getting his brew soon enough.

"You done me wrong. You done me wrong. You left me standing on my own far too long...." The music reached into his ears and mind. He thought back to his first love, Trisha Parks. It was his freshman year of college. Trisha was his partner in a sociology project. Her sparkling smile and contagious laugh had captivated his heart.

They spent many long hours together that semester, some working on the project, but many just getting to know each other. Though Ben was quite a playboy, he kept going back to Trisha. She seemed sincerely interested in him and was enchanted with his dream to become an anthropologist, even saying she could imagine accompanying him on some exotic dig in the jungles of Africa or South America.

Shortly after they began dating, Ben attended a crusade with his roommate. They planned to go just to study these far out 'born again-ers', but something in the message had touched a part of him he'd never even known existed. By the end of the evening, he was streaming down from the bleachers with thousands of others who were responding to the call to commit their lives to God.

Trisha couldn't understand this new side of Ben, and she definitely didn't want any part of it for herself.

Their relationship, which had been headed for serious physical involvement, now cooled noticeably as he dug into the scriptures and began reevaluating his priorities and values. Within a month, Trisha announced their relationship was at a dead end.

Ben mourned her departure, grieving his inability to persuade her to explore this new spiritual dimension. It had seemed like such a sacrifice at the time. Losing Trisha was like losing a dream for the future. But when he tried to seek her out one last time, she made it abundantly clear she wanted nothing to do with him or his God.

The next two years had been years of single focus for him as he sunk his roots deep into the heart of God. He spent every spare moment reading and studying scriptures. Sometimes he stayed up all night, poring over verses and commentaries while he downed cup after cup of coffee to keep going. He would stagger into class the following morning, his mind reeling with scriptures he had been reading. Somehow he'd manage to stay awake through the morning lectures and then would crash in his dorm room during the afternoon, often skipping lunch out of sheer exhaustion.

By his junior year, it was clear Ben was not destined to be an anthropologist. Though he loved to study about all the biblical digs and was fascinated about the idea of actually participating in one some day, he was certain God had a different plan in mind. He transferred from the state university to a Christian college and changed his major to theology. Now his studies matched his passion, and he voraciously devoured the scriptures.

One night at a worship gathering in the dorm, Ben found himself sitting next to a cute little redhead who introduced herself as Kelly McKinney. They chatted briefly before the worship songs began, and he enjoyed hearing her soft, melodic voice lifted heavenward as they sang together. When the evening drew to a close, several of his friends decided to go out for late night pizza. He casually asked Kelly if she'd like to join them and was pleasantly surprised when she said yes.

It turned out Kelly was the roommate of one of the first acquaintances Ben made at the school. Shannon was glad to see them getting along so well, especially since she had already mentioned to Kelly she thought they would make a cute couple. But Ben wouldn't find out about this until after he and Kelly started seriously dating a couple of months later.

All memories of Trisha faded into shallow recollections once Ben and Kelly realized the depth of their feelings for each other. Wanting this relationship to last, he was careful to honor Kelly and try to put her before himself. She responded with an open heart, and they became engaged after dating for a semester.

Chuckling to himself, he remembered how nervous he'd been to meet Kelly's dad and ask for her hand in marriage. He knew it seemed a little corny and old-fashioned, but he wanted to do this right.

Mr. McKinney, an articulate businessman who was also a devout Christian, appreciated Ben's gesture and considered it a sign that his little girl would be cherished and protected by this gallant young man. Ben was elated when he extended his hand in acceptance to his future son-in-law.

Kelly heard her husband's chuckle, and she lifted her head from its resting place. "What are you laughing about?" she asked with a smile.

"Oh, I was just remembering the day I asked your dad for your hand in marriage."

"You were so nervous," she recalled, giggling a little herself. "But it was really sweet of you to do that. Not many guys have that kind of respect anymore," she added.

"I don't know about that, but it sure was worth

the effort," he replied with a wink.

"I'd have to agree with you, Pastor."

"Would you quit calling me that? It makes me nervous every time you say it."

"No, I will not quit calling you that. You need to get used to it, Pastor," she added with special emphasis.

He looked, feigning a scowl. "You don't intimidate me," she said with a stern look in return. "Fine, Miss Unintimidated, are you ready for some breakfast?" he chided.

"As a matter of fact, I am. And a cup of coffee. I'm starting to get a headache from missing my caffeine fix this morning."

"I hear you. Me, too. There's a McDonald's two miles from here. I just saw a billboard for it."

"Sounds good," Kelly replied. Within minutes, they were pulling into the parking lot of the restaurant.

Ben found a booth near the door, where he could keep an eye on the truck while they devoured their meal. Kelly carefully removed the lid on her coffee to allow it to cool slightly before drinking. After stirring some creamer into it and blowing on the surface of the light brown liquid, she tentatively took a little sip. "Just right." She smiled with satisfaction.

"Set your coffee down for a second, kid," he said affectionately to her. Then he took her hand in his, and they bowed their heads while he blessed the meal and asked for God's safety on the remainder of their journey.

It didn't take long to finish their meal, and the two travelers were back on the road headed for Bridgeport.

CHAPTER EIGHT

The main lobby of the hospital was empty with the exception of one middle-aged man snoring softly in a corner seat with an open newspaper draped across his chest like a blanket. Ben and Kelly held hands as they approached the information desk.

"Can I help you?" a kind-faced woman in her sixties asked the young couple.

"We're here to see the family of John Ackerman," Ben explained.

"Ackerman. One moment, please." She typed the name into her computer. "He's in the ICU," she explained, pulling out a map and showing them the most direct route to that section of the hospital.

"Thank you," Kelly responded with a smile.

Ben led her through the various corridors outlined on the map until they found themselves at the nurse's station of the ICU. They were just about to ask for John's room, when Steve spotted them from inside the cubicle.

"There's Ben and Kelly," he said to Michelle, who was sitting at her father's bedside. "I'll be right back."

Michelle smiled. She leaned over her father. His eyes were closed, so she did not know if he was awake or asleep. "Our friends are here, Daddy," she told him softly. "We'll probably go out for a while, but Mom and Grandma should be back any minute."

Michelle's grandfather had come down with some

kind of stomach virus, which her grandmother insisted was food poisoning from all the fast food they had been eating lately. He was spending the day resting at the motel, while Sheila and Joan kept each other company.

Michelle could see no visible response from her dad, but she was convinced he heard every word she said. She leaned over and kissed him and was just standing to her feet when Steve returned with Ben and Kelly in tow.

"Hi, Ben," Michelle said, as she extended her arms to give him a hug. "You must be Kelly," she added reaching her hand out to clasp Kelly's.

Kelly returned her handshake and smile. "I've heard so much about you two," she said. "I'm glad to finally get to meet you."

"How's your dad doing?" Ben asked, glancing first over at John and then back to Michelle.

"He's doing great," she replied enthusiastically. She believed it was crucial to maintain an upbeat, optimistic attitude around her father. He needed to know he was doing great, even though he had such a long way yet to go.

Then she turned to see him just beginning to open his eyes. The noise in the cubicle had stirred him, and he winced as if in pain.

"You woke up, Daddy," she said cheerfully. He gave no response except the subtle shifting of his eyes as he searched for his daughter's face in the crowd. Moving closer to the bed, she leaned directly over him. "Steve's friend Ben and his wife Kelly are here. They stopped on their way to Sandy Cove. They're moving there to start a new church."

As John studied his daughter's face he appeared to be trying to process what she was saying. He kept his eyes intently focused on her as if she were his only bridge back to life and reality.

The doctor had explained his current existence as

a blur of dreams and sounds, but John seemed increasingly aware he could not move and desperately frustrated by his inability to talk or respond to her other than nodding his head.

Steve suggested perhaps John was being over-stimulated by everyone crowding into the cubicle. "Maybe we should wait outside," he said softly to Ben and Kelly. They nodded and followed him quietly out of the door and into the adjoining ICU lobby.

Feeling torn, Michelle didn't know what to do. She hated to leave her father alone now that he was obviously awake, but she had intended to spend the afternoon and evening with Steve, Ben, and Kelly. Her entire social life for the past few weeks had revolved around the ICU, her mother, grandparents, and nurses. She craved a time away from the whole hospital scene and an opportunity to reconnect with her husband in a social setting.

John winced again and peered intensely into her eyes.

"Daddy," Michelle began, "I need to leave for a little while. Will you be okay? Mom and Grandma should be back anytime now."

Gazing at her, as if willing himself to answer, he slowly rallied all his energy and nodded yes.

Her face relaxed with relief, and she smiled and leaned over to kiss him. "I love you," she said, looking him directly in the eye as she cupped his face in her hands. "I won't be gone long. Promise. And Mom will be here soon."

John closed his eyes again, and Michelle turned to leave. Walking out of the cubicle, she did not see the tear slide down his cheek.

Clark Christianson sat at his meticulously organized desk, rereading the briefs on John Ackerman's case. Ever since he first began practicing law fifteen years ago, Clark loved to represent the underdog. No matter how bleak the case might look, if he was convinced his client was being maligned, he would work night and day with a passion in order to prove his case and win.

This Ackerman situation was so similar to the case he had won six months ago that it was uncanny. The frame-up was nearly identical, and the charges were verbatim. Something was fishy. He could smell a link between the cases. Though his intellect told him he was probably crazy, his gut told him there was something there. Something very real. He was determined to weed it out.

He made a note on his day planner to have his secretary pull all the files on Harrison Brady. He'd go over them tomorrow night after he got home and see what he could uncover. This was one of the few consolations of being recently divorced. No one leaned over his shoulder nagging him to put his work away in the evenings. Now he found himself happily packing a full briefcase before he left his office each day.

"Guess you were right, Susan," he admitted to the air, as he thought about his ex-wife. "Law really is my first love."

He clicked open his burgundy cowhide briefcase and tossed John Ackerman's file inside. After adjusting the combination lock to protect from possible tampering, he walked out of his office and into the night air.

Phil moaned from the bed, struggling to sit up.

"You sound like you're dying," his wife, Joan observed.

"Come get me, Lord," he responded.

Joan sighed and shook her head as she glanced at Sheila. "These fast food places will kill us all eventually," she remarked.

Sheila just smiled, knowing it was pointless to argue with her mother's theories.

"Take this medicine, Phil," Joan urged as she held the small cup of creamy liquid. "It'll calm your cramping."

"I'll try," he muttered under his breath, clearly fighting waves of nausea. He managed to force down the chalky mixture and then fell back down against the pillow.

"We brought you some soda, too. I'll just leave an open can on the bedside table," Joan instructed. "Try to sip a little at a time. We don't want you getting dehydrated."

"Okay," he said, too weak to argue. He closed his eyes, with an expression of forced relaxation, willing the pain and nausea to subside. Joan adjusted his blankets, and then she and Sheila quietly crept out of the room to head back over to the hospital.

"I hope whatever Dad has is not contagious," Sheila said, thinking about her husband in the ICU.

"Don't be silly, Sheila. It's food poisoning. I've seen this before when your father sneaks out to those greasy hamburger joints. I'm telling you, they don't know how to cook in those places."

"Whatever you say, Mom," Sheila replied. She knew their stay in Bridgeport was taking a toll on her elderly parents, and she didn't want to create any more stress by getting into a debate with her mother. Still, she was glad they had strict rules about hand washing before entering the cubicles in the ICU. She wanted every possible precaution taken to protect her husband and speed his recovery.

Michelle, Steve, Ben, and Kelly were enjoying a stroll through downtown Bridgeport. The air was crisp and clear, and the streets were lined with a wide variety of interesting shops and restaurants.

At first they walked hand-in-hand with their spouses, but within a half hour, Ben and Steve were deep in a theological discussion, and Michelle and Kelly were enjoying slipping into the crafty tourist shops. They seemed to be hitting it off really well. Kelly was such an easygoing person and a great conversationalist. She knew how to draw Michelle out of the shell that usually encased her when she was around people she didn't know.

"What do you think?" she asked with a wink as they spotted their fourth antique store. Michelle smiled and nodded an affirmative.

Abandoning the men without a word, they detoured into the shop. Kelly was trying on a velvet hat with a feather plume when she spotted an aging basset hound watching her from beside the counter, his tail gently thumping on the floor when she made eye contact.

Putting the hat aside, she smiled at the owner and asked, "What's his name?"

"Archie," she replied with a smile.

Kelly held out her hand so he could sniff it before she slowly reached up and patted him on the head. His tail picked up speed, pounding the wood floor with fervor.

"Michelle, would you go outside and get Ben for a second?" she asked. "I want him to see this cutie-pie."

She found Steve and Ben perched on one of the park benches placed strategically along the main street. They both looked up at her. "Ben is wanted inside," she said, tipping her head toward the open door.

"Uh, oh," Ben moaned. "I hope this won't empty my wallet." Steve smiled. "Good luck, buddy."

Michelle swatted him playfully on the arm. "This isn't about money," she chided. "Kelly just wants Ben to see the owner's dog."

Ben's smiled, patting Steve on the knee as he rose from the bench. "Come on, pal. Let's go," he said.

"Okay, okay," he replied, draping his arm over Michelle's shoulder as they strolled inside.

After the appropriate small talk with the owner and lavishing affection on Archie, they managed to peel Kelly away and continue their stroll through town. As they walked on Michelle commented, "If you thought Archie was cute, you should see the babies at the hospital and the cute baby stuff in the gift shop."

"Sounds like fun," Kelly replied.

By now it was almost 5:30, the streetlights were coming on, and Steve was starving. "Anyone else ready for dinner?" he asked casually.

"Thought you'd never ask," Ben replied.

The girls agreed they could eat anytime, so the four of them began looking for an inviting place to dine. A couple of blocks from what they now fondly referred to as "Archie's Antique Store," they found a rib joint with a live banjo player and the delicious smell of barbecued ribs wafting out to the sidewalk.

"Let's go." Steve pointed, and the four of them scooted inside.

The place was packed, but Ben spotted a cozy, rounded booth up against the far wall. The rest of the party trailed him and slipped across the shiny red seats, retrieving the menus propped up between the tall salt and pepper shakers.

A young waitress appeared and introduced herself as Shawna, asking with a sweet smile, "Are you ready to order, or do you need more time?"

Steve glanced around the table. Everyone nodded in readiness. They placed unanimous orders of barbecued ribs with mashed potatoes and salad, even agreeing on their drinks -- tall, frosty root beers.

"Well this is sure a compatible group," Steve observed aloud. He was really pleased Michelle and Kelly were getting along so well. The Johnson's' move to Sandy Cove could be a great blessing for Michelle and him.

The evening passed quickly as they enjoyed their food and the pleasant conversation. Ben and Steve set aside their discussions about scriptures, and they all talked about Sandy Cove. Now that Michelle had been gone for a while, she realized she was getting attached to that beach community and their cozy home. She gave Kelly a description of the local shops and told her about her hopes to finish college at Pacific Northwest University.

"I was hoping to get started there in the fall, but I didn't make the application deadline" she explained. "Maybe spring semester, depending on how everything else goes," she added.

"Teaching is a great calling," Kelly responded with obvious admiration. "I've never really been very career-oriented. Guess I always just wanted to have a family and be a mom." She shrugged her shoulders and smiled.

It made Michelle feel special to have Kelly express such high regard for her career choice. She was really beginning to feel a kinship with Ben's wife and hoped they would spend a lot of time together once she was able to return to Sandy Cove. And who knew? Maybe if she and Steve decided to start a family soon, they might both be having kids at about the same time.

The motel was within walking distance, and they all agreed the exercise would do them good after stuffing themselves with ribs. A chill in the air nipped at Michelle, and she wished she had brought along an extra jacket or sweatshirt, but once they got moving, she warmed up a little.

As they neared the hospital, she wondered if she should go back in to see her dad. Then she remembered she and Kelly had talked about going by the gift shop. Although Steve and Ben were both beat, they agreed to indulge their wives in this one last venture of the day.

Michelle steered them to the back corner where the baby section was set up. Designer sleepers, blankets, and booties were carefully displayed, along with photo frames, footprint kits, bottles and nursing supplies.

Kelly immediately reached for one of the sleepers with tiny yellow ducks printed over the soft white background. The feet had appliquéd duck feet across the top and a matching cap sported a duck's bill and eyes.

"Aren't they precious?" Michelle asked.

"Makes you want to have a baby just so you can dress him in one of these outfits," Kelly replied. Turning to Michelle, she added, "Can't you just imagine having one of your own?"

Michelle nodded silently, her gaze traveling to Steve's face.

"We'd better get them out of here," Ben said to Steve with a wink.

"I'm with you. This could get out of hand. Come on, Michelle. Let's head over to the motel."

She sighed. "Okay. I'd like to stop by and check on my dad before we leave."

When they got to John's ICU cubicle, he was asleep, and Sheila was getting ready to leave. "Want to walk back to the motel with us?" Michelle asked.

"Okay," her mom replied, leaning over to kiss her

husband's forehead.

As they crossed the street and entered the motel lobby, Sheila told them all good night and headed to her room.

Ben had parked their truck in the extra parking lot behind the motel, and Steve accompanied him to retrieve their overnight bag while Michelle helped Kelly find their room.

Kelly took advantage of their brief time alone to ask Michelle a question. "Michelle," she began, "do you have a good doctor in Sandy Cove?"

"You mean a general doctor or a female doctor?"

"OB/GYN. I think I might be pregnant."

Michelle looked at her with surprise. "Really?"

"Really. It's a secret for right now. Ben is the only one who knows. I've already had one miscarriage, so we aren't talking about it much yet. This isn't exactly the ideal time to have a baby, but..."

"There's never a perfect time," Michelle said, finishing Kelly's thought.

"Exactly. Ever since the miscarriage last year, I've been really wanting to try again."

"That's how I've felt with everything happening with my dad. Going through this has really made me think about what's important. We'd planned I'd finish my degree first and then think about a family, but now...."

"Now you've changed your mind."

Michelle was amazed at how they were able to think alike and finish each other's sentences. It reminded her of her friendship with Kristin.

"I'm sure glad you live in Sandy Cove, Michelle. It'll be great to start out already having a friend in our new home."

Michelle smiled. "I'm glad, too. I've just started making friends there myself."

"So anyway, back to my question. Do you have a

doctor you like?"

"Actually, I haven't tried to find one yet. There are lots of doctors in Portland, but that's quite a drive. I noticed there is a women's clinic on Main Street at the north end of town. They mention something about infertility specialists on the sign."

"I'll check it out. Thanks," Kelly added with a smile.

"Sure. Let me know if you find a doctor there you like."

The guys walked into the open door. "Thanks for a great afternoon," Ben said, shaking Steve's hand, and then pulling him into a brotherly hug.

"Our pleasure," Steve replied with a smile, taking Michelle by the hand.

"Well, I guess we'd better let you get some rest," Michelle added.

They said their goodnights and made arrangements to share an early breakfast in the coffee shop the following morning before Ben and Kelly hit the road again on the last leg of their journey and Steve took off for the airport.

Once Michelle and Steve were back in their own room, Michelle eagerly popped the news about Kelly. "She just said she might be pregnant, so nothing's definite yet. But I'll bet you anything she is."

"Guess they beat us to it," Steve said jokingly.

"Maybe they haven't," Michelle quipped in return, a glint in her eye.

"What do you mean by that?" Steve asked, suddenly getting serious.

"I wasn't going to tell you this yet, but I'm actually a week late."

"You are?"

"It's probably just from the stress of everything about my dad," Michelle added.

"Did you tell Kelly about this?"

"No, I thought I should talk to you first."

"Thanks." Steve looked concerned. "So you'd be okay with this if you are pregnant?"

"Yeah, I would. Would you?" Michelle asked.

"I guess. I just thought we were going to talk more about it before we made that decision," he added.

"I know. But it isn't like I planned this or anything. If I haven't started by Wednesday, I'll do a home pregnancy test."

"Wednesday. I won't even be here on Wednesday," Steve said as he fidgeted with his water bottle.

"I'll call you right after I get the results," she promised, touching his face with her hand and breathing a silent prayer. *Dear God, please let it be so. Let this be the start of a new life within me.*

CHAPTER NINE

It was Monday morning, and Michelle was dragging. Usually she and her grandfather had breakfast together. He would pray and read the Bible with her, answering any of her questions. She savored those times and could see how God was using this season in Bridgeport to draw her into the Bible while she had an able instructor by her side.

But last week Phil had come down with an upset stomach, and now Michelle woke up feeling lousy.

"Aren't you meeting Grandpa at the coffee shop in half an hour?" her mother asked, when she noticed Michelle had rolled back over in bed.

"I'm feeling lousy," she moaned, secretly wondering if this could be early morning sickness.

"What's wrong?"

"It's my stomach and my head," she said, not wanting to roll back over to face her mother. Every move brought a new wave of nausea.

"Sounds like you might have what Grandpa had," Sheila observed. "I'll call their room and tell him you won't be meeting him this morning."

"Thanks, Mom," was all she could manage before forcing herself out of bed to make a run for the bathroom.

Sheila called her parents and explained Michelle's condition. "What did she eat?" was the first thing out of Joan's mouth.

"I don't know," Sheila replied impatiently, convinced her mother's theories about food poisoning were for the birds.

"I'll send your father over to your room with that medicine we got at the pharmacy. It seemed to really help him. Maybe it'll work for Michelle."

"Thanks, Mom."

"Do you want me to stay with her while you go over to the hospital this morning?" Joan asked.

"If you wouldn't mind, that would be great. She'll probably insist she'll be fine by herself, but she's in the bathroom right now, and she sounds horrible."

"I'll just grab a newspaper and a cup of coffee and come sit with her. Your dad can go with you to your meeting with Dr. Jeffries," Joan added.

"Oh, I'm glad you mentioned that. I've got to finish writing down my questions before we go," Sheila said, mostly to herself.

"We'll be over there in about fifteen minutes."

"You don't have to rush, Mom. My appointment isn't for another hour and a half."

"I know, but maybe you'll get a chance to eat a decent breakfast with your father before you go to the hospital. He needs to build his energy back up."

"I'm fine, Mother," Sheila could hear her father say in the background. She thought it was comical the way he called his wife "Mother" when she tried to parent him.

"You need to eat," Joan bantered back. Then she turned her attention back to the phone and Sheila. "Make sure he eats something," she instructed her daughter.

"Yes, Mom," Sheila replied, glad her mother couldn't see her shaking her head. Just then Michelle came out of the bathroom looking pale.

"I've gotta go," Sheila said into the phone. "See you when you get here."

After she hung up, she helped Michelle get settled back into bed. "Your grandma's coming over to sit with you while I go to the hospital. I've got that meeting with Dr. Jeffries this morning, or I'd stay here with you myself."

Michelle barely nodded her head.

"You just try to rest, honey. Grandpa's bringing over the medicine he took the other day. It seemed to help him. You can try a little if you're up to it."

Another faint nod was the only response she got. Sheila got dressed and sat down at the table by the window. She wanted to finish her list of questions for the doctor.

Soon Phil arrived with the medicine. But Michelle was sleeping, and Sheila didn't want to wake her. Joan followed Phil a moment later, newspaper and coffee in hand. She shooed them out the door with specific instructions to get a decent breakfast.

Phil just smiled at his wife, gave her a peck on the cheek, and offered his arm to his grown daughter, ushering her out of the quiet room and across the parking lot to the familiar coffee shop.

"Well, it looks like I have some encouraging news for you, Mrs. Ackerman," Dr. Jeffries began.

Sheila and Phil scooted forward in their seats as they leaned toward the doctor's desk.

"Your husband has stabilized quite nicely, and I think we can prepare him for a transfer from the ICU to the neurology wing on the third floor. We haven't had any more episodes since the middle of last week," he added, referring to the "Code Blue" that had required emergency intervention. "His intracranial pressure is stable, his vitals are strong, his neuro checks show his pupils to be equal and reactive, and he's even able to respond to some verbal commands regarding opening and closing his eyes, squeezing the nurse's hand, or nodding his head. These are all remarkable improvements that I, frankly, did not expect to see in this case."

Phil closed his eyes for a brief moment, and Sheila could guess he was thanking God for the doctor's words. He reached over and squeezed her hand, and she returned his smile then looked back at the doctor.

"He's still not completely out of the woods, Mrs. Ackerman. But I'd say your husband has a decent chance of recovery. We won't know the extent of the permanent damage for some time yet, but I'm optimistic he'll continue to improve slowly over the next few weeks. I'm encouraged by the fact he is making eye contact and is able to respond to some of our 'yes' and 'no' questions by moving his head up and down or side to side. This is a big step for someone with his injuries. It indicates he is not only hearing us, but processing the information and coming up with a fitting response."

"But doctor," Sheila cut in, "why does he sometimes just close his eyes instead of answering? It always scares me. Like he might slip back into a coma."

"Your husband is likely having great difficulty managing all the stimulation around him. In brain injuries like this, light and sound sensitivity are greatly increased. He is also probably in a lot of pain. Severe headaches are common for years, maybe his whole life, after a trauma like this."

Sheila looked at her list of questions. She was really excited about the news of John's pending transfer out of the ICU, but she wanted to be sure he would be well taken care of on the neurology wing.

Dr. Jeffries answered all her questions as well as he could, qualifying many of his answers with the statement "It is difficult to predict many of the points of recovery in brain injury patients." He reassured her that moving him from the ICU to neurology would not compromise John's care.

"How long do you think it will be before he can be safely moved down to Orange County?" Sheila asked.

"I'd like to observe him for at least another couple of weeks. He's still very weak, and that would be quite a trip for him to make. You're probably looking at a minimum of two to three weeks to build up his strength and get him ready for rehab. That would be the best time to make the transfer to another facility."

"Thank you, doctor," Phil said, as their meeting was about to conclude. "We really appreciate all that you have done and are doing for John."

"I'm just glad it has turned out this well so far," Dr. Jeffries said as he stood. "John's a lucky man."

"He's in God's hand," Phil stated in return.

By the time Sheila and her father got back to the motel, Michelle was sitting up in bed, gingerly sipping some soda Joan had brought for her. She looked a little better and even managed a weak smile as she asked her mom to tell her what the doctor had said.

Sheila explained about the good news of the imminent transfer to the neurology wing and the possibility of being transferred to Orange County. Michelle and Joan both looked relieved.

"That's great news!" Joan exclaimed, a smile brightening her face.

Sheila beamed. Her heart was feeling so much lighter after the meeting with Dr. Jeffries. "Why don't you two take a break and get a snack or some lunch," she suggested to her parents. "I'll stay here with Michelle."

"I'll be fine, Mom," Michelle said, forcing a weak smile. "There's nothing you can do for me anyway. I just have to wait this thing out."

"Are you sure, Mimi?"

"Positive."

"Okay, then I guess I'll go back over to the hospital and sit with your dad for a while."

"Oh, and Mom," Michelle began again, "that's great news about Dad. Give him a kiss for me and tell him I miss him."

"I will, baby. You try to get some rest," Sheila added with love.

As soon as the room was empty, Michelle sank back down under the covers. She yearned for Steve's arms to cradle her as she sought to get comfortable. When he had left the day before to go back home, it was as if a part of her went with him, leaving a huge void inside. She hadn't noticed it as much the first time he left because she was so wrapped up in the crisis with her father. But this time she felt lonely and a little lost without him. *Maybe after Dad gets settled into his new room, I'll take a week and go back home. Especially if I'm pregnant,* she thought to herself.

CHAPTER TEN

The next day was a better one for Michelle. Her stomach had calmed down quite a bit, reducing the likelihood it had been morning sickness, and she was starting to think about the plan for her father's eventual move to a facility in Orange County. When that occurred, she'd be able to go back to Sandy Cove.

No one seemed to know the extent of the rehab possible for her father or the duration of his future stay in such a facility, but Michelle knew her mother would be able to manage once she was back in her own home and had Tim readily accessible in the neighborhood. Of course, Michelle would still plan to make frequent trips down to see her parents, but she would be spending most of her time back at home with Steve.

Funny how Sandy Cove had become home to her. When she left Orange County less than a year ago, she wondered if she'd ever feel settled in Oregon. Now she craved her house, her husband, and even her cat.

Although she felt quite a bit better than the day before, Michelle and her mom thought it was in her dad's best interests for her to stay clear of him another day or two, just in case whatever had attacked her was contagious. Even Joan, who persisted in her food poisoning theory, supported their decision "just in case."

While Phil and Joan accompanied Sheila over to the hospital, Michelle made her own escape from the motel, slipping out and taking a short walk down to the nearby pharmacy to purchase a home pregnancy kit. Her cycle had not started, so she still hoped she might be pregnant. She felt embarrassed and awkward as she placed the blue and white box on the moving belt of the checkout stand, but the boy at the register did not even blink as he rang up her total.

Back in her room, she quickly opened the package and read the directions. She would wait till morning to perform the test since it advised using a small amount of the first urine of the day as a sample. Tucking the test kit away, she eagerly looked forward to discovering the results. She and her grandfather were not yet back on schedule for their morning prayers and Bible readings, so she planned to sneak into the bathroom and take the test before her mother even woke up.

The rest of the day dragged for her. She spent most of it channel surfing and looking through the stack of magazines her grandmother had purchased for her the day before. Knowing that she was still in the process of decorating her house, Joan had spotted several magazines with articles on the subject of remodeling and interior design, and she thought they would give her granddaughter a diversion while she was stuck in the motel room.

Michelle carefully folded down the corners of the pages that interested her, underlining some of the suggestions and circling pictures she wanted to show her mom to get her opinions. Later she opened her laptop and started a search for more community college courses but ended up on a website of baby names. She began a list of her favorites and was startled when a knock on the door announced the arrival of her grandmother bearing a light dinner of chicken noodle soup and crackers.

"This should help settle your tummy, dear," Joan said with a smile as she set the tray on the table.

Michelle closed the laptop and walked over,

giving her grandmother a hug. "Thanks, Grandma."

"You're welcome, baby." Joan glanced over at the unmade bed and the magazines strewn across one side. "Do you want me to straighten up a little here while you eat?"

"No. You just sit down and relax. Tell me about Dad. How's he doing?" she asked as she started sipping the soup and munching on a cracker.

"They finally transferred him to neurology around 3:45," Joan began. "We were waiting for the doctor to come by and sign the papers most of the day, but he got caught in an emergency surgery. Your dad looks great, Michelle," she added, patting her hand.

"So how does the neurology wing seem?" Michelle asked.

"I think it will be fine. The nurses are very nice. Guess who we saw there?"

"Who?"

"Sherrene. She's substituting for one of the regular night nurses. Isn't it wonderful how the Lord arranged that? She's such a sweet little gal, and your father already knows her, so it will make his first night in a new room easier."

"That's great, Grandma. Mom must be relieved."

"She was so glad to see him get out of the ICU. We all were." Joan looked into her granddaughter's eyes and smiled. "It's a sign, Michelle. Your dad's going to get well, I just know it."

"I love you, Grandma," Michelle replied with a hug. "You always look at things so positively."

"I love you, too, Mimi. I guess I've just learned over the years that it always helps to look on the bright side. When you've been through as much as I have, you begin to realize that no matter how bleak a situation looks, God's still in control. He can turn around even the most hopeless circumstances and bring blessings where they are least expected."

"I'm beginning to get that, Grandma. Grandpa's helping me start to go through the Bible. What's really interesting to me is how all those stories, that I used to love to listen to when I was little, are not seeming so much like stories anymore." Struggling to explain herself, she asked, "Know what I mean? Like I'm finally starting to get it."

Joan smiled broadly. "Yes, dear, you are. I think most children love to listen to Bible stories right along with all the other imaginary stories they read and listen to. Then one day that changes, and they realize they either have to accept those stories as truth or disregard them."

"Right. I'm really trying to understand everything Grandpa says, and I'm trying to pray a lot more. But I still have tons of questions."

"There's nothing wrong with questions, Michelle. This time you have with your grandfather is no coincidence in God's eyes. He knew all your questions before they even surfaced, and He's provided you with someone who can help you find the answers."

"That makes it almost sound like God planned for Dad to be here in the hospital, like He's partly responsible for Dad's injury so I could re-examine my beliefs and spend some time with Grandpa." Michelle wasn't sure she liked that idea.

"You know, honey, I can't fully explain all of God's role in this crisis with your father, but I do know His ways are always based on love. It would never be God's intent to set out to destroy your dad, but I believe He allowed this event to occur because He had a plan to turn it around for good."

"That reminds me of a verse Grandpa showed me the other day from the book of Romans," she commented.

"Romans 8:28," Joan replied, picking up the Bible

on the nightstand and flipping it open to the page with that verse. She handed it to Michelle, who read it over and nodded.

"Yep. That's the one. How do you guys know where all these verses are?" she asked with amazement.

"It's from spending lots and lots of time reading and studying His word. If you keep up with your own reading, you'll start to remember the passages that mean something special to you."

Michelle nodded, but felt a little skeptical.

"You need to get involved with a good, Bible-teaching church, Michelle. You'll be surprised how much you can learn in a short time. The more you study, the more you'll want to know. Believe me, it takes a lifetime to even scratch the surface of all the treasures in this book."

"I know what you mean. Sometimes I think I'll never even get through the gospel of John," she said with a twinge of impatience.

"I understand how you feel, sweetheart. When I first accepted the Lord into my heart and started studying the scriptures, I felt totally overwhelmed and frustrated. 'I'll never get through all this,' I used to say to myself, as I would thumb through the Old and New Testaments.

"Then God changed my perspective. He got me thinking about all the great books I had read and loved and about how disappointed I would be when each one ended and the story was over. I'd really miss the characters and reading about their lives. He helped me realize that wouldn't happen with the Bible because there is always more to read, study, and learn. The same verses I read two years ago can take on new and deeper meaning to me when I read them today. This is the only good book that never ends," she concluded with a smile.

"You'd make a great saleswoman, Grandma," Michelle teased.

"Humph!" Joan exclaimed, shaking her head. "You just think about what I said, sweetheart. The Bible will never disappoint you. Just keep digging and see what you discover."

"I will. Grandpa's got me hooked," she promised.

"Good. Now finish your soup before it gets cold," Joan replied.

On Wednesday morning, Michelle awoke before dawn. The bedside clock read 5:40. Sheila was sleeping soundly and did not stir as Michelle eased herself out of bed and snuck into the bathroom. Retrieving the pregnancy test from her cosmetic bag, she quickly reread the directions. Within minutes she was sitting on the side of the bathtub reading the results. Negative.

She picked up the insert and reread it, making sure she had followed all the directions correctly. In her heart, she hoped she'd taken the test too soon, but according to the information in the printout her hormone levels should be high enough by this time. Sighing, she carefully packed the materials away in the box and deposited it in the bathroom wastebasket under some other trash, so her mom wouldn't see the package.

After disposing of it, she sat there for a few moments feeling sad and disappointed. Even though she and Steve weren't planning on starting a family until she finished school, she felt unexplainably empty, almost as if she had lost a baby that never even existed. Twisting a strand of hair at the nape of her neck, she thought about her promise to call Steve with the results.

"We're just going to have to change our plans," she whispered to herself. Then she thought to pray. She poured out her heart to God, telling Him the depth of her new dream to be a mom and how seeing the newborns at the hospital had sparked a hope for good to come out of this trauma with her father.

Tears flowed freely as she prayed. Then a peace settled over her and she crept quietly back to bed.

CHAPTER ELEVEN

Steve was sitting at his desk drumming his pencil and staring at the clock. It was getting close to noon, and he still hadn't heard from Michelle. What was taking her? She'd told him she'd be doing the test early in the morning and would call him with the results. He thought she would call before he left for work, but by 8:15 he knew he had to get to the office and start working on the stack of paperwork awaiting him. In a last ditch idea, he thought about calling her himself, but they'd agreed she'd call when her mom was not around.

That must be the problem. For some reason, Michelle couldn't get to a phone by herself. Steve allowed his mind to wander, imagining her call and how he would respond when she told him the results were positive. Over the past few days, he'd gotten used to the idea and was even beginning to get a little excited.

His thoughts were interrupted by a buzz on the intercom. "Michelle's on the phone," his secretary announced.

Steve almost knocked over his coffee cup as he grabbed for the receiver. "Hi, babe."

"Hi, honey." Michelle sounded tired.

"Well?" Steve asked, trying to contain his curiosity.

"Negative." Then the phone was silent.

Steve thought he heard her crying. "Are you okay?" he asked tentatively, concern for his wife pushing aside his feelings of disappointment over the test results.

"No, not really." She sobbed as a floodgate of emotions overtook her.

Steve felt totally helpless. He yearned to take his wife in his arms and hold her, to tell her everything would be all right. But 500 miles separated them, and all he could do was to try to talk her through it.

"I'm sorry, Michelle," he offered feebly. No answer but her sniffling. "We'll have a baby. Don't worry, honey."

"It's not just the baby," she finally managed to say. "It's everything. My dad, missing you and Max, not being able to get into the university..."

"I know. I wish I could be there with you. God will get us through. He will."

"It just seems like nothing's ever going to be right or normal again."

"Maybe you need to come home for a week or so," Steve suggested.

"I've been thinking that myself."

"Talk to your mom. She'll understand, babe. She knows how hard it's been on you to see your dad like this and to be away from home so long."

"Okay. I guess you're right. I'll try to talk to her this afternoon. She's at the hospital right now, but we're supposed to have lunch together. We spent the morning getting Dad settled in his new room, so that's why I couldn't call you earlier. Besides, I wasn't looking forward to telling you I'm not pregnant, especially after how excited you've been sounding about it lately."

"Listen, Michelle. I'd have been thrilled if you were pregnant, but I don't want you feeling bad for me in the midst of all the other things on your mind. It's not like we'd been planning for a baby at this time anyway. Besides, like I said before, we'll have fun trying now."

"Funny, Steve." Her voice sounded lighter, and

Steve could imagine a small smile forming on her face.

"I'll call you tonight around 8:30, okay? We'll talk about getting you home for a while."

"Okay. Love you." Hanging up the phone, Steve let out a deep sigh.

Michelle flipped her phone shut and set it in the pocket of her purse. She twisted her hair as she planned out her talk with her mother. Tim was supposed to be back on Saturday with the mail, so it would be a good time to take off for a week and fly home. Her dad seemed comfortable in his new room. Hopefully he'd soon be ready for rehab and a transfer down to Orange County.

Locking the motel door, she headed across the parking lot to meet her mother at the coffee shop. She saw a woman just a little older than herself, being helped by her husband out of the front seat of a car. She looked like she was about seven or eight months pregnant, and although she did look a little awkward and tired, her face was glowing. A sudden sorrow engulfed Michelle. *What's wrong with me? Why is this suddenly such a big deal to me?*

Her mom was waiting for her in a corner booth, and Michelle wove her way through the familiar path to the table.

"Hi, Michelle," a young waitress called out from behind the counter as she poured coffee for a customer.

"Hi Becky," Michelle replied with a smile. This place was getting to be almost like a home away from home, with the hostesses, waitresses, and even busboys learning their names.

"She's such a sweet girl," Sheila commented, as she slipped into the booth.

"Yeah, she is. Everyone who works here is so friendly," Michelle agreed.

They didn't even have to look at the menu before ordering. While they waited for their food, Michelle decided to approach her mother on returning home for a week or so.

"I think that's a great idea, Mimi. Your dad is doing so well, and Tim will be back on Saturday for at least a few days. When you come back, I'm going to try to get Grandma and Grandpa to go home for a while. They need the rest and you know how Grandma is about her garden. Plus Grandpa is eager to get together with his Bible study group."

Michelle was relieved her mom understood and didn't have any hesitations about her going home. They agreed that Saturday would be the best day, and Tim could take her to the airport.

After lunch, Michelle went back to their room before returning to the hospital. She called the airline, reserving an afternoon flight. That way she and Steve could even have a little date night, maybe dinner out someplace quiet and romantic. She also called the clinic in Sandy Cove and made an appointment for the following week. Michelle wanted to find out why her period was so late and get more information about prenatal care.

Even though Steve had told her he'd call that night, Michelle decided to call him back herself right away. She caught him on the way out the door to a meeting and gave him the information about her flight and when to pick her up. He sounded elated, and she could hardly wait for Saturday.

Friday night Michelle stayed at the hospital later than usual. She knew her dad could sense something was different with her, and she wanted to explain to him about her return to Sandy Cove. He'd been asleep most of the afternoon, but he seemed to perk up for a while in the evening. Scooting her chair right up against the bed, she took his hand. He turned his head slowly toward her.

"Daddy," she began, groping for words. "I've got something to tell you."

John nodded his head up and down in what Michelle could tell was a laborious process of concentration.

"I'm going back to Oregon tomorrow for a short time. I miss Steve, and I need to get some things taken care of at home," she explained as she rubbed his hand between hers.

John studied her intently.

"I won't be gone long, Dad. Promise. I'll be back in a week, maybe sooner," she added, hoping to boost his spirits.

John gazed into his daughter's eyes. Then a tiny smile flickered for an instant on his lips. Michelle beamed in response. This newfound ability to smile back at them had just begun yesterday. Not only did it stand as more evidence of his improvement, but it also showed an element of emotional healing and contact.

"I love you, Daddy," Michelle said bending over and giving him a hug. She startled slightly when she felt his right hand come up haltingly and press against her back in return. He was actually hugging her back the best he could with the only functioning limb he had. Up until that moment, the most they had gotten from him was a squeeze of the hand. Now his arm had worked to embrace his daughter. Michelle didn't want to move. Her heart was pounding with joy and excitement. She held on for a moment longer and then felt his hand slip off of her back and fall back down onto the bed.

"You're telling me you love me, too, aren't you, Dad?" she said more as an observation than as a question.

John had only spoken one word since he was admitted to the hospital with a self-inflicted bullet wound.

Michelle recalled the decision the family had to make the first few days about whether or not to put her father on "no code." While they had been debating that decision, John had mumbled one word – Jesus. It was so out of character for him -- an avowed agnostic. But Michelle and her family believed it had to do with her grandfather's prayers at her dad's bedside. Since then, John had been silent. But the decision to keep him on any necessary life support was made based on this sign indicating he might speak again.

Another smile flickered momentarily on John's face. Then he took one last look at Michelle and closed his eyes. Exhaustion etched lines on his forehead.

The nurses had explained to them that even focusing his eyes on theirs required tremendous effort and not to expect too much too soon. But Michelle had witnessed another miracle, and she was overflowing with thanksgiving. Smoothing her father's sheets and blanket, she kissed him on the forehead and turned off the light, quietly slipping out of the room.

She took her usual detour out of the hospital, stopping at the gift shop, and going over to her favorite corner to check on the new baby items. A woman about her mom's age was holding up a precious little pink sleep sack with a ruffled bottom.

"That is so cute!" Michelle exclaimed.

The woman turned to her with a broad smile filling her face. "It's for my granddaughter," she said with pride.

"Is this your first?" Michelle asked.

"Yes, and we are so thankful. We weren't sure our daughter would be able to have kids. She postponed parenthood for quite a while after they got married because she was trying to get herself established in broadcast journalism. Then when they started trying for a baby, she couldn't get pregnant."

"Scary."

"Yeah. Thank heavens for modern medicine," the woman said as she picked up a matching pink receiving blanket. "They had to go through quite a bit of infertility procedures to get little Gracie."

"That must have been really hard."

The woman nodded. "Yes, but well worth it." She paused and then asked, "Do you have any children?"

"Not yet."

She looked into Michelle's eyes. "Don't wait too long. There's nothing like the joy of being a mom. I'm so glad it ended up working out for our daughter."

"Me, too," Michelle replied. "Congratulations." As she turned to leave, she remembered her conversation with her own mother and the tears of joy she'd seen in her mom's eyes when they'd talked about Michelle having a baby of her own.

CHAPTER TWELVE

Six days later Sandy Cove Women's Fertility Clinic

Michelle sat on the edge of the examining table talking to Dr. Foster. "So you're saying this kind of thing is normal?"

"Yes. A woman's cycle can easily be affected by stress, and from what you've told me, you've been through quite a lot this month. Since you still haven't started your period, and since you and your husband are interested in pursuing conception at this time, we could 'jump start' your system a little by putting you on a mild fertility pill if you'd like. It will put you back on a regular cycle and help you predict the most fertile part of your cycle. The pill I'd recommend is called Clomid. In low doses, it has few side effects.

"Well, I would like to get back to a normal cycle. I guess birth control pills would do that, too, but. . ."

"But since you're wanting to conceive, that wouldn't be your first choice," Dr. Foster finished Michelle's thought with an understanding smile. "I know it seems a little unusual for me to be offering you infertility medication at this early juncture, but it is the best alternative to birth control pills for regulating your cycle. And like I said, it will also help you determine your most fertile day or two of the month. The combination of accurate timing and the Clomid will give you a 75%

success rate."

Michelle tried to process all that information, but her puzzled expression communicated her need for a simplified summary.

"In other words, Michelle, if you use the Clomid for the next three months and follow the schedule I explained to you, you should conceive. Three months from now would be January. That would mean an October baby at the latest."

Now she nodded her head in understanding. "Sounds good to me."

"Okay. I'll just write up the prescription while you get dressed, and I'll also give you some literature on prenatal vitamins. Let's get you started on those right away."

"I'm really glad I came to see you today, Dr. Foster. And thanks for the prescription. I'd hate to have to wait much longer to get my cycle back in gear."

"You know, Michelle, these days most couples just don't want to wait months and months to conceive once they decide they are ready to have a baby. We are the instant generation, and technology has allowed us to expedite many of these processes."

Michelle just nodded her head in agreement.

"You get dressed and I'll meet you out by the front desk with your prescription." She left the examining room, and Michelle quickly dressed. It was obvious by the crowd in the waiting room that Dr. Foster had a busy morning ahead of her.

"Thanks again," she said as she took the prescription form and the vitamin information from her.

"You're welcome, Michelle. I'll look forward to hearing back from you sometime in the next three months," she added with a wink.

Michelle was just getting back into her car after filling the prescription at the pharmacy in Sandy Cove when a motorcycle pulled up beside her.

"Hey there, stranger," Trevor said with a pearly smile. "Monica told me you were back in town. We've missed you at class."

"Hi Trevor." Michelle's heart was racing. Why did this guy always have this adrenaline rush effect on her? "I'm only here for a week, then I've got to go back to be with my dad."

"How's he doing? I've been thinking about him a lot. Monica tries to keep me filled in." He seemed genuinely concerned.

"Well, I don't know what you heard last, but he's making eye contact and nodding his head for 'yes' and shaking it for 'no'. Before I left, he actually lifted his right hand and put it on my back to hug me." Michelle's eyes sparkled as she thought about all the miracles she had already seen with her father. Especially since Dr. Jeffries hadn't even expected him to survive.

"That's great, Michelle. Maybe those meditations helped."

"I think it was my grandparents' prayers," Michelle said, suddenly feeling awkward.

"Meditation, prayer, whatever. It's great that he's making progress," Trevor replied trying to allay her uneasiness.

She paused, and then started to reach for the door handle.

"Hey, before you go, can we set up a time to have coffee or something before you leave town again?"

"Maybe Thursday morning. Steve has a big meeting, so he'll be leaving for work early. How about the

Coffee Stop around 9:30 or 10:00."

"Sounds good. See you Thursday at 9:30." Trevor said with a grin; then he started his motorcycle and headed out of the parking lot.

"She said I could start taking them tonight," Michelle explained as she went over her doctor's appointment with Steve.

"Are you sure you're comfortable with all this? I mean it seems a little strange to start out with fertility pills," he said apprehensively.

"According to Dr. Foster, these will help reestablish a regular cycle and also help predict fertile periods of the month. She says they're really mild."

"But didn't she say something about twins?" He liked the idea of having a baby, but he wasn't sure he was ready for that.

"Very rare. She did say we should conceive within three months if I take these and we follow her schedule." Michelle held up the prescription and her chart.

"Well, I still think this is a little weird. We haven't even had time to really pray about this together. Don't you think when it's God's timing, it will happen?" Steve asked.

"Are you saying God might not want us to have a baby?"

"No. I'm just saying we want His timing."

"What would be wrong with this timing?" she asked defensively.

"Maybe nothing. But it seems a little premature to jump into all this fertility drug stuff."

Michelle was quiet, as she looked down at the package in her hand. Steve could tell she was upset. "I'm not saying I don't want a baby, Michelle. You understand that, right?"

"I don't know what I understand right now. It just sounded right when Dr. Foster recommended this." Michelle tossed the bag onto the kitchen table. She sank down into one of the chairs and could feel the tears welling up in her eyes. Maybe Steve was right. Maybe they should just wait and pray about it.

Steve's heart melted as he saw her tearful expression. "Okay babe. Let's go ahead and try it." He bent to kiss her.

Michelle stood and wrapped her arms around him. "I know it's hard for you to understand all this, but it's something that is really important to me right now. This next year is going to be so difficult for my parents and for Tim and me. A new baby in the family would be something special for us all to look forward to."

Steve nodded, drawing her up against his chest and kissing her forehead. Michelle was so happy to be home with him after the long separation in Bridgeport. Melting into his kiss, she felt almost euphoric thinking about her love for him and their new plan to have a baby. As they walked out of the kitchen and headed up to bed, she grabbed the prescription off the counter. Tonight would begin the three-month project!

Monica was dumb-founded as she sat across from Michelle trying to absorb all she was hearing. Though her head was a bit rattled, she was open and interested. She nodded frequently, encouraging her friend to continue.

"So anyway, Monica, I really think there is a lot more to the Bible than Trevor or Starla realize. It's not just some history book, or the writings of some interesting prophets. I'm really beginning to believe it was inspired by God Himself."

"But didn't Trevor say that God is the Universal Consciousness? Doesn't that mean He inspired all the writings of all the prophets, including Buddha, Mohammed, and all those other guys we've discussed?"

"That's what Trevor thinks. But I don't see it that way now. It's hard to explain, but if you could spend some time with someone like my grandfather, you'd know God is not some impersonal force. He is like a person, only bigger. More powerful, but very loving." It seemed she was grasping for words.

Monica didn't know what to think. "You think I'm nuts, don't you?" Michelle continued. "No. Not nuts. I'm just not sure I see it that way. God, I mean."

She was really confused now. Here she had gotten settled into their personal evolution class and was beginning to make sense of the universe, when Michelle threw this loop at her. Did all this mean Michelle wouldn't be going to class with her anymore? Would their friendship deteriorate? She decided to find out. "So does this mean you won't be taking Trevor's class anymore?"

"Probably not. It just seems so off from what I've been studying with my grandpa. I really think Christianity is more for me than most of the New Age stuff."

Monica was quiet. That was a first. "Well, I hope we are still going to be friends," she said softly, thinking about how their friendship had been forged through their yoga and personal evolution classes.

"Are you kidding? Of course we'll be friends." Michelle scooted around the booth and hugged her.

"All this heavy talk is making me hungry," she said with a grin.

"Me, too," Michelle replied. They both eyed the dessert menu in the clear plastic holder at the edge of the table. "Let's order something totally oinky," she said with a twinkle in her eye.

"Good idea." Monica smiled, relaxing and enjoying their usual camaraderie.

Steve had a light schedule on Wednesday, so Kelly and Ben invited Michelle and him to come over for dinner. They were eager to show them their house. Steve promised Michelle the evening would be very casual, explaining that Ben was rarely caught in anything other than jeans and a T-shirt, so she just put on her pale yellow sweatshirt with her jeans and surprised Steve by bringing a pair of matching yellow hi-top tennis shoes out of the closet. "Where'd those come from?" he asked.

"I got them at a discount store in Bridgeport," Michelle replied, slipping them on and lacing them up.

"Cute," Steve said approvingly.

"Thanks," she replied, rising from the edge of the bed and giving him a kiss. Steve wasn't about to let her get away with a little peck. He wrapped his arms around her and kissed her back.

"Hey, buddy -- we're supposed to be out of here," she reminded him.

Not yet releasing her from the embrace, he put his finger under her chin and looked into her eyes.

"What? Is there something wrong?" she asked.

"No. It's just that I'm going to miss you when you go back to Bridgeport."

"Hey," she began, pulling back from him a little, "don't forget our 'schedule'," she said, referring to the chart the doctor had given her. "I figure I'll have to see you again the following weekend," she added with a glint in her eye. "And for the next five days after that."

"So you're coming back next weekend?"

"If we can afford it," she said hopefully.

"No problem," Steve said, winking at her and drawing her back into another kiss. Michelle knew they were going to be late, but she didn't resist.

Ben and Kelly greeted them at the front door. Before they even got inside, Michelle could smell the fragrance of garlic wafting from the kitchen. "Something smells delicious," she remarked, returning Kelly's hug.

"Kelly made her special lemon-garlic chicken. You'll love it," Ben promised, gesturing them in.

Immediately Michelle was impressed with Kelly's decorating. It was clear they had very little money to work with, but Kelly had used her innovative ideas to begin decorating their house with common objects such as orange crates and old milk cans. Homemade decorative wreaths and birdhouses gave the living area a homey and cozy feel.

"Your house is adorable," Michelle exclaimed.

"Gee, thanks," Ben replied in a squeaky lady voice.

Kelly swatted him playfully and explained, "Ben thinks I overdo the decorating. He'd be happy with a plain sofa and coffee table and nothing on the walls."

Ben just grinned and shook his head. "It's a girl thing, I guess," he said to Steve as he led him into the kitchen. "Want some chips and salsa?"

"Sounds good," Steve replied, happy to see that Michelle and Kelly were already engaged in a conversation.

While the girls talked decorating, the guys discussed the new church and Ben's plans to reach out to the community. He shared about the Bible study he hoped to begin at the beginning of the month. "I really want to start before the holidays."

"Good idea. Lots of people get hungry for spiritual things this time of year. They see the commercialism and get turned off."

"My thoughts exactly," Ben replied. "I just hope people will be willing to fit it into their busy schedules."

"Some will; others may join in January. Michelle and I will be here whenever she's in town. I'll come by myself when she's not. Also, I asked my partner at the firm, Roger, and he said he'd like to give it a try. He'll probably bring his wife too, if they can get a sitter."

"Great! Hey, you should be my P.R. guy," Ben added with a smile.

"Seriously, Ben, if you need any fliers copied or anything, just give them to me and I'll take care of it. No use spending a lot of money on copying costs when I've got the equipment at the office. Roger won't mind. The secretary can run them off."

"Hey, thanks. That would be great. I've actually got one I wanted you to look at tonight while you're here." Ben stood up from the kitchen table where they had been munching on chips and salsa. "Be right back."

Kelly and Michelle came into the kitchen while he was gone. "Don't eat too many of those," Michelle warned Steve. "You'll ruin your appetite for that yummy smelling chicken."

"Yes, Mother," Steve said with a sly grin. Michelle blushed as she thought about the double meaning of his remark. Soon she might really be someone's mother. A wave of nervousness and excitement rolled over her.

"Speaking of 'mother'," Ben said as he reentered the room, "Kelly's got a surprise for you."

Kelly's expression told it all. She looked just like Michelle felt.

"You're pregnant?" Michelle asked excitedly.

"Seven weeks," Kelly replied with a smile.

"That's great!" Michelle replied. "I'm so excited for you guys." She reached out her arms to hug Kelly and pretty soon everyone was hugging each other as congratulations flowed from Steve and Michelle to their friends.

Michelle couldn't help imagining what it would be like when she could tell Kelly and Ben that she, too, was expecting a baby.

CHAPTER THIRTEEN

Trevor stared at Michelle as he chewed on his toothpick. Sitting across from him at the Coffee Stop, she was giving a blow-by-blow description of her father's treatment and progress. But Trevor could not hear half of what she was saying. His mind kept wandering to his persistent fantasies, and he was undressing her in his imagination, when she abruptly stopped talking.

"Are you listening, Trevor?" she asked with an expression of doubt mixed with embarrassment.

"Uh, yeah. You were just saying something about how they moved your dad out of the ICU."

"That was five minutes ago. Haven't you heard anything since then?"

"Hmmm," he hummed as he searched his brain for some clues to the rest of the conversation. "Guess I'm busted," he finally admitted, shrugging his shoulders and then tossing one of those irresistible boyish grins her way.

"This must be pretty boring for you," Michelle replied.

"It's not that. Really. I just get lost in your smile sometimes," Trevor confessed. "I love the way your eyes sparkle, and that little dimple on your right cheek always distracts me. Guess you're just too beautiful for your own good."

"Very funny. Why don't you talk for a while?" She looked down at her half-eaten Danish and cold cup of coffee.

"Okay. Let's see. I've been working on my thesis, and I should be finished by January," Trevor began as he pulled his thoughts together. "I'd like you to read it sometime."

"What's it on?" Michelle asked.

"It's on exploring the spiritual dimensions of anxiety disorders and depression. I've been incorporating a lot of the material we've been covering in our classes. You'd be able to appreciate how they can be used in therapy."

"Sounds interesting. When do I get to read it?" she asked, biting into her apricot pastry.

"Anytime. I'd be happy to show you what I've got so far and get your input," he said enthusiastically.

"Maybe I could take a copy back to Bridgeport. It gets a little boring in the evenings at the motel. I could read through it before I go to sleep at night."

Trevor's mind instantly pictured Michelle sitting in bed, propped up against a pillow, all alone. His body responded to the image, and he was momentarily out of the conversation again.

"Hello?" Michelle waved her hand in front of his eyes to get his attention.

He snapped back to the present. "Sorry about that. My mind wandered for just a second."

"Are you feeling okay?"

"Yeah. I'm fine. Anyway, so what were you saying?"

"I was saying I could read it while I'm in Bridgeport."

"Right. Good idea. I'll make a copy. When are you leaving again?"

"I'll be going back down there on Sunday and then coming back up here the following weekend."

"You're really raking in the frequent flyer miles,

aren't you?"

"Steve and I have some business to attend to the following weekend." Michelle smiled mysteriously. "And hopefully in a few more weeks my dad will be moved to a rehab facility in Orange County. Then I'll only go down once a month or so," she added.

"I see. Well if you'd like to take my thesis down to Bridgeport with you, I guess we'll just have to meet again tomorrow," Trevor replied with mock aggravation.

"I've been thinking of dropping by to say hi to Starla sometime tomorrow. Maybe you could just leave it with her," Michelle suggested.

"I'd really like to go over some of it with you when I give it to you," he said, groping for reasons to see her again.

"Okay. Give me a call in the morning, and I'll have a better idea what time I'll be going over there."

"Sounds like a plan. I really hope you'll like it," he added, imagining how his thesis would help draw Michelle back into the ideas of higher consciousness that she seemed to have lost during her time in Bridgeport. He was glad her stay there would soon be over. Obviously her grandparents were having a negative impact on all the progress she'd made in his classes.

Before she knew it, Sunday had arrived, and Michelle was packing her bags to head back to Bridgeport. The meeting with Starla and Trevor in the bookstore left her feeling a little uneasy. Though they outwardly appeared to be supportive of her exploration of Christianity, an undercurrent of patient anticipation communicated they believed she would soon abandon such a backward belief system and return to their "broader perspective" on spirituality.

How would her relationships in Sandy Cove be affected by her newfound faith? It seemed clear that her closest friendships, Monica, Trevor, and Starla all intended to remain friends. But would that hold true if Michelle continued to deepen her relationship with Jesus? Or would they fall by the wayside? At least she knew she had Kelly now. "Thank you, God," she whispered.

"What did you say?" Steve asked, walking into the bedroom from the hall.

"I was just thanking God for bringing Kelly and Ben to Sandy Cove," she explained.

Steve smiled and nodded. "What's all that paperwork you're packing?" he asked, pointing to the stack of pages she was placing on top of her clothes in the suitcase.

"It's Trevor's thesis."

"What thesis?" his voice concerned.

"His master's thesis. He's getting a marriage and family counseling license, and he needs a master's degree before he starts his internship," she explained, busying herself with her packing.

"So when did you see him?" he asked, trying to sound casual.

"Thursday morning. We had coffee together." She felt uneasy, not sure how he would respond.

"Since when are the two of you 'coffee partners'?" Steve asked with an edge to his voice.

"What's that supposed to mean?"

"I don't know. Never mind."

Michelle sighed. She wished she felt flattered by his apparent jealousy, but instead it made her uneasy and a little guilty. What was she supposed to do about Trevor? Pretend that he didn't exist? Ignore his requests to get together for coffee? She had so few friends in Sandy Cove, and she still couldn't shake the memory of how he had helped her understand her nightmares and resolve her fears.

"I don't want to leave on a bad note, Steve. If you're uncomfortable with me having coffee with Trevor, I won't do it again. He's really only a friend."

"Don't worry about it, babe. I trust you." He tried to sound reassuring as he walked around the bed and embraced her. "I'm sure gonna miss you this week," he added with a sigh.

"Me too. But at least we know we'll be together next weekend again."

"Yeah. This baby making project is paying off in more ways than one," he said with a wink.

After one more kiss, they pulled apart, knowing it was time to hit the road and get her to the airport. Before leaving, she carried Max down the stairs, giving him instructions on how to take care of Steve while she was gone. Then feeding him his favorite liver delight, she left him in the kitchen chomping away.

"Next time Michelle comes home, let's give her this book," Starla suggested, handing Trevor a copy of *My Path to Enlightenment Through Jesus*.

"Perfect."

"This guy really knows how to draw from scriptures and show the broader picture," Starla added, remembering when she'd heard the author speak at one of their conventions. "Hopefully his writings will be the bridge she needs to see the wisdom of incorporating what she has learned from her grandfather with what she has been learning from us."

Trevor nodded, but he didn't seem convinced. "Michelle's a bright girl, Trevor. Give her a chance. She'll figure it out. In the meantime, we need to keep meditating, tapping into the higher powers to reach her even when she's not with us."

Trevor agreed. That was something he could do whenever he thought about Michelle, which was more often than he'd like to admit.

Tim met Michelle at the airport in Bridgeport and filled her in on the latest news about their father. John had experienced a rather severe seizure, which required modification of his medication levels, but he had stabilized again quickly. The only other concern was potential problems with pneumonia if they couldn't get him moving more. The nurses had begun sitting him up in bed for part of each day, and he was having some physical therapy, but he seemed to tire quickly. His neurological responses continued to improve, although his interaction was still very limited, and he had not regained movement in his left limbs.

"So are they still thinking about moving him into a rehab facility soon?" Michelle asked hopefully.

"Yeah. After the seizure they seemed worried, but once they changed the levels of his meds, he was fine again. They'll probably move him in three or four more weeks."

"That sounds like what they were saying when I left."

"We just have to hope he doesn't get pneumonia. Otherwise, he'll definitely have to stay here longer," he warned.

"Don't those antibiotics they've been giving him prevent him from getting that?" she asked, realizing she was probably asking the wrong person.

"I don't know, 'Shell. I guess there's no guarantee, or they wouldn't be worried about it. Seems like the big deal is getting him upright more. Mom will be able to explain it to you better."

It was clear from his voice that Tim was ready to head back home. A week was more than he could take. Michelle felt a little guilty for taking off, knowing it had put some of the burden back on her brother. Brushing that thought aside, she reminded herself he had the life of a carefree bachelor most of the time. A little bit of responsibility wouldn't kill him. She was a little concerned about his job though. He had a hard enough time holding down a job, without taking lots of time off to be up in Bridgeport.

"How's work going?" she asked him tentatively.

"Slow. That's why they let me come up here this week."

At least he still has the job, she thought. As soon as they got to the motel, Michelle put her bags in her room and headed over to see her father. She knew she'd find her mom there, too. "Are Grandma and Grandpa with Mom?"

"Didn't you know?" Tim seemed surprised.

"Know what?"

"They went home on Wednesday. That's why I stayed for the rest of the week until you got back."

"I kind of thought they might need a break. I'm surprised Mom didn't say anything about it to me when we talked on the phone."

"She probably didn't want you to worry or change your mind and come back sooner." Tim held onto her arm as they crossed the busy highway, and Michelle felt a wave of warm affection wash over her. Tim was actually acting like a gentleman -- toward his sister no less.

She almost started to head toward the ICU, when Tim redirected her toward the corridor leading to neurology. "Auto pilot," she said apologetically.

"I know. I could navigate this place with my eyes closed," he replied.

Sheila looked up at them and smiled as they entered the room. John's bed was elevated at the head, and he looked directly at Michelle and Tim.

"Hi, Dad," Michelle said enthusiastically. John tried to smile. One side of his mouth turned up slightly.

Sheila stood and embraced her daughter. "It's good to have you back, Mimi."

Michelle hugged her mom back. "Dad looks great," she said.

"He's improving every day. They sit him up like this now."

"Tim was telling me that." She turned her attention to her father. "You'll be out of this bed in no time," she said with a smile as she reached out and squeezed his hand.

John nodded his head and smiled weakly.

CHAPTER FOURTEEN

The next few weeks were a blur for Michelle as she tried to juggle two lives -- one at her father's bedside, and the other focusing on her dream of starting a family with Steve. The unsettled feeling of living half her life in a motel in Bridgeport and the other half at home in Sandy Cove took its toll on her.

"You look exhausted," her mom commented one morning.

"I am, Mom," she admitted, her shoulders dropping as she let out a big sigh.

"Well, I have some good news for you," Sheila said with a smile.

"What?"

"They're moving your father back to Orange County on Thursday."

Michelle couldn't believe she was really hearing this. After all the trauma and waiting they had been through since her father's "accident," he was finally stable enough to begin rehab. "Oh, Mom," she said, her eyes filling with tears.

Sheila held out her arms and they embraced. "God is good," she said softly.

"Yes, He is," Michelle's voice revealed her relief. Her anthropology 106 course would be starting the following week, and she was glad she wouldn't have to drop it.

"Sit down with me and I'll show you the brochure

about the facility they are transferring him to," Sheila said as she led her over to the little table by the window.

They sat together and poured over the information. It looked good to Michelle. All the rooms had views of either gardens or courtyards. A large gymnasium overflowed with physical therapy machines and equipment as well as an Olympic size pool for water therapies. It was difficult to imagine her formerly strong, independent father in such a facility, but she was thankful he was alive, improving and had such a well-equipped rehab option.

"It looks great, Mom," she said enthusiastically. "How long will he be staying there?"

"The doctors couldn't give me an exact time frame. They said the plan is for him to stay as long as he continues to progress. When he plateaus, they send him home."

"Do they think he'll be able to walk again?"

"Dr. Jeffries seems guardedly optimistic about it. He explained to me about how they train brain cells that aren't damaged to take over for the ones that are. Your father may have a limp and require a cane for the rest of his life, but we are hoping and praying he will be able to regain his ability to walk." Sheila replied.

"We'll keep praying for him, too. He'll make it, Mom," she said, putting her hand over her mother's and giving it a squeeze.

That evening when Michelle talked to Steve on the phone, she was able to explain how she would be returning home permanently after her dad's pending transfer. With Thanksgiving coming up, Michelle still hoped to invite Kristin and Mark up for the holiday. They agreed to also include Ben and Kelly in their first Thanksgiving feast in Sandy Cove.

"You call Kristin and I'll talk to Ben," Steve suggested. "What about your mom and Tim? What will they be doing for the holiday?"

"Grandma and Grandpa will go down to Seal Beach and celebrate with them," Michelle replied. She felt a little sad to be spending her first Thanksgiving without her parents and Tim, but was excited about having a holiday dinner at their new home. After spending so much time with her family during the past month, she knew they would understand. Besides, they'd definitely be together for Christmas.

Wednesday night was a difficult one for Michelle. She sat by her father's bed and thought about all that had happened over the past weeks in Bridgeport. Looking at his gaunt face brought tears to her eyes. Would her father ever be the same? He'd survived a harrowing brush with death, but would he live to regret that fact? "Please, God, help him find the strength to keep going," she prayed quietly.

John opened his eyes and looked at her. His expression spoke volumes of love without saying a word.

"I'll miss you, Daddy," she whispered as she brushed a tear from the corner of her eye.

He nodded, his brows furrowed with concern.

"The rehab facility looks great. They'll be able to help you get back on your feet again," she added, hoping to sound encouraging.

"I'll........ be.........fine," John spoke haltingly. His voice sounded strange, almost ghostly, as if it came from somewhere far away.

Michelle gasped. "Daddy -- You're talking!" Her voice cracked and her eyes shimmered with tears.

"Dad," she began again. John's eyes fixed on hers. "There's something else I want to say. I don't know exactly how to put this, but... let God help you, okay?"

He studied her pleading expression then took a deep breath. "Okay," he said, the word seeming to echo from somewhere deep inside.

A wave of peace washed over Michelle, just like it had when she prayed in the chapel. God was real. She just knew it. Somehow she and her dad needed to find a way to build the kind of faith her grandparents had. At least they were both open. Walking back to the motel room, she felt an inner confidence that somehow everything would work out fine for her dad and for herself.

When Michelle returned to her husband's embrace at the Portland airport, she came bearing good news and bad news. Her father was improving in so many ways. She eagerly told Steve about their conversation from the night before. But she also had some disappointing news. She had not conceived that month.

"Hey, don't look so sad. It'll happen," Steve replied reassuringly. "This has been a stressful month. I'm sure it'll be different now that you're home. Besides, remember the doctor said to give it three months."

"I know, but I was really hoping I'd be pregnant before Thanksgiving. It sounds silly, but I just wanted to be able to have that to be thankful for."

"Let's just focus on being thankful your dad is doing so much better, and that you are back home," Steve suggested. He drew her into his arms, stroking her back.

Michelle suddenly felt childish and selfish.

"You're right," she replied.

They walked hand-in-hand to the car. All Michelle could think of was getting home and climbing into her own bed. She knew her husband was right, but she couldn't help feeling incredibly sad that she wasn't pregnant.

The drive home was quiet. Steve played some soft music on the radio, and Michelle allowed the gentle rhythm to lull her to sleep. Before she knew it, they were pulling into their driveway. *It's good to be home*, she realized, pushing all other thoughts out of her consciousness.

CHAPTER FIFTEEN

Michelle took her seat near the back of the class and surveyed the room. She watched as other students wandered in and sat down. An excitement surged through her as she glanced over the textbook on her desk. It felt good to be back in school.

Having experienced an array of professors at Cal State, she'd prescreened this one on ratemyprofessors.com. The student reviews were almost all five-star in their verbiage, praising his style as casual, entertaining, and highly informative.

While the students settled in, their professor entered the room with a leather laptop case slung over his shoulder and a tall takeout coffee cup in his hand. His sporty attire lent a friendly impression, but the words he scrolled on the whiteboard established his authority and intellectual prowess: Dr. Richard Chambers, Anthropology 101.

Focusing on his set up for class, he unzipped the case and began hooking up the cables to link his computer with the projector. He tested the projector, aligning the image, then moved the computer into sleep mode and looked up to face the class.

The students quieted down as they awaited his introductions and lecture.

"Good afternoon," Dr. Chambers began.

"Good afternoon," some of the students replied.

"An interesting greeting, wouldn't you say?" the

professor asked as he studied their faces. "Good afternoon. This two-word phrase is a statement on our culture. In a society where all are innocent until proven guilty, where freedom is treasured and tolerance is required, we choose as a society to view each new opportunity as good and to greet each other with recognition of that goodness as we link it to the immediate time and days in which we reside."

Michelle could see the students around her soaking in his words. His smooth presentation and friendly countenance reminded her of Trevor.

"My name is Rick Chambers, and I will be your anthropology professor this semester. It is my goal to lead you through a survey of society from the beginning of recorded history and to link the evolution of man's social interactions with the current society in which we live. Since it is impossible to give an in-depth look at the development of man in one short semester, I'll focus on those societies which were most key to bringing us to our culture, as we know it.

"Some of what I teach will be familiar to many of you, especially those with an interest in history. Some of you may find this class to be a challenge to what you have been taught to believe about man and culture. This will be particularly true for those of you who have resisted the evolution of our society into a post-Christian era.

"I welcome healthy debate and questioning in my class. Feel free to challenge me along the way, and let's see if we can explore and uncover the truths that have led to our current age of enlightenment."

Michelle could already feel the tension beginning to arise in her heart. She'd sat through a handful of classes at Cal State where Christian students had been mocked and derided by the professor, but that was at a time when she herself was questioning her beliefs. Sure, she'd always respected her grandparents' faith, but she knew they came from a different era, a simpler time. It seemed natural to question Christianity in the pluralistic environment of a college campus.

Today, it caused her heart to race.

What would Dr. Chambers preach in this class? Would she be called upon to agree with his views on Christianity? Would she have the courage to challenge things he said if they trampled on her newfound faith?

As if reading her mind, Dr. Chambers paused and made eye contact with her. He seemed to be looking into her very soul. His stare lasted a moment longer than was comfortable, then his face relaxed into a smile and he turned to look around the room.

"Today we will begin with a look into the most ancient civilization of recorded history – the Sumerians. Their story was recorded by the ancient Babylonians, known for their Code of Hammurabi, a writing in cuneiform tablet. The Sumerians never left any record. Their society vanished without a trace. But we know of their existence and culture through the writings of the Babylonians."

The professor powered up his laptop and began his PowerPoint presentation as the students quickly began taking notes. Michelle flipped open her spiral notebook and followed suit. She needed this class for her general education requirements and decided not to worry about what the professor had said in his introduction. She'd do her best to remain anonymous, take her notes, write her papers, and then move on to her teacher prep courses the following semester.

A baby was crying, the sound piercing Michelle's heart. Where were the desperate sobs coming from? Why wasn't someone helping the poor thing? She couldn't see through the thick darkness that engulfed her, but she struggled toward the pathetic cries. Her feet seemed to catch on invisible vines or ropes that grabbed her ankles. Then there was silence. A sickly silence, like death itself.

Michelle sat up in bed, her nightshirt soaked with sweat and her hair damp. She pushed off the covers and stood up. It was 2 A.M. The cries of the baby echoed in her mind as she walked into the closet and changed into a dry nightie. Knowing better than trying to go to back to sleep right away, she ran a brush through her tangled locks and threw on a robe before going downstairs.

This was the second dream she'd had about a baby crying. Both dreams ended with the same unsettling and eerie silence. She put the teakettle on the stove and wandered into the family room to look for her book on dreams. Finding it sitting on an end table, she carried it back into the kitchen and settled into the breakfast nook to drink her tea and read. As she scanned through the table of contents and index, she found several references to babies, but was disappointed to discover that none of them related to what she had dreamt.

Michelle thought about Trevor. He had helped her with her dreams before; maybe he'd help her again. She decided to call him in the morning but knew she wouldn't mention it to Steve, fearing he wouldn't understand.

Trevor was just heading out the door when the phone rang. He hesitated and decided to let the answering machine pick it up first. "Hi Trevor, it's Michelle," the soft voice on the other end began.

He reached for the phone. "Hi there. You caught

me on my way out the door."

"Oh. I can call back later," she replied, sounding a little uneasy.

"No, it's fine. Really. What's up?"

"Well, I wanted to return your thesis to you," she began, "and to talk to you about something."

"Want me to come by your house?" he asked.

"No," she answered quickly. "Let's meet at the Coffee Stop."

"Sounds good to me. What time did you have in mind?" he asked, knowing he'd change his schedule to meet hers.

"I was hoping we could meet for an early lunch. Like say around 11:00."

"Eleven is perfect. I'll be there," he promised. After they hung up, he glanced down at his watch. 10:00. Plenty of time to drop by the New World Bookstore and pick up the book Starla had suggested for Michelle. He smiled. This was going to be a better day than he'd anticipated.

Michelle sat across the table from Trevor. Her insides were somersaulting and she nervously twisted a piece of her hair. "Maybe this isn't such a good idea," she said, looking away.

"What do you mean?" Trevor asked, his face furrowed with concern.

"I mean us meeting like this. Something's not right about it."

"We're just having lunch, Michelle. Can't two friends meet for lunch?" His voice sounded impatient.

"I guess. It's just that I know Steve wouldn't be thrilled."

"Oh, so this is about Steve."

She looked up and made eye contact with Trevor. "How would you feel if you were him?"

"That's a loaded question. I'm not sure I can answer it. Hopefully I'd be understanding enough to let you get together for lunch with a friend." He paused for a moment and then wisely softened to her dilemma. "If you're really that uncomfortable, Michelle, maybe you should talk to him about it. You know, clear the air, and see what he thinks."

"Yeah. That's a good idea." Now she didn't know if she should excuse herself and leave or stay this one time and then talk to Steve about it for the future.

As if reading her mind, Trevor spoke, "Since we're already here, why don't you tell me what it was you wanted to talk to me about."

Sighing, she resumed twisting her hair around her finger and began explaining to him about her dreams about the crying baby. "It's so frustrating and upsetting, Trevor. I want to get to her, but I can't see in the darkness. Then, when it gets totally silent, it's almost like she's dead." Her anxiety mounted as she described the emotions connected with the dream.

"Okay. It's clear this is really upsetting you. Let's step back from it for a moment." Trevor placed his hand over her free one. "Take a deep breath, Michelle."

She obeyed, breathing slowly in through her nose and out through her mouth like she had learned in yoga and in the meditation exercises he taught.

"That's better. Now clear your mind of all distracting thoughts. Separate yourself from your emotions. Imagine you can put them into a paper bag and set them under the table. Are you with me?"

Michelle nodded, her eyes closing as her face relaxed.

"Good. Now direct your focus upward. Picture

the light of your higher self. Can you see the light?"

Again she nodded.

"Your higher self can tell you what this dream is about. What is it saying to you, Michelle?"

After a long pause, she spoke. "The baby is mine. It's the baby I will have someday. It is already calling me to be its mother." She paused, and then added, "That's all."

Opening her eyes, she was just looking up to read Trevor's response when she noticed someone striding toward their table. It was Steve. Quickly she pulled her hand out from under Trevor's.

"Fancy meeting you here," Steve said sarcastically as he glanced from Michelle to Trevor. "Hope I didn't interrupt anything."

Michelle's face was crimson. She stammered, trying to explain, "I was just giving Trevor his thesis back, and we got into a conversation about a dream I've been having."

Trevor stood up and extended his hand to Steve who ignored it. "Have a seat, Steve. I need to get going, anyway."

"Thanks, pal," Steve replied sarcastically.

Michelle cringed as Trevor winked at her over Steve's head. "It was good seeing you again. Thanks for your input on my thesis," he added before waving goodbye.

"Well that was a cozy little get-together," Steve commented caustically, as soon as Trevor was out of earshot.

"Are you okay?" Michelle asked tentatively.

"Swell," he replied with a scowl.

"Listen, Steve, it's really nothing. Trevor is just a friend. That's all."

"Do you always sit holding hands with your friends?" he asked pointedly.

"We weren't holding hands. Trevor was just trying to calm me down after I told him about a disturbing dream I've been having."

"Oh, is that all? How comforting." Steve was obviously reading more into it. "Since when do you confide your dreams to this guy?"

"He knows a lot about dreams. It has to do with his study of psychology." Michelle was grasping for a lifeline. "Remember when you told me you thought I should talk to someone professional about my dreams?"

"Yeah, but I never imagined you'd be sitting at some restaurant holding hands with your therapist. Besides, this guy isn't even a licensed counselor yet, right?"

"Yeah, but he knows how to help me sort through my nightmares -- how to make sense of them," she tried to explain.

"Have you ever thought about asking God to help you?" Though his question had validity, she could only respond to the hostility she heard in his voice.

"God may be able to answer all your questions, Steve, but I'm not there yet. I still need people to talk to, people who will really listen."

"Are you saying I don't listen?" It was clear her husband was not going to soften.

"At this point, I'd have to say no. If you could hear yourself, you'd know what I mean." Pushing her chair away from the table, she stood up. "I've lost my appetite," she said and headed for the door.

Michelle drove her car down to the beach. She pulled to the end of the road and turned off the engine. Staring out over the sand and sea, her eyes began to fill, blurring the horizon. Everything was such a mess. Her father was struggling to regain his life, her perspective on truth and God was radically changing, her friendships in Sandy Cove seemed to be in upheaval, and Steve was making her feel like some kind of cheat.

Was it wrong to be friends with Trevor? Hadn't he helped her through some confusing and troubling times? He seemed to genuinely care about her, to take a real interest in the issues of her life, while Steve seemed more interested in work.

And what about Monica? She acted more distant lately. It wasn't anything Michelle could really put her finger on, but the kinship they once shared just wasn't there.

She thought back to those first few weeks in Sandy Cove and remembered the homesickness and loneliness that had followed her through each day. Then she'd met Monica at the yoga class and it all turned around. Now she thought about the possibility of losing that friendship as well as those with Trevor and Starla.

She bit her lip and shook her head from side to side as the tears began to stream down her face. Why was this happening?

Hugging herself as she gently rocked back and forth and cried, Michelle began to pray. "Dear God, please help me. I feel so alone. I don't want to lose my friends, and Steve can't stand Trevor. Am I wrong to want him as a friend? I'm so confused. Please, God, show me what to do."

Michelle sat back against the seat and took a deep breath. She waited, hoping for some kind of answer. Nothing came except a memory of her grandfather's face as he had spoken to her in the hospital chapel saying, "If you are sincere about wanting to know the truth, God will show it to you." And God had met her in that chapel. Her spirit knew it. But today, He seemed silent.

A moment later she heard a tap on her window. Startled, she turned to see Steve leaning down and looking in at her, his face furrowed with concern. She took a deep breath and opened the door.

"Michelle.... I'm.." he began.

Before he could finish, she was out of the car and reaching for him. They stood hugging while both of them tried to apologize.

"I know I'm acting like a jealous jerk," he admitted. "But sometimes I get scared I'll lose you."

"Why would you think that? You know how much I love you. You're the only one I've ever loved."

"I just don't trust that guy, Michelle. There's something not quite right about him."

"You don't really know Trevor. He's not the way you think he is. He's honestly just a nice guy who cares about me like a friend," she tried to explain.

"I know guys, babe. Believe me, Trevor wants more than friendship."

She could feel herself starting to stiffen, but decided it would be better to change the subject. "Let's forget about Trevor and go get some lunch," she suggested, knowing Steve must be starving after leaving for work that morning without so much as a bowl of cereal or a piece of toast.

"Got your appetite back?" he teased with a wink.

Michelle just smiled and rolled her eyes. "Let's go home. I've got some lunchmeat from the deli. We can have sub sandwiches."

"Okay. See you back there," Steve said, closing her car door and walking back to his car.

After lunch, Steve went back to work, and

Michelle got on the phone to call Kristin. If only Kristin lived nearby. Then she'd have a great friend who really understood her -- someone to hang around with when Steve was busy. Well, for now she'd just have to settle for emails and phone calls.

Michelle was disappointed to get voicemail, but she figured Kristin had a lot to do these days what with planning a wedding. When she heard the beep, she said, "Hey, Kristin. It's me. Give me a call." Just as she was about to hang up, Kristin's voice sounded on the other end.

"Michelle? Is that you?"

"Kristin -- I'm so glad you picked up the phone," she said, elated to hear her friend's voice.

"I was just walking out the door. Appointment with the photographer."

"Oh. Well I won't keep you then. Are you and Mark still coming for Thanksgiving?" she asked hopefully.

"We wouldn't miss it," she replied enthusiastically.

"I'm so glad. I miss you, friend. There are so many things I want to talk to you about. Plus it will be good for Steve and Mark to get to know each other better."

"Mark is eager to get to know both of you. I talk about you all the time. Can you believe it, Michelle? Me marrying a pastor?"

"I think it's great. You deserve the best."

After a pause, Michelle spoke again, "Lots of stuff has been happening around here. I wish you were closer..."

"I know what you mean. Every time I go out looking at flowers or china or dresses for the wedding, I wish you were here with me." Kristin sighed and then added, "Maybe I'll kidnap you when we're up there and bring you back with me."

Michelle laughed. "Actually, I'd love that," she admitted softly.

"Hey, how's your dad doing?" Kristin asked.

"I call home every day, and so far Mom seems to think he's continuing to improve. But I can hear how tired she sounds. Wish I could be closer and help her. We'll be going down for Christmas."

"I'm sure they'll both be so glad to see you again, `Shell. It's such a miracle that your dad is doing this well."

"Yeah. Just pray for him to keep improving. He's got a long way to go, and if he plateaus for any extended period of time, they'll stop the therapy. Pray for my mom too. This is really hard on her. My dad was always the strong one."

"I'll pray. Mark too."

"Thanks."

"So is everything okay with you and Steve these days?" Kristin asked.

"I guess. We had a big fight today, but I think we got it straightened out. I'll tell you more about it when you're up here. I don't want to make you any later for your appointment."

"I can cancel the appointment if you need to talk, Michelle."

"No. It's okay. I can wait. It'll be better when we can talk face- to-face."

"Alright. Well, in the meantime, I'll be praying for you guys."

"Thanks, Kristin. I appreciate it. Really." Before they hung up, Kristin gave Michelle the information about their flight for Thanksgiving. "Steve can pick you guys up at the airport," Michelle added.

"No way. We'll just rent a car. I wish I could help with all that cooking. We tried to get a reservation for the night before, but everything was totally booked."

"I'll be fine. I'm just glad you'll be there to share the feast with us," Michelle replied. "Hopefully it'll be edible," she added with a grin.

CHAPTER SIXTEEN

Clark Christianson's eyes lit on a name. Marilyn Marlow. Why did that name seem so familiar? He rolled his chair over to the file cabinet and pulled out his file on Harrison Brady. Maybe this was the link he was looking for between Ackerman's case and Brady's.

"Bingo," he said with a smile as he spotted the same name on the roster of employees at Burksted's Technologies. "Now how does this Marilyn fit into the puzzle?" he asked himself aloud, knowing he was the only one burning the midnight oil at his office.

Scrolling through his contacts, he found Harrison Brady's home phone number. Punching it in, he pushed up the sleeve of his oxford shirt and glanced at his Rolex watch. 10:00. *Hope Brady isn't in bed*, he thought as he heard the phone begin to ring on the other end.

"Hello?" came a male voice. "Mr. Brady?"

"Speaking."

"This is Clark Christianson."

"Clark -- What a surprise!"

"Listen Brady, I hate to bother you so late at night," Clark began.

"No problem. What's up?" Harrison asked.

"Well, I'm working on another case very similar to yours, and I've stumbled across something that may link these two cases together."

"Really? What?"

"It's a name. A name that appears on both

companies' employment records. Do you remember someone named Marilyn Marlow?"

"Do I ever. That gal was something else. If you want my opinion, I think she had a thing for old Preston. But once it was uncovered that he was the one trying to frame me, she seemed to be totally disillusioned with him. A few months later, she turned in her resignation."

"So what makes you think she had something going with Preston?" Clark asked, his interest piqued.

"I didn't say she actually had something going with him. Preston was a pretty staunch family man. I don't think he'd fall for some floozy like Marlow. But she did hang around his office quite a bit, strutting in those tight sweaters and short skirts of hers."

"Thanks, Harrison. I really appreciate this. It could be just the lead I'm looking for," Clark commented halfway to himself.

"Happy to help in any way I can. And Clark," Harrison Brady added.

"Yeah?"

"I'll never forget what you did for me. You saved my life, pal. Thanks again."

The words reached into a part of Clark Christianson that very few people or things touched. It was moments like this that made his job his passion.

"Don't mention it, Brady. I was just doing what you hired me to do," he replied, covering all traces of emotion.

The next morning, Clark Christianson decided to take a little trip over to John Ackerman's office at Mather's, Inc. He wanted to meet this Marilyn Marlow and see what he could find out about her.

Entering the glass doors to the downstairs lobby, he was impressed by the simple, yet dramatic entry. Gleaming white marble flooring complemented the soaring, tinted glass windows and mirrored elevators. In the front left corner, black leather furniture and a sleek glass and steel coffee table provided a general waiting area, rarely used since each department had its own reception room.

Off center and to the right was an imposing, markedly uncluttered cherry-wood desk. Void of any type of paperwork, it boasted a handsome matching cherry-wood set comprised of a large blotter, a gracefully carved pencil holder, and a simple, but elegant, daily calendar. The attractive woman stationed behind this fortress wore a headset for the telephones. It was clear her only responsibility was to channel incoming calls and visitors.

Her white teeth sparkling against her mahogany skin, she offered Clark a smile and asked if she could help him.

"I'm looking for one of your employees, a Marilyn Marlow. I believe she has worked here for close to a year."

"Ms. Marlow is no longer with us," the receptionist replied matter- of-factly.

Clark's face registered his obvious disappointment.

"Are you a personal friend of Marilyn's?" she asked in response to his expression.

"No. It was a business matter," Clark replied.

"Would you like to talk to her replacement?" the woman offered.

"I don't think that would help me. Any idea where she might be working now?" he asked, hoping it would be somewhere in the area.

"Perhaps they could help you in personnel. They're on the third floor."

"Thanks. I'll try that." Clark smiled, nodding to her as he strolled past her desk to the elevator.

"Marilyn Marlow. Now there's an interesting character," Chad Jenkins said, shaking his head as if continuing to be puzzled by her.

"When did she leave Mather's?" Clark asked.

"Tell me again why you're looking for her?" Chad requested. "We don't usually give out information on our employees without their permission."

"I'm working on a case right now, and I think Ms. Marlow may have some critical information for me. Since the case is confidential, I can't really go into any more details. I could subpoena the information, but I was hoping you'd help me avoid the hassle."

"Well, I guess it wouldn't hurt to tell you when she left. It was a month ago. We were all surprised when she gave us notice. Lots of the guys were really bummed to see her go, if you know what I mean. Marilyn's quite the babe. But she seemed to have a thing going with some guy in accounting. He left around the same time she did. Lucky cuss. Bart Thomas was his name. Never could figure out what she saw in him."

Clark smiled. Very interesting. Ms. Marlow disappears with someone from accounting while John Ackerman is framed for embezzlement. The pieces were all coming together. "Hey, thanks, Mr....Uh..."

"Jenkins. Chad Jenkins."

"Mr. Jenkins. Right. Thanks again. You've been most helpful." Clark extended his hand and grasped Chad's in a firm handshake.

"Glad I could help you out. Hope you find Marilyn," Chad added with a wink.

Clark just smiled, turned, and walked to the elevator.

Sheila hurried to open the front door, her arms loaded with groceries and her heart racing as she heard the phone ringing in the kitchen. Ever since John's "accident" she felt her anxiety levels rise whenever the phone rang. Though part of her was relieved to be back home, in some ways life in Bridgeport had been simpler. Her days had been filled with her bedside vigil in John's hospital room.

Now she was thrust back into the daily routine of life -- keeping up with the mail and bills, housework, grocery shopping, laundry -- all the activities that occupied a normal homemaker. In addition to those obligations, she was immersed in helping to clear her husband from the embezzlement charges that had driven him to attempt to kill himself in a lonely motel in Bridgeport.

Dropping the groceries on the counter, she grabbed the phone from its resting place. "Hello?" she asked breathlessly.

"Mrs. Ackerman?"

"Yes," she replied.

"This is Clark Christianson."

"Mr. Christianson -- I'm so glad to hear from you." She pulled up a chair and sat down as she cradled the phone to her ear. Please let this be good news, she hoped silently.

"I've found a lead I'd like to discuss with you and your husband. Is it possible for me to meet with you both at the rehab center this evening?" Clark knew he might be rushing his conclusion, but a gut-level instinct told him he'd found the key player in John's case. He was eager to get John's reaction to the names he'd gathered from personnel at Mather's.

"Tonight? Well, I guess that would be fine," Sheila said tentatively. She knew John was exhausted at the end of each day of intense therapy, and she wasn't sure if he'd be up to any kind of meeting with his attorney. But she also knew that the resolution of the lawsuit could be just the healing balm her husband needed.

"What would be a good time?" Clark asked.

"How about 7:00? He'll be finished with dinner by then. Hopefully he'll still be awake and alert. Therapy takes a lot out of him," she explained.

"7:00 will be fine. Room 121, right?"

"Right. At the end of the hall on your left."

"Okay. I'll see you there," Clark said, and then added, "I really think this is the break we've been looking for."

Sheila sighed as she sank further down into the chair. "I hope you're right." Hanging up the phone, she began putting the groceries away.

Boxes of frozen meals made up much of her purchases these days. She didn't feel motivated to cook for just herself.

Tim usually came over on Wednesdays and Sundays, and she fixed something for the two of them those nights. The remainder of the week, Sheila had a hard enough time forcing herself to microwave a frozen entrée before heading back to her husband's side at Rancho Vista Rehab Center.

She tried to stay and eat with John the first night he was there, but his frustration over the mess he made trying to feed himself resulted in the therapist asking her to take a break at dinner time and go home to eat. It made for lonely meals, but seemed to help John focus on his retraining process rather than wrestling with embarrassment.

With Thanksgiving right around the corner, Sheila was glad her parents were coming down for a visit. Their presence would fill the house with companionship and hope. They always brought a feeling of peace with them that she desperately needed. This whole trauma with her husband had her reconsidering her own beliefs and yearning to go back to her childhood faith. *I guess I loved John so much, I was willing to throw that all away for him,* she thought. *Now maybe I need to grab a hold of it again for his sake as well as my own.*

Shuffling through the frozen dinners, she selected a casserole. While it cooked, she continued putting the remainder of the groceries away.

A few minutes later, she sat at the kitchen table and ate her instant dinner while opening the day's mail. This was her new routine. Read the mail while eating dinner. It helped keep her mind off the empty place setting across the table.

Finishing up, she decided to go to the hospital earlier than usual in order to prepare John for Clark's arrival. Perhaps she could help him stay focused and alert for their evening meeting.

Clark walked down the long hall off the foyer of the rehab center. When he entered John's room, Sheila was adjusting the covers on the bed and helping him get into a more upright position. This was only the second time Clark had seen John, but he noticed an improvement in his coordination right away.

"Hello, John. Sheila."

Sheila turned to face him and smiled. "Hello. We

were just getting ready for your visit." John simply nodded his head in acknowledgement, his eyes narrowing to study Clark's face.

"Well, John, I think I may have a lead."

"What?" John asked after a moment's hesitation.

"There appears to be a link between your case and another similar case I won last year. It involves a person who worked at my prior client's company and at yours."

John was listening intently. Sheila held his hand as she, too, eagerly awaited the information.

"Do you know someone by the name of Marilyn Marlow?" Clark asked John.

Immediately John closed his eyes and turned his head away from Sheila. "What is it, John?" she asked him. He did not reply. She turned to look at Clark and shrugged her shoulders.

"Could I have a few minutes alone with your husband?" he asked.

Sheila stood up, looking very puzzled, and nodded as she walked out of the room.

CHAPTER SEVENTEEN

Steve, look what I found at the Stork's Nest," Michelle said as she pulled a lamp with a Noah's ark base out of a bag.

"What's that for?"

"For the baby's room, doofus. I've decided to start collecting things as I find them. I'd really like to do a Noah's ark theme in there."

Steve put his notepad aside. "Michelle, we don't have a baby yet."

"I know, but I was shopping with Kelly today for their nursery, and I couldn't resist this. It was on clearance. It might have been gone by the time I got pregnant."

"It just seems a little premature, honey. We'll have plenty of time to find baby stuff."

"So do you want me to take it back?" Michelle asked defensively, turning her face away from him to hide the tears beginning to well up. *Why does everything have to be such a big deal?* she thought to herself.

As if he realized he'd crossed the line with her, he said gently, "Come on, Michelle. This isn't worth crying about. If it's that important to you, go ahead and buy whatever you want."

Michelle just nodded her head. After composing herself, she said, "You're right. I'm getting ahead of myself here. Seems like I'm always either worrying about

Dad or obsessing about a baby. It just gives me hope when I focus on stuff about the baby."

Steve got up from the table, rinsed out his coffee mug, and walked over to give her a hug. "That's fine. Just don't go overboard with buying stuff until we know we're really going to have a baby." He paused and then added, "I've got to work on the notes for my briefing tomorrow. Are you and Monica still going out for a while tonight?"

"Yeah. She'll be here in a few minutes."

"Do you need any money?"

"No, I've got enough." She hesitated for a moment and then added, "Sorry I snapped at you."

"It's okay. You've got a lot on your mind. If it's any consolation, I really think this Christianson guy is going to be able to resolve your dad's legal battle."

"That's what Mom says, too. She has a lot of confidence in him."

The doorbell rang and Michelle leaned down, picked up Max from his resting place on the chair, and walked out of the kitchen. "That's Monica, Max. You remember her? She bought you all those toys."

"Hey girl," Michelle said as she swung open the front door.

"Michelle -- It's so good to have you back. Let me hold that baby for a minute." Monica reached out to Max, who showed no resistance as he was handed into her arms. " I miss you, Maxie," she said in a high-pitched, singsong tone.

"You spoiled him, Monica."

"I know. But I had fun doing it." She released Max, who had spotted his toy mouse on the floor. "Are you ready to go?"

"Yep. Just let me grab my coat. Bye, Steve," she called over her shoulder.

"Have fun," he replied.

After spending a laborious half-hour with John, Clark now understood why Marilyn Marlow's name brought such a reaction from him. John did not want his wife or kids to ever know about his fling with Marilyn. Clark would have to approach this carefully.

The added difficulty with this case was John's physical limitations. His speech was still very hesitant and hard to understand; yet Clark knew he deserved the same chance to fully tell his story and to be able to do it confidentially.

While Sheila could understand everything John said, she could not participate in these sessions. Clark had tried to explain to her the delicate issues involved in any corporate case involving money and frame-ups. He hoped he had successfully explained the need to talk to John privately without arousing her suspicions.

His next step was to begin his search for Marilyn. Perhaps a visit to the man found responsible for Brady's charges would give him some more insight into Ms Marlow. Preston was serving time at a low security facility just outside the county line. Clark phoned ahead to request a meeting with him and set an appointment for the following day. Now he had one more delicate call to make.

Harrison Brady picked up on the first ring. "Harrison? It's Clark."

"I was just thinking about you."

"Really? You must be psychic." Both men chuckled.

"What's up? How's the case going?" Brady asked.

"It's going fine."

"Good. I hope you nail whoever's after that guy. I remember that feeling." Harrison's voice shuddered at the fear that had invaded his life and family.

"Listen, Harrison, I've got to ask you something personal. Are you alone right now?"

"Yep. Just me and a stack of work that's been staring at me all morning." Harrison took a deep breath before adding, "Talk to me."

"You remember me mentioning Marilyn Marlow."

"Yes."

"I've got to know if there was any connection between you and her —- anything personal." The phone line was silent. "Harrison, are you there?"

"I'm here."

"Well? I know this may seem like it's none of my business, especially since your case has been settled and put behind you, but it could really help me piece things together at this end with my new client."

"You know I'd do anything to help you, Clark. I don't know where I'd be today without your expertise." Harrison paused and then continued, "I've rebuilt my life here. I have a good family and I intend to protect them. Understand?"

"Yes."

"Anything you repeat about what I'm going to tell you now, I will deny ever saying."

"Understood. This is completely confidential."

"Marilyn and I knew each other, intimately, for a very short season. When she first came to Burksted's, I had just been turned down for a key promotion. Things were not going well at home, either. Sharon was struggling with her interior design business and had very little time for me. Marilyn was temporarily assigned as my assistant on a project we were working in Dallas. We spent three weeks together installing a system for a research lab."

"And that is when you and Marilyn had an

affair?"

"If you could call it that. She was so focused on me, so appreciative of my skills and knowledge, and she let me know it." Harrison paused and sighed. "Guess I let my ego get the best of me. You understand why I didn't tell you this when you called last time? Sharon was in the next room. It would kill her to know about Marilyn and me. She's already been through enough, and we've got a solid marriage now."

"Sure. I understand. Who broke off the relationship between you and Marilyn?"

"I did. Even in the short span of three weeks together, I could see she had big plans for us. There was no way I was going to break up my family."

"How did she react?"

"Surprisingly calm. She said she understood and that everything would work out for the best in the long run."

"Doesn't sound like a woman scorned."

"That's what I thought, but I figured I was lucky to get off so easy."

"You might not have gotten off so easy after all."

"What do you mean?"

"I mean, I think Marilyn is behind Preston's plan that backfired."

"You're serious?"

"Dead serious. I think she used Preston as a pawn in your case." Harrison could see the pieces of the puzzle coming together.

"So that's why she left Burksted's right after Preston was arrested?"

"Yes."

"But why wouldn't Preston turn her in?"

"He had more to lose by doing that. He'd already been proven guilty of the legal issues involved. Why would he risk losing his marriage too? If I recall, his wife was clearly stationed at his side throughout the trial and swore to stand by him in spite of his 'mistake'."

"You're right. Tami would never tolerate infidelity." Harrison whistled softly in amazement. "So you think the whole thing was Marilyn getting back at me?"

"Yep. And I think that's what's happening with my other client now."

"Can you pin anything on her?"

Clark hesitated and then said, "I don't know, Harrison. She's shrewd. She knows the men she's 'punishing' have more to lose by blowing the whistle on her than they do by turning the other cheek. The beauty of her plan is she uses her charm to involve an accomplice, who ends up doing most of the dirty work for her and who takes the fall if the frame-up collapses. My guess is that she purposely involves them in a sexual relationship with her too, so they have more vested interest in keeping her name out of the picture."

"I have to give her credit," Brady admitted. "I never would have thought she had the brains."

"Here's the real clincher. In the case I'm working on now, both she and her accomplice actually got away with the money. At least for now, that is."

"Great. Well, I hope you track her down and serve her what she deserves."

"Thanks. I'm working on a way to do that."

"Remember what I said about this conversation, Clark. It's just between the two of us. I hope it helps you solve your new case, but please respect that my case is over."

"Gotcha," Clark replied. "Give Sharon my best."

"Okay, I will. Call me anytime if you think I can help. But if it's about Marilyn, don't call at home."

"Will do. Bye."

Clark sat at his desk thoughtfully gazing out the

window, his elbows resting on the arms of the chair and his fingertips pressed together in a steeple. In all of his years of practice, he'd never seen such an intricate web of deception. The fact that these two cases were linked made him wonder how many other men were falling victim to this woman's ploys. How much money had she managed to embezzle from companies without being caught? Was she off on some tropical island sipping margaritas with Bart Thomas, celebrating John's demise while they squandered the money he was accused of stealing?

Steve pushed aside his notepad and scrubbed his hands over his face. He was starting to see double from working on this briefing. Standing up, he walked over to the fridge and got out some milk. Michelle had baked cookies that afternoon and cold milk would be perfect with those chocolate chips.

Max immediately noticed the jug of milk and began to prance around mewing.

"The vet said this stuff isn't really that good for you, Max."

Not to be diverted from his goal, Max only wailed louder, beginning to rub against Steve's legs in a ritual that had always brought success in the past.

"Okay, okay. I'll give you just a little sip. But don't tell Mom," he said.

Max seemed satisfied with the small saucer of milk. After licking the last drop, he strolled out to the family room where Steve had settled on the couch with his snack. In a graceful leap, he landed on Steve's lap and began sniffing at a cookie in his hand.

"No way, Max. These are all mine." Steve gently nudged the cat off his lap. Max took the hint and relocated himself on the rocking chair where he began kneading an afghan draped over the arm.

After finishing eating, Steve picked up his Bible. He thought about Michelle and how much she wanted a baby. *Lord,* he prayed silently, *Is this your will? I want your timing here.* Thumbing through the pages of scripture, his eye fell on a verse in the book of Psalms. "Delight yourself in the Lord, and He will give you the desires of your heart." It seemed to be a confirmation. It was certainly Michelle's desire to have a baby now, and he was getting attached to the idea, too.

In his relief that he had found confirmation about their 'project', Steve missed the first part of the verse, not realizing the key it held.

CHAPTER EIGHTEEN

Clark's conversation with Preston the following day held no big surprises. Preston refused to answer any questions about Marilyn Marlow, clearly preferring to serve his time and put the whole thing behind him.

Next Clark used his contacts with the police department to put out a tracer on the whereabouts of Bart Thomas. He was located within a day, residing now in the coastal community of Oceanside. Jotting down his address, Clark decided to pay Mr. Thomas a surprise visit. He strode out to his Lexus and climbed in. Popping up his GPS screen, he punched in the address of Bart's home. These things still amazed him. Looking at a navigational map with step-by-step driving instructions from his immediate location to Bart Thomas's front door, he started the motor and pulled out of the lot.

Although the air held a cool November chill, the sun was shining and the sky was clear. It was one of those gorgeous fall days in Southern California, with an off-shore breeze that tickled the treetops and invigorated pedestrians. Clark was looking forward to his drive along the coast. Opening his sunroof, he reclined the seat a bit more and readjusted the rearview mirror accordingly. His stereo system oozed a jazz CD he had started listening to on his way to the office that morning.

One of the songs transported him back in time to a tiny coffeehouse in Santa Barbara where he and his ex used to spend many evenings when they stayed at his father's ranch outside of Montecito. He felt an old emotion resurfacing as he pictured her smiling face, framed in a halo of blond curls. *Wonder how Susan's doing these days*, he thought to himself, trying to picture her living on her own up in Washington as she pursued her dream of becoming a writer. Maybe I'll give her a call tonight.

Time flew quickly, and soon he was pulling up to the front of a picturesque new house with a beautiful view of the coastline. He glanced down at the legal pad on the passenger seat and replayed in his mind some of the questions he wanted to ask.

A short man of slight build with brown hair and wire rimmed glasses responded to Clark's rap on the door. "Can I help you?" he asked.

"Who is it?" called a female voice from somewhere inside. Within a moment the source of the voice was revealed, as a very curvaceous young lady with long blonde hair appeared behind the man, resting one hand on his shoulder.

"I'm looking for Bart Thomas," Clark began as he reached into the pocket of his sport's coat and pulled out a business card.

The man scrutinized the card for a moment and then said, "I don't remember calling for an attorney." The woman behind him squinted her eyes, giving Clark a piercing stare.

"I'd like to talk to you for a few minutes, if you have the time," Clark began, ignoring the obvious hostility he was confronting.

"About what?"

"I'm John Ackerman's attorney. I'm trying to piece together what happened at Mather's."

"He embezzled some money. That's what happened. There's not much else to tell." The man began to close the door.

It was clear they were not about to cooperate with him. Clark decided to try one last ditch effort. "Apparently you haven't heard what happened to Mr. Ackerman."

"What? He went to jail?" the man and woman both laughed.

"No. Actually, he shot himself."

Their expressions changed momentarily, the woman withdrawing her hand as the man glanced back at her. "He what?" the woman asked.

"He shot himself in the head."

"But I thought you said you were his attorney?" the man asked, puzzled.

"I am. He survived. But he's pretty messed up – can't walk, can barely talk. He's in rehab right now at Rancho Vista Hospital. The man's life is pretty much over." Clark could see he was making some headway. The woman in particular looked guilty as sin, and her fellow wasn't looking too good either.

"Listen, Mr. Christianson, I'd like to help you and I'm sorry to hear about John. But there's nothing I can really tell you. We worked together at Mather's, but that's about the extent of it." The blond nodded her head in agreement. "Now, if you'll excuse us, we were just about to go out."

Clark noticed the surprised look on the woman's face, but she quickly backed him up by saying, "We're meeting some friends. We're already late."

Clark nodded. "Maybe some other time."

"Yeah. Another time."

As the door closed on him, Clark's mind was ticking. *Pretty clear what we have going on here. Marilyn's found herself a sucker.* He turned and strolled back to his car, pulling away from the curb and driving down the street to re-park where he could watch and see if they were really leaving. Twenty minutes later, with no action coming from their house, he pulled out and drove away. *Time to get the police back on this case*, he thought. *But how do I protect Brady and Ackerman from the secrets Marilyn might reveal?*

Waving goodbye to Monica, Michelle walked into the family room and found Steve asleep on the couch with Max snuggled in his lap. She went over to wake Steve up to go to bed. His Bible was open on the coffee table and a verse was underlined.

" 'Delight yourself in the Lord, and He will give you the desires of your heart.' That's pretty cool," she said softly. *There are lots of great sayings in here*, she observed to herself.

Steve started to stir. "Are you talking to me?" he asked sleepily.

She smiled and inclined her head toward the open book. "Just reading your Bible."

"What time is it?"

"It's 10:30. Come on. Let's go to bed," she said, reaching for his hand to help him up.

"How was your evening with Monica?" he asked as they climbed the stairs, connected to each other by intertwined fingers.

"It was good. We had a lot of catching up to do." Michelle hesitated and then continued. "I told her about our little 'project'."

"You what?"

"I told her we've decided to start a family."

"Are you sure you should be talking about that? Don't you think it would be better to just wait until you're pregnant?"

Michelle withdrew her hand from his. "It's a girl thing, Steve. We like to share our hopes and dreams and plans."

"I see."

"You do?"

"Look, Michelle. You can tell Monica anything you'd like. This just seems like something kind of personal, between you and me, not the whole world."

"Monica won't tell anyone. She promised."

"Okay. Whatever. Let's just go to bed. I'm beat." He headed straight for the closet and began unbuttoning his shirt.

I wonder if I'm pregnant right now, she thought to herself. She'd already had one disappointing month. In a few more days she'd know if she'd conceived this month. With Thanksgiving only a week away, she hoped she'd be able to tell everyone some exciting news – a new baby to be thankful for.

Sheila could tell something was really troubling her husband. John seemed to be withdrawing again and his therapy was slowing to a near halt. She did not know what to do. Every time she tried to reach out to him or to ask him what was troubling him, he would just turn away and close his eyes — the closest he could come to walking away from her.

Phil and Joan had arrived the day before to be with their daughter and grandson for Thanksgiving. "What's the matter, Sheila?" her mom asked as she watched her daughter staring out the window over the kitchen sink.

"I don't know, Mom. Something's up with John. He's been very quiet ever since our attorney visited him the last time. Clark asked me to leave the room for a while. When I came back, I could tell something was upsetting John."

"Do you think Clark is concerned he might not win the case?"

"He hasn't indicated anything like that to me. He seems very confident whenever we discuss it."

"And you don't know what they talked about while you were out of the room?"

"Something that Clark said was delicate in relation to the company where John works. He seemed to be alluding to something about other personnel at Mather's."

"Maybe he has a pretty good idea of who's been framing John and it upset him when he heard who Clark thinks it is."

"That's possible. I just hate to see him lose any footing he's gained in therapy. It's really important for him to be focused on the future now. On rebuilding his strength and his life."

"Do you think it might help if your father went over to talk to him alone?" Phil had such a calming affect on their son-in-law up in the hospital in Bridgeport. Maybe he'd have the words to speak to John's issues or concerns, whatever they might be.

"Actually, I was just considering asking Dad if he'd mind doing that."

"Mind doing what?" Phil asked as he entered the kitchen with the newspaper in one hand and a glass of water in the other.

Joan replied, "Talking to John. Something's troubling him and Sheila can't seem to get it out of him."

"And you two think he might open up to me?"

"It's possible. He seemed to gain a lot of strength from your visits in the ICU," Joan offered.

"He did, Dad. You were the only one who seemed to really help him when he got agitated." Sheila studied her father, noticing the twinkle in his eye that belied his age. In spite of his wrinkles and gray hair, he had a certain youthful spark she'd always admired. Even when he was faced with big issues or concerns, an underlying current of peace and joy permeated his countenance.

"Okay. I'll go over to Rancho and see what I can do."

"Thanks, Dad," Sheila said, already beginning to feel better.

"Anything for my princess," Phil replied, drawing her into a father's embrace.

Later that night, as Phil was praying for the words to reach John and to uncover what was troubling his son-in-law, Marilyn Marlow was driving up the coast to see John herself.

CHAPTER NINETEEN

Phil stood outside the door to John's room, taken aback by the sound of a female voice speaking in a threatening tone.

"You are pitiful, John Ackerman. Look at the mess you've got yourself in now. What were you thinking? Obviously you weren't. Just like you weren't when you gave me the shaft after Dallas. You better listen carefully and start thinking now. I will not be dragged into your mess. Tell your lawyer friend, Clark, to back off, or I'll be making a little call to your precious wife."

Phil cleared his throat to signal his entrance. Standing by John's bed was a tall, well-built woman in her thirties. She was dressed in a clinging black dress that stopped several inches above her knees, revealing slender legs and black high heel shoes. "Excuse me, miss..."

"Marlow. Marilyn Marlow." She spoke in short, clipped words. "I don't believe we've met."

"No, and it's not likely we ever will again." She took one last look at John, making eye contact, before she turned and strutted out of the room.

As soon as she was gone, Phil sat down beside the bed and studied John's face. He was clearly distressed and angry. "Want to tell me what that was about?" Phil asked after a few moments of silence.

John shook his head and turned away from Phil.

"It's hard to run away when your trapped in a bed, isn't it?" Phil observed. He could tell by John's glance back over his shoulder that he'd caught him off guard. "Listen, John, I heard what Ms. Marlow was saying to you before I walked in. It doesn't take a rocket scientist to figure out what she was alluding to. You had an affair with her while you were in Dallas, didn't you?"

John turned to face him and gave him a cold stare.

"You can be angry with me if you'd like, but my hunch is that deep down inside it's yourself you're really mad at."

John just squinted his eyes and continued to stare, almost as if to try to figure out what was coming next.

"Does this Marilyn gal have something to do with your frame- up?"

John's face remained stoic.

"I'll take that as a 'yes'. This is quite a mess, isn't it? It just keeps getting bigger and bigger." Phil stood up, walked over to window, and looked out, his hands in his pockets absentmindedly fiddling with some coins. He turned back around and stood over John.

"Well, John, since you're not talking to me tonight, I guess I'll just sit and talk to you for a while. Ever since we first met you that night you and Sheila went to the drive-in movies together, I've been praying for you. Guess you've probably heard that before. Do you know what I've prayed?"

No response.

"I've prayed for you to figure out you can't make it through this world without God, that we all need Him at some point or other, even if it's not until we look death in the face." Phil paused. John was staring at the ceiling.

"Throughout the years, Joan and I have loved you and accepted you as a part of our family, even though you rejected our beliefs and essentially pulled Sheila away from them in the process. Now it appears you were also unfaithful to her and to your marriage vows. But that's not what this lecture is about.

"Whether you've known it or not, we've covered you both in our prayers. And now I believe God is answering those prayers in a very unexpected way."

John looked around the hospital room as tears began to pool in his eyes.

"You've just got to surrender, John. Give your life over to the Lord. Let him take these burdens and straighten out this mess. Give up your self-sufficiency and pride and let Him take over."

"I . . . don't . . . know. . . how." John's face matched the frustration in his voice.

"How is the easy part, being willing is the hurdle. Are you ready to lay this all down?" Phil gestured to the room as a symbol of John's dilemma.

John closed his eyes, forcing a tear out of the corner of one. As it trickled down his face, he just nodded and sighed deeply.

Phil looked heavenward for a moment. Then he placed his hand on John's shoulder and led him in a simple prayer of repentance and surrender. When John opened his eyes again, his frown relaxed. A new peace was finding its way into his head and heart.

"Ready to talk now?" Phil asked, sitting down on the chair beside the bed.

John took a deep breath and nodded. "I was right about you and Marilyn in Dallas, wasn't I?"

"Yes."

"And Clark thinks she is tied to your embezzlement charges?"

"Yes."

"Well, this is how I see it, John. Truth is always the best path to choose. It's not always the easiest, as I'm sure you can see from your current vantage point, but it is ultimately the best."

"What . . . are . . . you . . .saying?" John

concentrated hard to speak every word clearly.

"I'm saying you can't cover up this Marlow thing and uncover the truth at the same time."

"But . . .what . . .about . . . Sheila?"

"Well, that's a tough one. It'll really hurt her. But the truth is the truth. She'll have to accept it, John. There's no excusing what you did, but at least you were able to realize your mistake and cut off the relationship."

"Yes."

"The other side of this picture is the fact that it will hurt Sheila tremendously if you are convicted."

"True. What . . . a . . . mess. . ."

"Well, some of this is out of your hands now. You made a choice to turn this over to God and that limits your options. It's clear from His word that you've got to tell the truth. Covering up your sins from the past will not solve anything."

John cringed and nodded. "Okay."

Phil could see what a struggle each word was for John to form. "Do you want me to talk to Sheila for you?"

He shook his head. "No . . .I . . .will . . .tell . . .her."

"All right. She'll be here pretty soon. Do you want me to stay?"

"No. Thanks. Please...pray."

"You know I'll be doing that, Son. God will give you the strength."

John's focus shifted to the window. It was clear he was beginning to think about how to tell Sheila everything. Phil squeezed his shoulder gently, before turning and walking out of the room.

Michelle flipped through a catalog of baby furniture and was startled when Max pounced on her lap. "You scared me," she said, ruffling his fur. "I'm looking at pictures of furniture for the nursery. See?"

Max seemed unimpressed. He nudged her hand with his head. "Okay, okay." She set aside the catalog and cradled him in her arms, scratching under his chin while he purred contentedly.

"Maybe we don't need a baby after all," Steve said as he came down the stairs. Looks like you've already got one."

"Yes, little Max is my baby, aren't you Max? But that doesn't change anything about little Joey."

"Joey?"

"Yeah. I like that name for a boy."

"Oh, so now we're naming the baby too." Steve shook his head.

"That's right. It's part of getting ready. So what do you think?"

"About what?" He sat down on the couch beside her and draped his arm over her shoulder.

"Names, Steve. What names do you like?"

"I don't know. I haven't given it much thought."

"Well, start thinking. What do you think of Madison for a girl's name?"

"It sounds like a last name to me."

"But that's what makes it so cute," she explained with a smile.

"Lots of girls have names that used to be last names."

"Really? I hadn't noticed."

"Why are guys so clueless?" Michelle asked herself aloud.

"Hey. If we were all so 'clueless' there wouldn't be any babies, would there?"

"Funny, Steve. We aren't talking about that."

"Well, I am." He pulled her close and used his free hand to begin tickling her.

Max quickly wiggled free and fled the scene while Michelle was laughing and trying to fight her way out of Steve's grip. Finally, she collapsed exhausted and admitted defeat.

"You know I love you, honey," Steve whispered into her hair.

"I love you, too," she said softly in reply.

He turned her face toward him and studied her for a moment.

"What?" Michelle asked.

"Our baby is going to be so beautiful. I hope she looks just like you."

Smiling, she reached to touch his cheek. He leaned forward and kissed her gently at first and then more passionately. "Let's skip dinner tonight," he whispered in a throaty voice.

"Okay," she agreed. They rose and walked upstairs with their arms wrapped around each other.

John watched Sheila as she fussed over his bed, adjusting the covers and fluffing the pillows. "Do you want to watch some TV tonight?" she asked, reaching for the remote control.

"No," John replied as he placed his hand over hers. "We . . . need . . . to . . . talk."

Sheila stopped and looked into John's eyes. She could see the worry written across his face. "What is it, sweetheart?"

"Sit . . .down."

Pulling the chair up to his bedside and taking his hand in hers, Sheila began again. "Tell me, John. What's troubling you?"

He studied her face. How could he explain Marilyn to his faithful, loving wife? He grasped for words. "A mistake."

"A mistake? What mistake?"

"I . . . don't . . . want. . .to. . .hurt . . .you."

"Is this about your accident, John?" She still could not get herself to use the word suicide, even though that had been the intent behind his injury. Accident somehow softened the blow.

John thought for a moment. "Yes…. No."

Sheila could see he was wrestling with his words as well as with whatever he needed to tell her. Trying to help him, she said, "It's kind of about what happened in Bridgeport, but not totally?"

He nodded. Then he took a deep breath and sighed, closing his eyes momentarily as if to shut out the truth.

"We don't have to talk about this right now." She could tell he was exhausted.

John opened his eyes and struggled to sit upright in the bed.

"Here. Let me help you." Sheila stood up and readjusted the pillows again, supporting John at the elbow as he scooted up.

"I . . . am . . . so. . .sorry," he began again.

"It's okay. You'll be fine. Just give it time."

"No." He paused, took another breath and continued. "About . . . Marilyn."

Sheila's pulse quickened. She hadn't heard that name in quite a while. Her mind flashed back to the first time she met Marilyn Marlow at a company Christmas party. She had the appearance of a lingerie model — sultry and seductive in her clinging, low-cut black cocktail dress.

When Sheila had learned about Marilyn being

John's assistant in the Dallas project, it had taken all her reserve and trust to resist protesting jealously. But John had always been a family man, and he'd never given her any reason to question his faithfulness.

"What are you talking about? What about Marilyn?"

"She . . . framed . . .me."

"How do you know? Did Clark figure this out?"

"Yes."

"But why? What did she have to gain?"

"Money . . . and . . . re . . .revenge."

"Revenge for what?" She could see this was taking a great toll on her husband, but it was clear he needed to get it off his shoulders.

"For . . . telling . . .her. . . no . . . more."

"No more?"

"No . . . more . . .us." John let out a deep sigh. His eyes were full of sorrow and regret.

"Are you telling me you and Marilyn had a relationship?"

"Yes. Three. . . weeks. Dallas." A tear rolled down his face.

Sheila released his hand and stood up. She walked over to the window and looked out over the sprawling lawn and rose garden that flanked the west side of the hospital. Her heart was squeezed in a vise, and her vision was blurring from the tears that threatened to spill. *Dear God, help me. What do I say to him?*

Running her fingers under her eyes, she wiped the tears away before turning to face her husband again. Sitting back down, she reached over and gently touched his hand. He turned and looked at her. His eyes were deep pools of expression. She could see compassion, regret, love, and surrender.

"I don't know what to say," she began, grasping for words. "You know I'd love to deck you," she added with a slight smile, "but it looks like you're already flat on your back."

He squeezed her hand and smiled his crooked smile, one side of his face remaining frozen in paralysis from his injury. "I . . .have. . .always. . .loved. . .you." His earnest expression touched her heart.

"I believe you, John. I have always loved you, too." She could not bring herself to say anymore than that.

"Call . . . Clark."

"Okay, I will." A few moments later, he was asleep — the exhaustion from the afternoon taking a huge toll on his already depleted reserves. Sheila leaned over, kissed him gently on the forehead as was her usual nighttime routine at the hospital, and then walked quietly out of the room.

When she arrived home, the phone was ringing. Before she could get to it, the answering machine picked up and she heard Michelle's voice on the other end.

"Hi, Mom. It's me. Just checking in to see how Dad's doing today. Give me a call when you get this message."

Sheila sunk into the soft cushion of the sofa and sighed. It meant so much to her that the kids checked in daily. But she didn't have the energy to call her daughter back tonight. Besides, she needed time to think — to process what she had learned tonight and decide how to put it all behind her. The kids must never know about John's affair. It would crush them, and maybe turn their hearts away from a father who so desperately needed their love now more than ever.

CHAPTER TWENTY

Steve woke up and reached across the bed to find his wife's side empty. Hearing muffled sniffling from the next room, he threw off the covers, raked his hand through his hair, and walked into the bathroom. Michelle was sitting on the edge of the bathtub in her robe, tears streaming down her face.

"What's wrong, babe? Did you have another nightmare?" he asked.

"No. I'm okay," she replied, turning away. Her voice was thick with emotion as she rubbed the back of her hand across her eyes.

Steve sat down beside her. He spotted the pregnancy test on the counter by the sink. Putting his arm around her, he gently pulled her head down onto his shoulder. Not quite sure what to say, he hesitated to speak. Instead, he took her hand off her lap and laced his fingers through hers. "It'll happen, Michelle. We just have to give it time. This is only the second month."

Her shoulders shuddered as a stray sob escaped. "The doctor said it shouldn't take more than three months," she began.

"So we still have another month left," he said, rubbing her back. "We can wait four more weeks, can't we?"

"Yeah, I guess," she replied softly. "Come back to bed. It's lonely in there without you."

She turned and looked at him. "I was thinking of

going downstairs and making a pot of tea. Maybe I'll read the Bible for a while."

"Want company?"

"No. I'll be okay."

He stood up with her and gave her a warm hug. "Be patient, okay?"

"Okay. I'll try." Giving him a peck on the cheek, she headed for the kitchen.

As Steve climbed back in bed, he saw Max curled up in the covers. "Move over, buddy. This is my side of the bed," he said as he scooted the cat out of the way. Pulling the quilt up over his shoulders, he heard the sound of the teakettle beginning to whistle as he drifted off to sleep.

Michelle poured herself some tea, added a little honey, and took it into the family room. She wrapped herself in the afghan and sat at the end of the couch, pulling her feet up underneath her and cradling the warm cup in her hands.

God, You know how much this baby means to me. You promised to give us the desires of our hearts. Please give us this one thing we so desire.

She could feel God's presence. It was almost as if He were sitting on the couch right beside her that very moment. She closed her eyes and listened with her heart, but all she could hear was a silent voice telling her, *Wait. Wait for My timing.*

She shook off her impression. Not wanting to hear anymore about waiting, she went to the kitchen, wearing the afghan like a cape. Then she reread the scripture she had posted on the refrigerator, "Delight yourself in the Lord and He will give you the desires of your heart."

Michelle glanced over at the Noah's ark lamp, sitting on the counter, and smiled as she imagined her baby's nursery all decorated.

Like Steve said, I can wait one more month. With that thought settled, she went upstairs and crawled back into bed, allowing Max to snuggle under the covers with her.

In twenty-five more minutes, the alarm clock would ring for Steve to get up. She wanted to get up with him and make a good breakfast before he took off for work. Pretty soon she'd have a baby to care for and wouldn't have as much time or energy to give her husband.

As she was starting breakfast, she remembered her mother hadn't returned her call from the night before. Yesterday was the first day she hadn't talked to her since her dad had been transferred to rehab. Michelle's mind started racing with possible scenarios.

What if her dad had suddenly relapsed? What if they were back in the hospital? Surely her mom would call her, wouldn't she?

It was early, and she hated to wake her mom if there was nothing wrong. On the other hand, her fears were escalating. They'd come so close to losing her dad. His safety and well-being were on Michelle's mind throughout each day.

She picked up the phone and dialed home. On the third ring, she heard her mother's somewhat garbled voice. "Hello?"

"Mom?"

"Mimi, is that you? Is something wrong?"

"That's what I was wondering. You didn't call me back last night. Is Dad okay?"

Her mom cleared her throat and replied, "Everything's, okay, honey. It was late when I got back. I didn't want to wake you."

"Don't ever worry about that, Mom. I need to talk to you everyday. I need to know you guys are alright."

"I'm sorry, honey. Please try not to worry. I

promise I'll call you if your dad has a setback, no matter what the time."

"Okay. Sorry if I woke you up."

"It's no problem. I need to get going anyway. And thanks for calling and checking. I really look forward to your calls everyday. It was just a late night last night, but everything's fine."

"Okay. Love you, Mom. Talk to you tomorrow."

"I love you too, Mimi."

Turning back to the breakfast preparations, Michelle heard Steve come barreling down the stairs. *Better hurry, or he'll leave hungry*, she thought as she grabbed some bread and threw it in the toaster.

Thanksgiving arrived two days later with a torrential downpour that threatened to close the highway. Michelle wondered if there would be a problem with Kristin and Mark flying into Portland, but Steve reassured her that only small private planes would be restricted from landing in the low visibility caused by the storm.

Michelle spent a half hour between preparations calling home and talking to her mom and grandparents. They had brought her dad home for the day, and she was able to speak with him briefly.

"Hi....honey," his voice struggled to communicate.

"Hi, Daddy. How are you?"

There was a long pause and then, "Okay. They....take....care....of ....me."

Michelle's heart ached. She wanted to be there to give him a hug and tell him how much he meant to her. He seemed so vulnerable. Would he ever recover the strength he had once possessed? Or would his life be a daily struggle just to say and do the simplest things?

"Daddy, you know how much I love you, right?" she asked, forcing her voice to be steady and calm.

"Love...you...too...Mi –chelle."

"Have a wonderful Thanksgiving. I miss you so much."

"You...too."

The next thing she knew, her mother's voice was on the other line. "Were you done talking, Mimi? He just handed me the phone."

"Yeah. I guess. Give him a big hug for me, Mom. Wish I could be there."

"Christmas is around the corner, sweetheart. We'll all be together then," her mother said reassuringly.

Ben and Kelly arrived in the late afternoon, bringing Kelly's special scalloped potato casserole. The fragrance of the turkey cooking in the oven and the warm glow of the fire in the fireplace gave a cozy and festive air to Steve and Michelle's house. "Smells great," Ben commented as he helped Kelly out of her raincoat.

Michelle noticed a slight bulge at Kelly's waistline. "Are you starting to show already?" she asked with amazement.

Kelly smiled. "I'm thirteen weeks now. First trimester is about over, but it seems like it will be forever until June 6th. I feel really sick if I don't keep something in my stomach. Most of this is probably just fat," she replied as she patted her tummy.

"What's your excuse?" Steve asked as he glanced at Ben's stomach, which also looked larger than usual.

"Sympathy pains," he explained. "Whenever I see her eating, I have to join in. You know, to keep her company."

"Right."

"Okay. Enough talk about stomachs," Michelle piped up. "Why don't you guys just make yourselves comfortable out here, and Kelly and I will go finish the feast in the kitchen," she said, smiling at Kelly.

"Sounds good to me," Ben replied. "Let us know if you need any help."

"Yeah. Let Ben know if you need any help," Steve said as he reached for the remote control and flipped on the football game.

"You guys listen for Kristin and Mark. They should be here anytime."

"Will do," Steve replied without taking his eyes off the game.

Michelle and Kelly retreated to the kitchen. As they cooked, they talked about their plans. Kelly was waiting to decorate her nursery until she made it halfway into her second trimester.

"I should probably wait, too, especially since I'm not even pregnant yet," Michelle replied. "But I keep finding all this cute stuff for my Noah's ark theme." She showed Kelly the lamp and some pictures from the baby store catalog.

Kelly didn't want to put a wet blanket on Michelle's plans, but she felt concerned about how determined Michelle was to make this all happen. "Michelle," she began carefully, "have you been praying about all this?"

"Yeah. Why?"

"Well, I'm just wondering if you are certain this is God's timing for you and Steve to start a family."

"I guess. It feels right. Wouldn't God take away this desire if it wasn't His timing?"

"Maybe. I just know I've gotten ahead of God a few times in my own life, and it's always ended up adding lots of extra grief."

"So how do you know when it's His timing?"

"Just pray and then wait to see what happens. But don't stress over it. By the way, I love the lamp," she added.

"Thanks," Michelle replied, her frown relaxing into a smile.

Suddenly the lights flickered and went out, leaving them standing in the dark.

"Hold on a sec," Steve called as he eased himself into the kitchen, sliding his feet carefully along the smooth flooring to avoid tripping over Max or any other obstacles. It was totally dark everywhere, indicating it was not just a power outage in this one residence but also affected the surrounding area, including the street lamps.

"What happened?" the girls asked in unison.

"A transformer must have gotten knocked out by the storm," he answered, retrieving a flashlight from the utility drawer. "Why don't you two come out to the family room with us."

"What about the turkey?" Michelle asked.

"It should be fine. No reason for the gas to go out too," Steve said.

"Oh yeah. Good thing we don't have electric like my parents."

The four of them sat in the family room. Steve lit a few candles on the mantle and the coffee table. "This is cozy," he said, trying to reassure his wife, who wasn't fond of storms.

"I'm getting worried about Mark and Kristin. What time is it? They should be here by now."

"It's 5:30," Steve replied.

"There were probably delays at the airport because of the weather," Kelly offered.

Ben suggested they pray. "Good idea," Steve agreed. "Would you like to do the honors?"

"No problem."

The four of them bowed their heads as Ben began, "Lord, we want to lift up Kristin and Mark to you right now. We know you can calm any storm. Wherever Kristin and Mark are at this moment, please protect and give them a harbor from the wind and rain. Bring them safely here, in your timing. We ask this in Jesus' name. Amen."

"Speaking of timing, I'd better get those potatoes in the oven," Kelly said.

"I'll help you," Ben offered, reaching for the flashlight to lead her through the darkness.

CHAPTER TWENTY-ONE

Kristin and Mark were sitting by the side of the road, their rental car having sputtered to a stop. The rain was pelting the windshield and the wind howled through the trees.

"I can't believe I left my cell phone at home," Mark said for the fourth time.

"Don't worry about it." Kristin flipped open her phone again. "Still no service on mine."

"I'm really sorry about this, honey. We should never have accepted this car. It didn't sound right when we were pulling out of the lot."

"It was the only one they had left, remember? Thanksgiving's just a crazy time to travel."

"Wish I knew more about cars," he said.

Just as he was about to step out into the pouring rain, an old Chevy truck pulled up beside them. "Need a lift?" an elderly man called through the downpour.

Mark looked at Kristin. He seemed like a nice enough fellow. Which would be safer — to be stuck out here in the storm or to accept a ride with a stranger? "What do you think?" he asked her.

Kristin peered down at the lit up face of her cell phone. 5:45. Michelle would be really worried. "Let's take it," Kristin said, something in her spirit sensing this man's good intentions.

"Yeah, thanks!" Mark called back as they grabbed their bags and dashed through the downpour to the passenger door.

"Jim Morgan," the man said, extending his hand to Mark.

"Mark Fisher. And this is Kristin," he said as he shook the driver's calloused hand.

"Where're you folks headed?" Jim asked as he pulled back out onto the highway.

"Sandy Cove," Kristin said quickly, "to see some friends."

"That's quite a ways. How'd you get stuck out here in the middle of nowhere on Thanksgiving night?"

"Our plane was delayed and there was only one rental car left," Mark began, trying to explain.

"We don't want to ruin any plans you have," Kristin added, noticing the man was wearing a tie under his old yellow raincoat.

"Well, I was actually on my way to my sister's house, just down the road a piece. If you folks don't mind pulling in there for a spell, we could phone ahead to your friends."

"That would be great," Mark replied.

"Steve could probably drive out and pick us up," Kristin suggested.

"I heard that part of the highway was flooded up ahead. Might not be a good night to travel through to the coast."

"Are there any motels nearby?" Mark asked.

"No need for a motel, young man. LouEllen will be happy to put you up for the night. Even though it's just the two of us, I'll wager she's made enough turkey dinner for an army. Never did know how to put a limit on her cooking. Hold tight," he said as he pulled off the road onto a winding driveway that led back into the trees.

The house was a simple, A-frame wooden structure with a large front porch and a welcoming warm glow reaching out through the lace covered windows.

They hurried from the truck up the front steps.

Jim rapped on the door twice in warning and then threw it open. Their senses were immediately bombarded by the warmth of the fire blazing in a brick fireplace dominating one wall of the living room. Heavenly aromas from the kitchen competed for their attention. Jim quickly closed the door behind them. "LouEllen?"

"I hear you, Jimmy. I'm just pulling the turkey out of the oven."

"You two folks wait here. I'll be back in a wink." Jim headed in the direction of the kitchen.

As he walked through the swinging door into the kitchen, Mark and Kristin could hear a female voice calling out, "Give me a hand with this, would you, Jimmy?"

"Look," Kristin said to Mark as she pointed to the painting on the wall over the buffet. It was a picture of an older man, his head bowed in prayer over a chunk of bread and bowl of soup. Underneath it was a scripture, "In everything, give thanks."

"I kind of sensed they might be Christians from the way Jim was so willing to take us in," Mark commented, relieved he had made the right choice in going with this man.

Just then, a plump woman in an old fashioned floral dress burst into the room with a smile. "Name's LouEllen," she offered as she wiped her hands on her apron. "Jimmy told me about your rental car. Never did trust those loaners myself," she added as she shook her head. "Let's get you two dried off a bit." She disappeared for a moment and returned with two large towels.

"It was very kind of your brother to help us out," Mark began, as he and Kristin used the towels to blot at their damp clothing.

"Nonsense. No problem at all. Least we could do with all the good Lord's done for us." LouEllen steered them over to the fireplace. "You two stand here and let the fire warm you up. Wish I had some dry clothes to offer you, but me and Jim – well let's just say we aren't as slim as we once were."

Mark smiled. "Well thanks just the same."

"I hate to ask you for another favor," Kristin began, "but would it be possible to use your phone to call our friends out in Sandy Cove. We'd be happy to pay for any long distance charges."

"You just come with me, darlin'. And don't you worry about any charges." LouEllen took Kristin by the hand and led her into the kitchen.

The room reminded Kristin of her grandparents' kitchen up in their cabin in the mountains. The appliances were old, but clean. A round wooden table sat in the middle of the floor and was currently loaded with ingredients used in the dinner. The old linoleum beneath their feet was yellowed and worn with a dark shadow by the sink where some water damage or just continuous standing had stained a spot.

The aromas were mouthwatering. A golden brown turkey rested on the cutting board on the counter, a bubbling hot sweet potato casserole sat next to it, and a pumpkin pie had been set on the adjacent counter. Jim was stirring the gravy and sneaking bites of the mashed potatoes in the pan next to him.

"Jimmy," LouEllen scolded. "Get your paws outta the taters."

"Oh, relax, Lulu. I'm just making sure they've been mashed through and through."

LouEllen shook her head, a scowl on her face melting back into a smile as she saw Kristin's expression. "Don't you mind us. We've been going at it like this since we were kids."

Kristin nodded her head and returned the warm smile. "Everything smells great."

"Let's just hope there'll be some left when it comes time to eat." LouEllen cocked her head in Jim's direction, and they both chuckled.

"Here's the phone, sweetie."

"Wow. I've never used one of these," Kristin said, looking at the old black phone with its dial mechanism.

Jimmy laughed. "I told you to get a new phone, Lou."

"Now why should I do that when this one works perfectly well?"

Kristin picked up the receiver, inserted her finger into the first hole and turned the dial until it hit the stop.

"You see, Jimmy, she's got it right down already." LouEllen said with a smile.

Kristin could hear the phone ringing and then Steve's voice on the other end. "Hello?"

"Hi Steve, it's Kristin."

"Where are you guys? Are you okay?"

"Yeah. We had a little car trouble with the rental we picked up at the airport, but a nice gentleman gave us a ride. We're at his sister's house. Apparently the highway is flooded between here and the coast, so we'll probably need to stay here overnight."

"Bummer. Here, let me put Michelle on." Kristin could hear Steve quickly explain what was happening as he handed Michelle the phone.

"Kristin, are you sure you're okay? Steve could try to drive out there and get you guys if you give us your location."

"I think we'd better wait 'til the rain lets up, 'Shell. It's really pouring here. How's it in Sandy Cove?"

"Pouring. The power went out, too. Fortunately the oven and stove are gas, so we should be okay for the dinner."

"That's good."

"Oh, Kristin. Dinner — what will you guys do

181

about Thanksgiving dinner?"

"The folks who took us in are offering to let us eat with them and stay the night here."

"Are you sure you're okay with that? I mean, spending Thanksgiving with strangers..."

"Actually, they're really nice people and the food looks delicious." Kristin noticed LouEllen and Jim had both gone into the dining room. "They're Christians, `Shell. We'll be fine here overnight. I'm just sorry to mess up your holiday."

"Don't worry about that. I'll put Steve back on the phone and maybe someone there can give him directions to pick you guys up tomorrow."

Jim talked to Steve and explained that he would be happy to drive Kristin and Mark out to Sandy Cove in the morning. Steve tried to convince him it wasn't necessary and he'd drive out there at first light, but Jim wouldn't take no for an answer. As soon as the phone conversation ended, Kristin and Mark followed him back into the dining room.

Sitting down at the festive table laden with a wonderful feast, Jim reached out in both directions in a gesture of prayer. As the four of them joined hands, he bowed his head and prayed, "Lord, we are thankful for this food we are about to eat. And we thank you for keeping Mark and Kristin safe and bringing them here to share this holiday with us. Bless their friends in Sandy Cove and give them a good Thanksgiving as well. In your name we pray. Amen."

"Amen," the rest of them echoed.

At the same time, Steve, Michelle, Ben, and Kelly were bowing their heads and thanking God for their shared meal. As they started to pass the food around the candlelit table, the lights and music came back on. "That's better," Steve said with a smile.

Later that night, after Ben and Kelly had gone

home and Steve was upstairs getting ready for bed, Michelle sat down with her Bible. It seems like things never turn out the way I want them to. I really wanted to be pregnant before Thanksgiving, and I was looking forward to seeing Kristin and Mark and introducing them to Ben and Kelly. She opened her Bible to the passage marked in Psalm 37. Delight yourself in the Lord and He will give you the desires of your heart.

Michelle could feel the tears starting again. Do you really keep your promises, Lord? She closed the Bible and headed upstairs.

CHAPTER TWENTY-TWO

The sun was streaming into their bedroom the next morning when Michelle woke up. She could hear Steve in the shower and smelled fresh brewed coffee. Glancing over, she saw a steaming cup sitting on the bedside table. What a sweetie to bring me coffee in bed. Her heart swelled with love for her husband.

Propping herself up against the headboard, she cupped the warm mug in her hands as she thought about a dream she'd had just before awakening. It seemed so real. She was in a hospital and a nurse was handing her a tiny newborn baby girl wrapped in a pink receiving blanket. Her mother and Steve were at her side, both joyously welcoming the new member of their family. As she continued thinking about the dream, she could almost feel the tiny bundle in her arms and see the baby's blue eyes gazing into hers.

Maybe it was a sign from God that this really was her time to become a mom.

She sipped her coffee and gazed out the window at the deep blue sky and white, puffy clouds as she thought about her day ahead. Kristin and Mark would be there soon. She was thankful for the change in weather. *A sunny day – finally. Maybe Kristin and I will go down and take a walk at the beach.*

"Hey there, gorgeous," Steve said, breaking her reverie. His hair was wet and tousled, a towel secured around his waist.

"Did you leave me any hot water?" Michelle asked with a grin.

"Nope. You should have joined me in there." He winked in reply.

She climbed out of bed, placing the coffee mug on the nightstand. "Thanks for the coffee."

"Anytime." He looked out the window. "Looks like a great day. Kristin and Mark should be here anytime."

"Yeah. I'd better hurry and get my shower."

"Need any help?"

"Funny." Michelle tossed a pillow at him, but he ducked, leaving it on the floor where it landed.

"Just thought I'd offer," he countered with a grin.

"I know exactly what you thought. We don't have time."

"Okay. Whatever you say."

Smiling, she said, "Later, babe."

"Right. Later." Turning toward the closet, he added under his breath, "I'll just check the schedule."

A knife pierced Michelle's heart. It was just another reminder she wasn't pregnant yet. Rather than trying to appease him, she ignored his remark and went into the bathroom.

When she got out of the shower, she could hear voices downstairs. Hurrying to get dressed, she headed down to greet Kristin and Mark.

"You're here!" she exclaimed as she raced over and hugged Kristin. "And this must be Mark," she added with a smile. Over her shoulder she could see an older man with a straw hat clutched in his hand.

"Michelle, this is my fiancé, Mark, and this is Jim Morgan." Kristin gestured toward Jim who nodded his greeting.

"Thank you so much for everything," Michelle said as she extended her hand to Jim.

185

He seemed to feel a bit awkward shaking hands with a woman, but his grasp was warm and firm. "You're welcome. It was nothing, really. We were blessed to have `em join us for Thanksgiving dinner."

"You've got to get to know these folks, Steve," Mark commented. "Jim's sister's quite a cook."

Jim smiled and blushed.

"I was telling them about your friends, Ben and Kelly, and the church they are planting here," Mark continued.

"We'd like to help in any way we can," Jim offered.

"Well, I'll tell Ben. They are planning to start with a weekly Bible study and see what develops from there."

"You just let us know when and where they'll be holdin' their meetings and we'll be there. We don't got a lot of money or anything like that, but we can bring some homemade muffins."

"I'm sure they'd appreciate that. Isn't it quite a way for you to drive, though?"

"It ain't that far. LouEllen would love to be part of a new church getting started. She's been sayin' for a long time that she wants me to start takin' her to Portland again on Sundays, but the drive out here is much nicer. Lots less traffic."

"Great. Just leave me your phone number, and we'll contact you in a week or two." Steve handed him a small pad of paper and pen.

Jim scrawled his number down. "Well, I'll be off and let you folks get on with your visit."

"Thanks again, Jim," Mark said, shaking his hand. Kristin gave him a hug, causing him to blush again.

"You two take care now, you hear?" Jim said, smiling fondly at Mark and Kristin. "You be sure to send us an invite to that wedding of yours," he added with a wink.

After he had left, Michelle and Steve led Mark and Kristin into the kitchen. They sat down at the table and shared coffee and stories about their Thanksgiving dinner adventures. Eventually the conversation drifted to Sandy Cove and the new church Ben was hoping to start.

Mark seemed very interested to meet Ben and learn more about the church planting process.

"Let me give him a call and see what he's up to. Maybe we could just drive over to their house and I could introduce you guys," Steve suggested.

When they called, Ben was just sitting around reading the newspaper, so Steve and Mark decided to drive over.

"Want to go for a walk on the beach while they're gone?" Michelle asked Kristin.

"That would be great. It's such a pretty day."

"Yeah, and that's rare around here. Let me just dry my hair, and I'll be ready to go."

"Okay. I'll wait here and play with your kitty," Kristin said, scooping Max up into her arms.

"He'll keep you entertained," Michelle said with a smile. "Be right back."

Soon they were climbing out of Michelle's car and walking out onto the sand, which was still damp from the downpour the night before. The air felt crisp and the wind bit their faces, but the water was sparkling and the sky was a brilliant shade of blue. Michelle and Kristin linked arms, like they had all their lives, as they walked toward the water's edge.

"So how are the wedding plans coming along?" Michelle asked.

"Great. I still can't believe it's true. Mark was so worth waiting for."

"He seems to adore you," Michelle observed.

"Feeling's mutual," she replied. "How are things with you and Steve? You said you guys had a fight the other night. Is everything okay?"

Michelle sighed. "Oh, Kristin. I've been wanting to talk to you about so many things. I'm not sure where to start." They stopped walking and sat down on some rocks. The sound of the waves crashing and the seagulls overhead took them back to all the times they had spent at Seal Beach listening to each other's hopes, dreams, and disappointments.

"Well, why don't you start by telling me what you were fighting about?" Kristin suggested.

"How do I explain all this? I guess it started at the hospital with my dad." She paused, staring out over the water. "Seeing the tiny infants...."

Kristin smiled, nodding. "They sure are cute, aren't they? All bundled up in their little blankets."

"I fell in love with every one of them." Michelle sighed. "Anyway, it kind of got me dreaming about having a baby of my own." She paused again for a minute. "Then I thought I might be pregnant because my period was late, but it turned out to be just from the stress of everything with my dad."

Kristin reached over and squeezed her hand. Michelle could feel her tears starting to well up again. She took a deep breath and continued. "So Steve and I had a talk and decided it was okay to start trying to get pregnant."

"That's so exciting, Michelle," Kristin said hopefully.

"Well, it's not quite that simple. I went to the doctor and she put me on a mild fertility pill to get my cycles back in gear. She said I should get pregnant in the next three months if I follow this schedule she gave me."

"And?"

"And it's been two months. No luck." Michelle looked Kristin in the eye. "What's wrong with me? I keep praying and doing what the doctor said, and nothing's working." A tear slipped down her cheek.

"Sometimes things take time, `Shell." Kristin wrapped her arm around her shoulder and pulled her close. "It'll work out. In God's timing."

"What does that mean? That God might not want us to have a baby right now?"

"I really don't know what God's plan is for you guys. But I do know He will give you the desires of your heart, if you just trust Him and be patient."

"It's funny you should say that. The verse in the Bible I keep reading is in Psalm 37 where it says, 'Delight yourself in the Lord,'"

"...and He will give you the desires of your heart," Kristin joined in to finish the verse. "He will, `Shell. I know He will. Have you studied that entire Psalm?"

Michelle looked a little puzzled. "What do you mean?"

"I mean the other verses around that verse. The ones that talk about trusting God, committing your way to Him, and waiting patiently."

"I'm trying to be patient, Kristin. But Steve and I get edgy with each other pretty easily, and I can't figure out why nothing works out the way I plan for it to. I mean school... the baby...and just look at last night. I couldn't even have the Thanksgiving dinner that I planned for weeks, without the power going out and my best friend getting stuck at some strangers' house." She paused and then added, "On top of that, every time the phone rings, I wonder if it's Mom calling to tell me Dad's had a set back, or worse. There was one day when I couldn't get a hold of her, and I was so worried. It's like I'm on edge all the time. Bet Steve is thrilled to be married to such a basket case." She pushed herself up from the rock and started walking, wiping her tears on the back of her jacket sleeve.

Kristin stood and took off down the beach after

her.

CHAPTER TWENTY-THREE

When Kristin caught up to Michelle, she simply draped her arm around her shoulder and fell into step beside her as they silently continued down the beach.

Michelle was still sniffling, but she had stopped crying. "I'm sorry, Kristin. I hate how I've been getting so emotional lately about everything."

"Don't apologize, `Shell. You've been through a lot." Kristin hesitated and then added, "Everything with your dad – I can't imagine how hard that must be for you. Calling home everyday just to find out if he's okay. And all the worry about your mom and how she's handling all of it, too. Then to have this other concern start to worry you...

"Believe me, I know how hard it is to wait for something you really want. It was hard for me when all my friends were either seriously dating someone or getting married, and there I was, the single girl no one wanted.

"I watched you and Steve preparing for your wedding. It was all so romantic. Even though I was happy for you, I couldn't help being a little jealous and wondering what was the matter with me. Why didn't any guy want me?"

Michelle looked over at Kristin and her heart ached for the pain her friend had gone through. Pain she'd been unaware of because she was so caught up in her own excitement. "I'm so sorry, Kristin. I didn't know."

Kristin looked into her eyes and smiled softly. "I'm not telling you this to get you to feel sorry for me. I just want you to know I really do understand what it's like to want something so bad that it hurts and have no guarantee of when you will get it. We all have seasons when we have to just wait."

"Yeah."

"How is Steve handling all this? Is he wanting a baby as much as you do?"

"I don't know. He seems fine with the idea, but it's really my thing more than his. He has work, his career. I just keep picturing how sweet it would be for the whole family if we had a baby now. It would bring so much excitement and hope for all of us."

Kristin just nodded, studying her face.

"I guess Steve would be fine waiting for it to all just happen in what he calls 'God's timing.' Sometimes he makes me feel bad about our little fertility schedule. At first he was all hyped when it meant I'd be coming home from Bridgeport more often. But now that Dad is back in Southern California, and I'm home to stay, he seems really put out by the whole schedule thing."

"Maybe he just feels like some of the spark is lost," Kristin offered.

"Probably."

"Is that what you had the fight about the other day?"

Michelle flashed back to the scene at the coffee shop with Trevor. "No. It was something else."

"Want to talk about it?"

"I guess. But you'll probably be on his side."

Kristin looked at her with a puzzled expression. "Why do you say that?"

"Because most people wouldn't understand."

"Most people? How about your best friend

forever?" Kristin playfully slugged Michelle's shoulder.

"Okay. I'll tell you. Just don't think I'm a horrible person."

"I would never think that of you. You know me better than that." This time she was completely serious.

"Want to sit down?" Michelle asked, taking her by the hand and leading her down to a large driftwood log that faced out over the water.

As they watched the waves roll in one after the other, she told Kristin all about her friendship with Trevor – how they met, the class she took from him, the special attention he showed her, their weekend at the New Age conference and the unexpected kiss. She explained the way he always seemed to understand her and help her through times of confusion or fear, and their last meeting at the coffee shop when Steve had walked in and seen Trevor's hand holding hers.

"So anyway, that is what we had the fight about."

"I can see why," Kristin responded.

"I told you you'd be on Steve's side."

"I'm not taking sides. I'm just saying I can understand why that would lead to a fight. If I ever saw some girl sitting across a table from Mark holding his hand, I'd be pretty upset too."

"Even if they were just friends?"

"From what you've told me, your relationship with Trevor has crossed over the line of friendship more than once."

"But I just think of him as a friend, Kristin. Seriously."

"You might think of him as a friend, but how does he think of you?"

"That's exactly what Steve said. He thinks Trevor is all hot for me or something."

"And that's so impossible?"

"Come on, Kristin. He knows I'm a married

woman. It's not like I'm leading him on or anything."

"You might not be meaning to lead him on, but personally I think he sees more in you than just friendship."

"Why would you say that? You don't even know him."

"I know guys, Michelle. Come on. Think about it. He kisses you in your hotel room at the conference and then pretends you two are just pals? Why do you think he waited while you got off the plane ahead of him so Steve wouldn't see the two of you together? And why do you think he put his hand over yours at the restaurant? This guy likes you, Michelle, and I don't mean like a buddy."

"You think so?"

"I really do."

"So what do I do now? Just quit being his friend?"

"Yeah. That's exactly what you need to do. You just told me, you're a married woman. A happily married woman, from what I could tell from your emails and our phone conversations."

"I am happily married. You know I love Steve. He just doesn't always understand me."

"Like Trevor does?" Kristin asked.

"Yeah. Like Trevor does. Is that such a sin?" Kristin searched Michelle's face.

"What do you think?"

"I don't have that many friends in Sandy Cove, Kristin."

"And if the tables were turned?" Kristin asked.

"What? If Steve had a female friend?"

"Yeah. How would you feel then?"

"Steve is surrounded by women in the office where he works.He and Roger have a cute secretary and many female clients. That doesn't matter to me."

"That's different, `Shell, and you know it. If you

knew Steve had kissed someone else while he was gone on a weekend business trip, I doubt you'd be okay with him having lunch with her and sitting across the table from her holding hands."

Michelle eyes misted over. She sighed. "Yeah. I guess you're right."

"Everybody feels insecure at times, Michelle. Maybe that's why Trevor's friendship appeals to you so much – he makes you feel so special and understood. But think of it from Steve's side, and I think you'll realize you've got to give up this relationship with Trevor."

"But I really only have three friends here in Sandy Cove – Monica, Starla, and Trevor."

"What about Kelly? Isn't she your friend?"

"I guess, but we're just starting to get to know each other."

"Well, why don't you invest some time in that relationship for a while. Kelly must be kind of lonely, too. And you have a lot in common, with both of you coming from Southern California and your husbands being friends. Plus you have the bond of being Christians. It doesn't sound like you have that with Trevor or Starla or Monica."

"Actually, that part kind of intimidates me. All this Christianity stuff is really new to me, Kristin. I'm still sorting through all of it and trying to figure out what to do with all the New Age things I was learning before this."

"It's pretty new to me, too. But the only way to really grow in your relationship with God is to just dig in, study the Bible, and spend time with other people who have the same beliefs."

Michelle looked at her. "I guess Mark has really helped you in that area."

"Yeah. He's so patient with me, but he keeps challenging me one step at a time, to keep learning and growing in my faith."

"I can tell. You're different."

"Good different or bad different?" Kristin asked.

"Good, of course." Michelle smiled and squeezed her hand.

"Want to walk some more?"

"Okay."

As they strolled down the shore, the smell of the salt air and the cries of the seagulls helped them both relax. They continued to talk about the issues on their minds and hearts. Michelle agreed to spend more time seeking God and waiting patiently for the baby she wanted, and Kristin promised to pray for her to have wisdom about Trevor and for God to give her and Steve a beautiful baby.

Before going to bed that night, Michelle got out her Bible and read the other verses in Psalm 37 that Kristin had been talking about.

"Trust in the Lord and do good; dwell in the land and enjoy safe pasture. Delight yourself in the Lord and He will give you the desires of your heart. Commit your way to the Lord; trust in Him and He will do this."

Help me be patient, God. Help me to be thankful for what I have and to trust you.

Steve strolled into the bedroom. "You look so serious. Everything okay?"

Glancing up, she just nodded, patting the bed beside her. A grin softened her expression as she asked, "Coming to bed?"

The next morning Michelle was reading her Bible again when Kristin came into the kitchen.

"Good morning, `Shell," her friend said

cheerfully. "Oh, sorry. I didn't mean to interrupt your reading."

"Don't be silly," she replied, returning her warm smile. "Want some coffee?"

"Yeah. That sounds great. Where are the guys?"

"They went out to look at a commercial building for rent. Ben wanted their opinion about leasing it for the church."

"I'll bet Mark is loving this," Kristin said thoughtfully. "He's always wanted to be part of a church planting team."

"Really? You guys should move here and help Ben. Isn't Mark a youth pastor? I'm sure Ben will be needing one with all the teens around here."

"Wouldn't that be great? We could be neighbors." They both grinned as they sipped their coffee.

"You should have Mark talk to Ben about it," Michelle suggested.

"I'll mention it to him, but he's pretty committed to the kids he works with right now. I'm not sure he'd be willing to leave that position."

"Well, it's something we could pray about," Michelle said with a big smile.

"Speaking of Mark being a pastor and about praying," Kristin began. "I could really use your prayers for me, too."

"Why? What's up?"

"It's just a little scary thinking about becoming a pastor's wife. I feel like I should know so much more about the Bible and everything."

"I'm sure you'll be fine, Kristin. Like I said yesterday, I can really see the difference your faith is making in who you are and the way you look at life. Plus you have Mark there to answer all your questions about the Bible when you aren't sure of something."

"I know, but still...just pray for me, okay?" Kristin

asked.

"Sure. You know I will. Just remember I'm kind of a novice at this prayer thing."

"I don't think that matters to God," Kristin replied with a grin.

"I hope not 'cause I've got a lot resting on Him answering a few of my prayers."

"He will, `Shell. Just give Him time."

"There's that four letter word again. Time." Michelle shrugged and grabbed some bread out of the refrigerator to make toast. "Sourdough, right?"

"With strawberry jam."

"With strawberry jam. Coming right up."

CHAPTER TWENTY-FOUR

Rick Chambers looked over the sea of faces in the lecture hall. Today would be his favorite class of the semester, the one where any "born again-ers" would likely surface. It was his opportunity to begin challenging them personally, to help them see the archaic nature of their Christian beliefs, and to broaden their viewpoint to one of contemporary humanism. He'd been successful in this endeavor in the past, and he saw it as one of his critical roles as an intellectual leader and guide.

He usually began this session in a casual discussion format to loosen up the dialogue he hoped would naturally unfold. Pushing aside his computer and lecture notes, he greeted the students and hiked himself onto the table, straddling the front corner with one leg resting on the ground, the other dangling freely in front of him. Setting his coffee cup at his side, he smiled at the group and began.

"I'd like to start out the day with a discussion of your reading assignment about the Phoenician culture. What did you find most inspiring about their accomplishments?"

Several students raised their hands and offered answers reflective of the text.

"Yes. Can you see how those advances have benefited our culture today?"

Nods of affirmation indicated his point was well taken.

"What were some evidences from the Phoenician culture that indicated their attachment to paganism?"

A student from the back of the room raised his hand. "David?" Dr. Chambers responded.

"The worship of the god of Moloch."

"Yes. Good example. What did you learn about Moloch and the Phoenicians?" Dr. Chambers lobbed the question to the class.

A girl raised her hand and answered, "That they sacrificed their infant children to him."

"Sadly, yes. They would heat the statue of Moloch with fire and then place a newborn in his arms and watch it burn to death."

Michelle felt nauseous as she recalled this description. Her mind traveled back to the babies she'd seen at the hospital – such tiny, helpless infants nestled in their mothers' arms. How could anyone sacrifice one of these precious little ones to a god of stone?

"What might have been a good outcome of this ritual for the evolution of society and man?" Dr. Chambers asked.

The class was silent.

"No one can think of anything good that might have come from this?" Dr. Chambers probed.

Again silence in the room. Michelle squirmed inside. Where was he going with this?

"Allow me to give you a hint. As we know, Moloch was the god of the Phoenicians. He represented the religious focus of their time. Was religion a force for good or evil?"

The girl next to Michelle raised her hand.

"Kate?"

"Evil?"

"Exactly. And how does that apply to religion today?"

Michelle heard someone stand behind her. The

class turned to look at the young man in the back of the room who had spoken earlier. "Professor?"

"Yes, David."

"I believe your goal here is to lead us to an assumption that religion is a negative factor in society."

"Interesting perspective. Go on."

"On the first day of class, you invited us to challenge you. I'd like to pose a challenge."

Dr. Chambers was standing now. He crossed his arms and walked closer to the front row. "Be my guest," he replied with a smile.

"While pagan religions such as the worship of Moloch were barbaric and detrimental to society, isn't it true that Christianity is the opposite?"

"Continue."

"Well, for example, doesn't Christianity take a stand in opposition to the sacrifice of babies which occurs today in the form of abortion?"

Michelle could feel her heart racing. This guy was saying exactly what was on her mind.

Dr. Chambers raised his eyebrows. "Interesting comment. How many of you would compare the infant sacrifices to Moloch to our modern day medical practice of terminating an unwanted pregnancy?"

Michelle wanted to raise her hand, but no one was responding. She felt badly for the young man who had courageously challenged Dr. Chambers, but she lacked her own courage to stand with him.

"Well, David, as you can see, you are alone in your perspective and defense of religion. I think we'll move forward with a glimpse into the practices of Christians during the crusades. Perhaps that will help you rethink your position."

Dr. Chambers flipped open his laptop. An image of a vicious looking man on horseback wearing a cross on his shield as he plunged a sword into the chest of an unarmed man on the ground was entitled: The Crusades of Christ, a Dark Era in Mankind's Evolution.

As Michelle walked out of class, she noticed David talking to another student. Finally finding the courage she'd lack in the lecture hall, she walked up and waited for their conversation to end.

David turned to acknowledge her, and she began, "Thanks for speaking up in there. I wish I would have had the courage to say something, too."

"No worries. I'm used to professors like Chambers. They seem to be running the show at universities these days. But as the head of Campus Crusade for Christ at this campus, there's no way I can let those guys blow hot air without at least challenging the other students to think for themselves," he explained.

"What's Campus Crusade for Christ?" Michelle asked, her interest piqued by this possible link to her new faith.

"It's an organization for Christians on college campuses. A place where like-minded believers can support each other as well as share their faith with non-believers." David paused and reached into his backpack, pulling out a flyer. He extended it toward her. "Here. This explains more about us."

Michelle took the flyer and looked it over.

"If you're interested, we're meeting tomorrow night to discuss an outreach to the local family planning clinic," David offered.

"Really? That's appropriate. Especially after the Moloch lecture today," Michelle added with a cringe.

"Yeah. Great timing, huh? God seems to be the master of that. Timing, I mean." David smiled. "Wanna join us?"

"Maybe. I'll talk to my husband about it and let you know," she replied, noting his phone number and email address.

David smiled and extended his hand. "David." She reached out and shook it. "Michelle."

"Great to meet you, Michelle. Hope to see you tomorrow night. You can just show up. No need to call first."

Michelle smiled, nodding. A sense of peace and purpose surged within. What a great opportunity for her to grow in her faith and to be used for God at the same time. "Okay, thanks."

The group of students sat together on a grassy hillside of the park that sloped down to the sidewalk below. Michelle hugged her knees to her chest as a cool breeze wafted past them. Across the street, the clinic was in full swing with several cars in the parking lot and an open door extended to the public.

David stood and faced the group, his back to the clinic. "Let's pray," he began. Michelle bowed her head along with the others. "Father, we are here to serve you today. Those who come to this place are hurting, Lord. They are looking for answers. Help us to share the hope that only you can offer them. Give us wisdom, gentle and compassionate spirits, and the right words. Save lives today. In Jesus' name, amen."

"Amen," echoed the students surrounding Michelle.

David and a girl named Traci started walking down the slope to the street. "You guys be praying," David called over his shoulder.

"What will they do?" Michelle asked Alise, the girl sitting next to her.

"They'll stand over by the parking lot and wait for someone to show up at the clinic. When they see a girl coming, they'll try to talk to her about options and other possible resources many of them don't even know about," Alise replied.

"But aren't there lots of girls who come here just for birth control or other health needs?" Michelle asked.

"Sometimes. But usually they are coming because of an unwanted pregnancy. The clinic is mostly for abortions."

Michelle felt sick. She wanted a baby so badly and she knew in her heart she could easily love any one of those babies like her own. How could someone not understand the wonder of a new life growing inside?

"What about adoption?" she asked. "Why don't they consider adopting out those babies?"

Alise looked at her and smiled sadly. "Abortion is a big money maker, Michelle. These clinics aren't going to encourage women to look at alternatives like adoption. Besides, most of these women have no idea about the actual stages of development of their unborn babies. They're told their babies are just unformed masses of tissue and an abortion will solve their problems." She shook her head and then added, "They're scared, Michelle. I guess for most this seems like their only choice."

Tears filled Michelle's eyes. Oh, God. Please help David and Traci to make a difference for at least one baby today. She thought back to the meeting at David's place the night before. He'd shown them a website which kept a running count of the number of abortions performed that year worldwide. The number had increased every second. And Michelle had tried not to think about each of the precious babies at the hospital as her eyes filled with tears for the millions of infants losing their lives this very year.

"What was David saying the other night about safe haven laws?" Michelle asked Alise.

"Safe haven or safe surrender laws give mothers who can't care for their babies a chance to turn them over to a safe location like a fire department or police department without facing abandonment charges."

"Do they tell them about that option?" Michelle asked as she gestured to the clinic across the street.

"I doubt it, Michelle. The people who run these clinics really believe their clients should not go through with an unplanned or unwanted pregnancy."

"But what about the babies? Don't they care about them?"

"Their business is with the pregnant women. They don't consider a fetus to be a baby unless it is wanted or planned."

Michelle couldn't help wondering how many women would consider allowing their infants to survive if they knew they had a safe haven option. From what David had told them, only a handful of women exercised this option compared to the throngs who were persuaded to abort. It seemed like such a tragedy that convenience was preached as trumping the value of human life.

And where did that mindset leave couples like her and Steve, who might not ever be able to have children of their own? Couldn't these women understand that couples from many good homes were waiting to take in and raise their unwanted babies? Michelle's grandmother had spoken of the days before abortion was legal. She'd talked of the handful of adoptions in her own circle of friends and the joy those babies had brought to the eager couples who gave them a family and a future.

She could almost understand the desperation of a woman who found herself pregnant as the result of a rape. But even then, she wondered at the fact that the rapist would not be eligible for capital punishment, yet the life of the innocent baby could be legally terminated. And when David had given them the statistics on motivation for abortion, only a fraction had to do with rape, incest, or the health of the mother.

Images of the sacrifices to Moloch mingled with what she knew was taking place in the clinic across the street. A physical ache pressed upon Michelle's heart as a lump in her throat made it difficult to swallow.

Alise nudged her. "Look," she pointed across the street. A girl who appeared to be in her teens was climbing out of the front seat of a beat up van. David and Traci walked in her direction. "Let's pray," Alise said as she reached over and put her hand on Michelle's.

"How'd it go?" Steve asked as Michelle came into the kitchen several hours later.

She walked over to him and put her arms around his waist, burying her face in his chest.

"Hey. What's up? Are you okay?" he asked sounding concerned.

"I just... Oh Steve, I just can't believe how many girls were there." She pulled back and looked into his eyes. "At least 10 babies lost their chance for life at that clinic today." She shook her head. "Only two girls changed their minds after listening to David and Traci. Two."

"Well, that's two more babies who will live, honey. You guys made a difference for those two," he said, hoping to sound encouraging.

"But what about the rest?"

"They're in God's hands, Michelle." He guided

her over to the table and they sat down.

"It seems so unfair. We really want a baby and can't seem to get pregnant. Meanwhile that clinic is encouraging women to terminate pregnancies everyday. Many of the girls don't even know their babies already have arms, legs, hands, feet..."

Steve felt so frustrated and helpless. "I know. It's hard to understand."

Michelle gazed out the window, looking lost.

"What are you thinking?" he asked.

"I was thinking of the babies at the hospital. Just looking at them in their little blankets, I felt like I could have loved any one of them as my own," she explained.

"Yeah. I remember you saying that."

"Can we at least think about the possibility of adoption?"

"We can pray about it, but don't get your hopes up. Private adoption is really expensive." She leaned over and hugged him. "Okay, thanks," she replied.

Steve turned to put some paperwork into his briefcase, and she went into the other room to call her mom. She was eager for Christmas to come so she could actually see everyone in person again. Many times, when her thoughts went to her dad, all she could picture were scenes from the hospital — the tubes and monitors, the fear in his eyes when he tried to speak and couldn't find the words. She wanted to see him at home again, and see for herself that he was really, truly on the road to recovery.

Her mom tried to sound optimistic, but Michelle knew she was battling worries of her own. And she had the feeling her mom was carrying burdens she wasn't sharing with her.

Their conversation went the same as always. Michelle asked about her dad's day, and Sheila reported the therapy and any progress he'd had.

"Is there anything else, Mom?" Michelle asked after the report.

"Like what, dear?"

"I don't know. You just seem kind of worried lately. Like things aren't going as well as you hoped."

"Everything's right on schedule, honey. Don't worry. I'm just tired by the end of the day."

As Michelle climbed into bed that night, she thought back over her day and thanked God for the chance to support the team at the clinic that morning and for the change in Steve's attitude about the possibility of adoption. As she was about to drift off to sleep, she pictured the tiny infants in the hospital, and these words crept into her mind. *Try every door, Michelle.*

What did it mean?

The few short weeks between Thanksgiving and Christmas flew by. Michelle and Steve had a flight down to Southern California on the twenty-third of December. She was so eager to see her family again and be able to hug her mom and dad.

The night before their departure, Michelle started feeling the familiar cramping that signaled the end of another cycle.

In the past three weeks since Kristin's visit, Michelle had tried fervently to spend more time with God praying and reading her Bible. Though she drew comfort from some of the verses she read, she still had a hard time accepting and understanding the idea that it might not be in God's plan for her to have a baby right now.

Everywhere she went, she seemed to run into pregnant women or women pushing baby strollers. When she did her Christmas shopping, she gravitated to all the baby departments, oohing and ahhing at the cute little dresses for girls and overalls for boys. She even stopped in a maternity clothes store and checked out the latest fashions. In her heart, she felt certain this was the time to start a family. Besides, wouldn't it help to cement the bond between her and Steve that her friendship with Trevor had threatened to fracture?

At first she tried to deny the cramping and continue with her packing. Finally she gave in to another month of disappointment and sat down on the bed to pray. Clutching a teddy bear Steve had gotten her in Bridgeport, she poured out her heart to God.

Okay, God. Here we go again. Another month. You know my heart. Please help me be strong for Steve and for my family. Help me not let this disappointment ruin our Christmas.

She sat back against the headboard, cradling the teddy bear to her breast like a baby. Carrying it downstairs, she went into the kitchen and sat down at the table to read through the mail.

Opening a card from Jim Morgan and his sister LouEllen, Michelle gazed at the serene picture of Mary and Joseph with little baby Jesus. "The best Christmas gift ever was the gift of a precious baby that first Christmas morn." She closed her eyes and allowed a tear to trickle down her cheek. *How pathetic am I? Here Jim and LouEllen don't even have spouses, but they have joy and peace. Meanwhile, I've got a man who loves me and here I sit wallowing in pity.* Michelle made a mental note to try to spend time with the Morgans after she got back home. Maybe she could learn some things about contentment.

The sound of the garage door opening pulled her back to the moment. As Steve entered the kitchen carrying his briefcase, he asked, "How's the packing coming? Are you almost done? We should get to bed early since we've got to be out of here by 5:00 tomorrow morning."

"Yeah," she replied, but her voice lacked enthusiasm

"What's wrong?"

"We're not pregnant. It didn't work."

Steve sighed. He stood up and gently helped her up into his embrace. "I'm sorry hon. I know this means a lot to you."

"To me? What about to you? Am I the only one who really wants this baby?"

"Come on, Michelle. You know I care."

"It seems like you only care because I do," she said.

"Whatever the reason, I care. I'd love to have a baby with you." Reaching out, he lifted her chin with his finger. "Just because it's taking some time, doesn't mean God doesn't want us to have a family. We just have to be patient."

"Maybe," she replied. "But we have no guarantee we will actually ever have a baby."

"Life doesn't hold many guarantees. You know that."

"I was just kind of banking on what the doctor said about three months."

"The doctor isn't God. She's only giving you the odds. Maybe next month will be the winner."

"I think we should go back after the first of the year and see what she says."

"Fine. I have no problem with that." He hesitated and then added, "Let's just try to enjoy the Christmas holiday with your family. Your mom and dad really need us to be there for them."

"I know. You're right. I've got to pull myself out of this before we get there."

"We'll talk about going to the doctor in January and see what she says. In the meantime, let's try to be patient and see what happens."

"Okay." She perked up a little. "But you did say we could even consider looking into adoption, too, right?" She wrapped her arms around his waist and looked up into his eyes.

Steve bent down and kissed her gently. "I think you're getting way ahead of yourself there. Let's just give all this some time. Adoption is really expensive. Until you get your credential and start teaching, we've got to watch our money, too."

"Okay. Let's just keep every option open." She pulled him closer and kissed him deeply. "I love you, Steve." Before he could respond, she kissed him again.

"Whoa, girl. We won't get any packing finished at this rate."

She smiled and released him. "I've got the big suitcase ready to go downstairs. I'll finish packing the bathroom bag and make sure all the gifts are labeled." She walked out of the kitchen carrying the teddy bear, with Steve close behind.

As Michelle and Steve walked into her parents' home the next afternoon, a wave of nostalgia rolled over her. Everything looked and smelled like it did every year at Christmas. The only difference was the fact that her dad was not standing at the door to greet her. Instead it was her grandfather who ushered them into the house as Tim followed from behind, helping to carry their luggage.

"How's my favorite granddaughter?" Phil asked as he gave her a squeeze. He was wearing the dark green cardigan he wore every Christmas and smelled of Old Spice aftershave.

"Great, Grandpa. How are you?"

211

"Fit as a fiddle and hankering for your grandmother's turkey dinner," he replied with a wink as he nodded toward the kitchen where they could hear Joan and Sheila busily working away. "The kids are here," he called out to them, and they quickly abandoned their cooking and rushed out to greet them.

"You look wonderful, Mimi," her mom exclaimed, as she held both of Michelle's hands and looked her in the eyes.

"You too, Mom. Hi Grandma."

"Hi baby. Oh it's so good to see you both," Joan said with a beaming smile.

"Where's Dad?" Michelle asked as the men carried their luggage into Michelle's old bedroom.

"He's asleep, dear. We'll get him up pretty soon. You can take a peek at him if you'd like." Sheila gestured toward the master bedroom.

Michelle quietly opened their bedroom door. Her father was stretched out on the bed, but his eyes were open. "Dad?" she whispered.

"Prin —cess," he said in a strained voice as he lifted a shaking hand to reach out to her.

"Oh, Daddy — it's so good to see you home!" Michelle rushed over and took his hand in hers, trying to stop the shaking.

"You.... are.... a..... sight.... for... sore.... eyes," John said through his labored breathing. "I've.... missed.... you... Michelle."

"I've missed you too, Daddy." She leaned over, hugging him. "You look great."

"Not.... really...." he answered and then added, "but... I'm... working... on... it."

"I thought I heard you two talking," Sheila said, as she entered the room. "Are you ready to get up?"

John just nodded.

"I'll get Tim. Just a minute." She came back a

moment later with Tim and Steve in tow.

Rolling the wheelchair over from the corner of the room, she explained to Steve how they helped John into the chair. Tim took a hold of his father's hand, supporting him behind the elbow as well as he helped him to sit up. Sheila lifted his legs and gently set his feet down on the floor. Then Steve and Tim each took one of John's arms to help him stand up and get into his chair.

"Thanks for helping, Steve. My back hasn't been doing so well today," Sheila explained.

"No thanks needed, Mom," Steve replied. They both seemed to enjoy the familiarity and closeness of that term, especially since Steve had been without a mother for so long.

Michelle's heart ached to see her dad so weak, so dependent on others just to get up from the bed. Her mind flashed back to her childhood and the ways he'd always taken such good care of the whole family. Now he needed to be taken care of himself.

She watched Steve help her dad and suddenly felt so proud to be married to him. He really was a great guy. As soon as the holidays were over, she was going to have a little talk with Trevor and put an end to their friendship just like Kristin had suggested.

As the afternoon settled over them, Michelle spotted her grandfather sitting on the back patio, deep in thought. Steve was occupied, shooting hoops out front with Tim, and her father was napping in his chair while the ladies fussed over the final meal preparations in the kitchen.

Michelle went over to join Phil, sitting down close to him. "Penny for your thoughts, Grandpa," she said with a smile.

He glanced over at her, nodding, as a warm grin spread over his face. "Got me, didn't you."

She laughed.

"Okay. I was thinking about your father and all the things God has done recently in our lives. So many miracles and breakthroughs. It's been tough, but good in so many ways."

She nodded in agreement. "Seems like all our lives are different now," she observed. "I'm noticing that I look at life from a whole new perspective."

"I know, pumpkin. Me, too."

A comfortable pause filled the air as they gazed out toward the distance.

"Grandpa?" she asked.

"Yes?"

"Can I get your advice on something?"

He turned to look her in the eye. "Sure. What's up?"

"Well, you know I've started back to school, right?"

"Yep. Your mother tells me you're taking an anthropology class.

How's it going?" he asked.

"That's what I need your advice on."

"I'm not much for anthropology, kid, but fire away," he replied with a smile.

"It's not the anthropology part I'm struggling with, Grandpa. It's the professor. He's got some kind of vendetta against Christians, and he keeps interjecting his thoughts and opinions about it during lectures." She studied her grandfather's face, hoping his wisdom would guide her future responses to Dr. Chambers.

Phil shook his head and sighed. "You know, I've heard about this several times in the past couple of years. Seems to be the trend with many college professors these days to try to discredit our beliefs."

She nodded. "Why, Grandpa? What's the point?"

"I think a lot of it is just a matter of pride, honey. Lots of these professors are pretty puffed up with their own sense of self- importance. They crave accolades and want to appear to be above the masses in their intellectual prowess. And they love to stimulate debate, so they'll do whatever they think will challenge their students to rethink issues and the things they've been taught in the past."

"But it doesn't seem like they challenge other belief systems, Grandpa. It's only the Christians who are attacked."

"I think there are two reasons for that. First, Jesus is the name that divides. You can find that truth in scripture. For example, Jesus talked about being the only way to God. He also said anyone who was not with Him was against Him. No middle ground, Michelle. That troubles a lot of people because it forces them to take a stand on one side or the other.

"I also think it has a lot to do with the politically correct atmosphere of our culture. You know, tolerance with a capital T. Because Christians really believe and embrace Jesus' teachings about only one way to heaven, they are seen as intolerant. So, some professors make it their politically correct mission to stamp out that mindset." He patted her on the shoulder. "Scripture warned us that in the last days there would be mockers. You're seeing that."

"Yeah. I guess you're right."

"Here's something for you to consider, sweetheart," he added. "What do you think is the root of intellectual arrogance?"

She thought for a moment. "I don't know. Pride?"

"Yeah. I think that is a big part of it. But I also

think it comes from insecurity."

"What do you mean?" she asked.

"I mean the need to be the smartest, the best, to outwit others – it comes from a basic insecurity, a need to somehow be significant. It's just off track from the root of real significance – being linked with the all-powerful God of the universe and having Him as your Father and friend."

"I never thought of that."

"Most guys with big egos are really hiding insecurity, honey."

"So what should I do, Grandpa? I want to stand up to the guy, but I don't think I know enough about scripture or about history and anthropology to make a strong argument. Like when he brings up the Crusades and the brutality of Christians during that time period, I don't know what to say in response."

"You know, the most important thing you can do is to start praying for that professor. He may be bugging and offending you with his comments, but ultimately he's taking a stand against God and His word. That's a mighty fearful place for anyone to be, even if he's totally unaware of his own personal eternal danger. He needs your prayers more than your debates, pumpkin."

"I never thought of that, but I guess you're right. It's just hard to pray for someone who's such a jerk," she added.

"I understand, honey. But think of Jesus when He was hanging on the cross. What did He pray? 'Father, forgive them for they know not what they do.' His life and death are an example for us. God's ways are always higher than man's."

"What about the guys who stand up to Dr. Chambers? Like there's this one guy named David who is pretty bold."

"Good for him. But he has a responsibility to

pray for Dr. Chambers too."

Michelle sat silently, thinking about everything her grandfather was telling her. "One more thing, Grandpa."

"Yes?"

"What about things like the Crusades? What do you think about those brutal attacks in the name of Christianity?"

He shook his head. "Lots of wars and acts of violence or terror have been committed under a false banner of religion that were really cloaking other motives. The crusaders were not warring to spread Christianity. Even if they were, Christianity is not something that comes through conquest. It is a spiritual adoption that can only come when God personally touches the hearts of individuals, and they respond to His love.

"The truth is that most crusaders were 'Christian' in name only. They fought for fame, glory, riches, and power. Leaders throughout history have used religion to stir up emotion and passion for war.

Don't fall for your professor's false portrayal of these marauders as men attempting to spread the gospel."

"Well, that's not how Dr. Chambers portrays it. He makes a big deal over the fact they were crusades – like the brutality was motivated by their Christianity."

"I know it's frustrating, and I agree it seems wrong to have professors be able to lecture based on a biased mindset. But think of it this way. Maybe there is a good side to having teachers like Dr. Chambers in colleges. His lectures force Christian students to really sink their roots deep into their faith and not rely on a surface understanding of their beliefs. Those who have truly made a commitment to God have the opportunity to get that much stronger. Those who flounder and succumb to Dr. Chambers and others like him may think they are embracing a more rational, thought-based perspective, but actually they are sheep, who have not exercised enough discernment and courage to stand their ground. It takes a greater mind to see the deception of pseudo intellectuals like your professor and be willing to stand up to them rather than allowing insecurities to lead you down the same path of arrogance and pride."

She studied his face and nodded.

"Don't try to argue with him about his anthropology claims, Michelle. He's spent years perfecting his arguments with regard to his field of study. Instead, share what your experience with God has been. He can't argue with that. Pray for such an opportunity. You might even want to tell him about what your father has been going through. God can use that horrible experience to touch others. Who knows? Dr. Chambers might be one of them."

Michelle was quiet for a moment as she pondered what he had said. Looking at her grandfather, she reached over to squeeze his hand. "Grandpa?"

"Yes?"

"I love you."

"I love you, too, kid." He planted a big kiss on her cheek.

"Now let's go check on those ladies in the kitchen and see if they could use a hand."

That evening after dinner, they all retired to the living room. The Christmas tree looked so beautiful with its sparkling white lights and myriad of sentimental ornaments. Michelle stood drinking it in and remembering her childhood Christmases in this room with so many of these same decorations. She recalled sitting under the tree every day for what seemed like months on end, waiting for Santa to come and deliver all the packages.

"The tree looks great," Steve exclaimed, settling on the couch beside her.

"Thanks," Sheila replied. "I had help from Tim."

Michelle noticed a faraway look in her father's eyes. "I'm so glad you are here to share Christmas with us, Dad," she said as she reached over and put her hand on his arm.

He just nodded, but his expression looked weary and very distant.

"Are you getting tired, dear?" Sheila asked.

He nodded again, closing his eyes. As if on cue, Tim rose and nodded to Steve, who immediately joined him to help John back into the bedroom and onto the bed.

After they were out of earshot, Michelle asked softly, "Is he always this tired?"

"Pretty much," her mom replied with a sigh.

"You have to realize how much effort this takes," Phil said, leaning forward in his chair. "Your father has to work hard to say every word, to chew his food and swallow it correctly, to keep himself upright and focused on the events around him. It will take time, Michelle, but he'll get there."

"We're praying for him continuously," Joan added with a hopeful voice.

"Me, too," Michelle replied.

Steve and Tim walked back into the room. "He's pretty much settled for the night," Tim said matter-of-factly, as if he were accustomed to caring for his father every day.

"You are so good with him, Tim," Michelle said with a smile. "I'm sure it means a lot to Dad to have you around helping out like this."

"Did Tim tell you he moved back in?" Sheila asked.

"You did? You gave up your apartment?" Michelle was impressed with her younger brother's sense of responsibility and willingness to help.

"I figured Dad has done plenty for me over the years. It's the least I could do for him."

"Good man," Steve said, patting him on the back.

"Thanks," he replied with a shrug. He looked embarrassed by all the attention.

"Well, I don't know about the rest of you, but I'm beat," said Phil as he stood up and stretched. "Come on, Mrs. Claus, let's hit the hay." He reached over, taking Joan's hand and helping her to her feet.

"Goodnight, everyone," Joan said with a weary but contented smile.

As they headed for the guest room, Tim asked Steve if he wanted to have some more pie with him. Steve patted his stomach and smiled. "You're on," he said, as he followed his brother-in-law into the kitchen.

"So will you and Steve be okay in your old room? I know it's only a double bed."

"We'll be fine, Mom. Steve will love sleeping under my lavender comforter," she added with a grin.

"I guess I could have changed the décor in there a little," Sheila began.

"Don't you dare. It wouldn't be home without my lavender room."

Sheila smiled. "That's how I felt, too."

They chuckled together. Then Michelle asked, "So tell me how everything is going with Dad, really."

"He's doing fine. It just takes time."

"That seems to be the theme to life these days," Michelle said.

"What?"

"Nothing, Mom. What do the doctors say about his progress?"

"They're all very pleased with how far he's come.

They've been working on getting him up and walking. He can walk between the two parallel bars at the rehab gym, and they are getting him going with a walker."

"That's great. So why is he still in the wheelchair?"

"He's embarrassed about the walker. Says it makes him look like an old man."

"When do they think he'll be home to stay?"

"We really don't know. As long as he's making progress, they want to keep him at Rancho. But I think it's really good for him to be home here for Christmas. It will give him more motivation to keep working hard to get well."

"How's he doing psychologically?"

"He's come to terms with what happened, I think. He seems to want to make things right. But his physical struggles are really hard for him. You know your father. Always so independent."

"Yeah, I know. It's hard to see him like this." She paused, staring at the tree. On the piano next to it, she could see a family portrait taken the year she had graduated from high school. Her dad looked so handsome and strong.

Her mom came over and sat next to her on the couch. "I know what you mean, honey. We just have to believe he'll recover completely."

"Yep. We have to keep hoping and praying."

"Did I tell you about the lawsuit?" Sheila asked.

"What about it?"

"That attorney Steve found for us thinks he has solved the case. He discovered who forged your father's signature on the transfers of funds."

"Really? Why didn't you call me and tell me?"

"I guess I've been a bit overwhelmed with everything. Besides, I wasn't quite sure what to tell you."

"What do you mean?"

"I mean, I can't give you any details about it. But I wanted you to know it looks pretty certain the charges against your dad will be dropped in a matter of weeks."

"That's great, Mom." Why was her mom being so evasive and mysterious about this? Maybe she wasn't allowed to say anything until the evidence was presented in court. "Well that should take a load off of Dad's shoulders."

"Yes." Sheila turned to her, taking her hand. "Tell me about you, `Shell. What's going on in your life lately?"

CHAPTER TWENTY-FIVE

The stereo system played traditional Christmas songs and the smell of pine mingled with the magical effects of the twinkling lights. Christmas. Michelle was so glad to be home with her family.

She felt an overwhelming urge to confide in her mother. It had been a long time since they had talked about anything other than her father. Sitting there in the living room of her childhood home, she thought of all the conversations she had shared with her mom on this very couch. She could remember the first time she told her mom about Steve – how nervous she had felt and how hopeful that her mother would like him.

Sheila studied Michelle's face and waited for her answer. She seemed genuinely interested in hearing whatever it was she had to say.

"Well, Mom," Michelle began as she reached up and started twisting a piece of her hair, "Steve and I have started working on a special project."

"A project?"

"That's what we're calling it," she said rather mysteriously.

"What is it?"

"We've decided to try to have a baby." She watched her mother's expression to see how she would react.

"A baby — that is so exciting! But are you sure you want to do that before you finish your education?"

"I'm sure, Mom. I've really given it a lot of thought. Ever since Bridgeport, I've been wanting to do this."

"How does Steve feel about it? I'm surprised he would go along with this so early in your marriage."

Michelle nodded and smiled. "Actually, Steve is really supportive. He knows how much it means to me."

"Well, I'm very happy for you, Mimi. There is nothing like having your first child. I'll never forget my pregnancy with you and the moment I first saw your tiny face."

She seemed lost in thought, and Michelle didn't want to interrupt her memories, but she was eager to know if her mom had any problems getting pregnant. "Mom?" she asked.

"Yes?"

"Did you and Dad have any problems getting pregnant?"

"No. In fact, you were a bit of a surprise for us because we had only been trying for one month."

"Really?"

"Yeah. I remember how surprised your father was when I called him and told him." She glanced over at a photo on the piano of her and John taken in their early days of marriage.

"Oh." Michelle didn't know what to say.

"Why do you ask, dear? Are you and Steve having some kind of problem?"

Michelle sighed. She could feel the tears coming to the surface again. "Kind of."

"Oh, baby," her mom said softly as she wrapped her arms around Michelle. "You have to give it some time."

"That's what everyone says, but we've been trying for three months now and I've even been taking fertility pills."

"Fertility pills? Why?"

"Because my cycle got all messed up when everything happened with Dad. I went to the doctor and told her we had decided to try to get pregnant, and she said the fertility pills would help me get my normal cycle back and also help us get pregnant quickly. She said most people conceive within three months." Michelle's vision began to blur and her eyes filled to overflowing with tears.

"So now you're worried because it's been three months and no baby."

She just nodded.

"I wish I had the answers for you, honey. I'm sure you and Steve will have a baby."

"We've talked about doing some tests starting in January. We've even talked about maybe adopting at some point." She wiped her eyes with the tissue her mother handed her.

"I really doubt there is anything wrong. It just takes time for some people. But if it makes you feel better to do the tests, then I say go for it. Adoption is a big decision, though. You two will make great parents, and I know you'll figure out what's best." She studied Michelle's face and gave her another squeeze. "Let's go have another slice of grandma's pie. That'll make you feel better."

Michelle smiled at her mother through the tears and nodded. "Sorry I'm putting this on you, with all you've got on your mind with Dad."

"Don't you worry about that, dear. Things are looking up down here, and a mother's heart is always ready to listen."

"Love you, Mom," Michelle said as she gave her mom a hug.

"Love you too, Mimi. You'll be a great mom one of these days. I just know it."

Christmas morning passed with a flurry of gifts and grandma's delicious Swedish pancakes. John seemed more alert than he had the night before and pleased to have the family together once again. Michelle and Steve had bought him a gray cashmere vest; one that Michelle thought would look great with his silver hair and light blue eyes.

After helping him to open the package, Michelle lifted it out and held it up for him to see. "What do you think, Dad?"

John gazed at the vest and then looked into his daughter's eyes. "Beautiful," he said slowly.

She placed it on his lap and he caressed the plush knit with his useable hand. "Soft," he added with a smile.

After all the packages had been opened and they had eaten their breakfast, Michelle got a call from Kristin. They made plans to spend some time together the following morning. Steve and Michelle would be heading back to Oregon in a couple of days, and they wanted to squeeze in another short visit. Kristin had a lot of wedding plans to discuss with her matron of honor.

The sky was clear, but the air quite cool as the girls walked down the pier, heading for their favorite high school hang-out – Ruby's Diner, a fifties style hamburger and shakes restaurant sitting at the far end, surrounded by the Pacific Ocean. Michelle pulled her parka tight and hugged herself against the biting ocean breezes. It was difficult to carry on a conversation with the wind stealing their words and carrying them away.

"Pretty day," Kristin shouted.

Michelle nodded her head. "Wish we got more sun like this up in Sandy Cove," she replied.

"What?"

"More sun. I wish we got more up there," she repeated loudly.

They hurried into the entrance to the restaurant with their cheeks and noses pink and their hair tousled.

"Whew! That wind is strong today," Kristin said with a grin.

"You should see your hair," Michelle said.

"My hair? What about yours?" They both laughed as they tried to tame their locks with their fingers.

The restaurant was pretty empty, so they didn't have to wait. They requested a window and were ushered to a table with a great view. Michelle soaked in the familiar surroundings. Shiny, cherry red vinyl upholstered booths and chairs, gleaming white tabletops with thick, grooved chrome edges. Everything was retro – very authentic fifties — right down to the music playing in the background.

After ordering their customary burgers, fries, and shakes, they began discussing the details about Kristin's upcoming wedding. She showed Michelle pictures of the dresses she was considering for her attendants, and Michelle gave her feedback on the ones she liked best.

"Are you still planning to come down the week before the ceremony?" Kristin asked hopefully.

"Of course. I wouldn't miss watching you go crazy with last minute stuff. This will be so fun, Kristin. I'm really excited for you."

"Me, too. And I'm really glad you'll be here to help."

"No problem. That's the matron of honor deal,

remember?" Michelle replied, thinking back to Kristin's participation at her wedding. It had really helped to have her there running errands and making last minute phone calls, not to mention taking her out to the movies and for walks on the beach to calm her nerves.

"Just think, `Shell, you might be pregnant by then. Hope you don't get morning sickness."

Michelle smiled. "I just hope I get pregnant."

"You will. I know you will. You and Steve will make the best parents. I can just see you guys with some little boy in overalls chasing your cat around the house."

"A boy, huh? I was thinking maybe a girl."

"Boy. Girl. Either way. You guys have what it takes to be a great family. Especially now that you both have started building a spiritual base, too."

Michelle nodded. She gazed out the window and sighed.

"What are you thinking about?" Kristin asked.

"I was thinking about a talk Steve and I had before we came down here."

"About?"

"About not getting pregnant the first three months like the doctor said we probably would."

"That seems like quite a promise, especially coming from a doctor."

"It wasn't exactly a promise," Michelle said. "She just said that 75 percent of the people who use this drug and follow this particular schedule conceive within three months."

"Well, don't get discouraged. Give God time. I know He'll give you that baby in His perfect timing."

"So do you think we should just wait and see?" Michelle asked.

"What else would you do?"

"We were thinking of looking into adoption and going back to the doctor in January to start some tests."

"What kind of tests?"

"Whatever kind she recommends. I guess there are tons of tests to find out if there is anything wrong."

"Do you really think there is?"

"I don't know what to think." Michelle sipped on her vanilla shake, discouragement written all over her face.

In a soft voice, Kristin asked, "What does Steve think about all this?"

"He thinks we should pray about it and wait and see."

"But you don't agree?"

"I don't know. What would you do? I know I'm kind of obsessing on getting pregnant. It's suddenly become so important to me. I think it has something to do with the jolt I got with my dad. It's like I don't want to put things off anymore."

Her friend reached over and squeezed her hand. "I honestly don't know what I would do, `Shell. I don't think there's anything wrong with seeking medical advice. And adoption is a wonderful gift for a child needing a home. I'm just not sure you've given this enough time. But I understand what you mean about not wanting to put things off, especially after almost losing your dad like that."

Michelle was clearly focused on everything she was saying, looking for direction and affirmation about the decision to pursue the tests. "So you think it would be okay to go ahead with the tests and look into adoption?"

"Yes, but I also think you need to get to the place where you can trust God with this whole thing and believe He'll give you a child in His timing."

"That's a hard one for me," Michelle admitted with a sigh.

"Yeah. When you really want something, it's hard for most people. Mark's been a Christian for a long time, and he still wrestles with that all the time."

"Really? About what?"

"About expanding his ministry and becoming involved in something like what Ben is doing. He's had a dream about starting a church for a long time now. His job down here is good, but he wants to do more. He loves the kids and all, but he has a bigger vision."

"Maybe you guys really will end up in Sandy Cove," she said with a smile that erased her earlier frown.

"Maybe we will," Kristin replied as she studied the horizon. "I know Mark is keeping in touch with Ben, so we just have to keep praying for the Lord's will."

"I'll pray for you guys about Mark's dream, and you pray for us for a baby."

"Deal," Kristin said, as the girls both gave each other the thumbs up sign.

Later that afternoon, Tim showed up to help take John back to his residential rehab facility. Steve and Tim worked smoothly as a team helping John to maneuver himself into the front passenger seat of the car. Phil rested his hand on John's shoulder and said a quick prayer before they closed the door.

"I'm going with you," Michelle said, climbing into the back seat beside Steve.

"Okay," Tim replied. "It'll be good for you to see this place. It's a great facility."

John was very quiet on the fifteen-minute ride. Michelle and Steve made small talk with Tim, commenting on the new mall that had just gone in before Christmas and the lack of traffic on the freeway.

When they pulled up in front, an automatic glass door opened and a large, black woman in a nurse's uniform came strutting out to meet them.

"John — it's so good to see you. We've missed you around here."

She smiled and winked at Michelle. "Is this beautiful thing your daughter?"

John nodded. "Mi —chelle."

"It's nice to meet you, Michelle," the woman said warmly.

"Michelle, this is Samantha," Tim said, gesturing to the woman while she helped their father out of the car.

"Now don't you go calling me Samantha like that, young man. You know all my friends call me Sammy," the woman scolded with a glint in her eye.

"Right. Sammy. Sorry about that." Tim smiled.

"I'll forgive you this time. Just don't let it happen again." She stood there waiting. "So, are you going to get his chair outta the trunk, or do I have to do that?"

"Oh, right. We'll get it," Tim replied, rolling his eyes as he played along with her exasperation. Unloading it, he started helping his father into the chair.

"Now you wait just a minute, young man. Let's see what your father can do for himself," Sammy said loud and clear. "Come on, John, let's try this. Here. Put your right hand on the doorjamb. Good. Now put your other hand over here on the dashboard."

John did not move. His face showed intense concentration with his forehead drawn downward and his jaws clenched. But his left arm hung at his side.

Sammy waited a minute. "Try again."

John's hand flickered and jerked, but he could not lift it off the seat.

"Okay. Here. Let me help." Sammy reached into the car and placed John's left hand on the dashboard. "Now try to push yourself up. Straighten your elbows."

John's right arm straightened, but his left collapsed and he fell sideways against the dashboard.

"That was a good try, John. You'll get there."
Sammy helped him sit up straight again. "Okay, boys.
You're on."

Tim and Steve came over to the open door and
helped John out, carefully turning his body and guiding
him into the wheelchair.

"Shall we take them on a tour?" Sammy asked as
she leaned over and smiled at John. "By the way, who's
that handsome fellow who keeps making eyes at your
daughter?"

"Steve," John answered gesturing toward his son-
in-law with his right hand.

"Hi, Sammy. I'm Michelle's husband, Steve."

"Nice to meet you, Steve," she said with a friendly
grin. "Okay, hold on tight. Here we go."

"I'll park the car and meet you guys inside," Tim
said as he climbed back into the driver's seat.

Sammy wheeled John into the building through
the open doors with Michelle and Steve close behind.
Michelle could feel her stomach tighten as she inhaled the
antiseptic in the air and saw a variety of residents sitting
in wheelchairs in the open living area adjacent to the
lobby. Several were strapped into their chairs and only
two of those present even looked her direction as they
passed.

A television attached to the ceiling in the far
corner of the room droned the play-by-play account of a
sporting event, which some of the residents appeared to
be watching. Off in one corner, two pajama-clad men sat
at a round table playing checkers.

Looking at her father, Michelle tried to imagine
what it must be like for him to live in a place like this.
Completely stripped of his self-sufficiency and pride, who
was left behind in the shell of his body? She noticed he
looked straight ahead as they moved into the hallway.

"Your dad doesn't like to mingle with the guys,"

Sammy explained, then blew a kiss into the room full of men.

"Does he have any friends here?" Michelle asked.

"Why don't you ask him yourself, sugar." Sammy stopped pushing the chair and nodded toward John with her head.

"Dad? Do you have any friends here?" Michelle felt awkward talking to her father as if he was a child.

"I...don't...need...friends. I'm...going...home...soon." His jaw was firmly clenched, as was his right fist. "Take...me...to...my... room," he added, closing his eyes.

Sammy sighed and patted him on the shoulder. She gave Michelle a reassuring smile and began pushing the chair down the long hallway with its gleaming white linoleum floors.

Tim joined them in the room John shared with an old fisherman named Bill, who had spinal damage due to a fall. Although Bill's greeting was jovial, John merely acknowledged his presence with a nod.

After getting him settled in an upright position on his bed, Sammy left to give them an opportunity to visit. They introduced themselves to Bill, chatted with him for a few minutes, and then turned their attention to John.

"Daddy," Michelle said softly as she reached out and took his hand, "I'm so glad we got to be together for Christmas."

John nodded and smiled at her tenderly.

"Steve and I are leaving tomorrow to go back to Oregon. I'll be back soon to help Kristin get ready for the wedding."

"Okay...honey."

"You take care now. Work hard at your therapy so you can go home."

"I'll make sure he does," Tim said. He looked at John with compassion. Michelle couldn't remember seeing such maturity in her brother before. He certainly was changed by all of this. It was good to see a new bond developing between her brother and their father.

"We'll be praying for you, Dad," Steve said as he extended his hand to John, who weakly shook it.

"Thanks...son."

Michelle kissed her father. "I love you, Daddy," she whispered in his ear.

He looked into her eyes as if seeing her clearly for the first time. "Thank...you."

As they walked out of the facility, she prayed that her father would find the strength to rebuild his life – a better life than he had before.

CHAPTER TWENTY-SIX

Michelle stared at the phone. She nervously twisted a piece of her hair and tried to coach herself through the phone call she was about to make.

Hi, Trevor. We need to talk. Can you meet me at the Coffee Stop?

It was simple enough. Why was she shaking like this? Lord, help me do this.

She picked up the receiver and punched in the number. Her heart was pounding and she could feel her throat tightening like it was in a noose.

"Hello?" Trevor's voice sounded a little sleepy.

"Did I wake you up?"

"Michelle, is that you?"

"Yeah. Did I catch you at a bad time?"

"No. Not at all. I was just looking over some information Starla gave me. What's up? How was your Christmas?"

"It was fine." She hesitated for a moment and then jumped in. "Trevor, we need to talk."

"Okay. About what?"

"Just some stuff that's been on my mind. Could you meet me at the Coffee Stop?"

"Sure. What time?"

"How about in half an hour?"

"I'll be there," he promised. "It'll be good to see you again, Michelle. I've missed you."

"Okay, well, I'll see you there."

Michelle's hand was visibly shaking as she hung up the phone. *What is the matter with me? I've got to get a grip before I see him.* She looked over at the coffee table and saw her Bible lying open. She picked it up and read the verse she had highlighted earlier that morning in the book of Joshua.

"Have I not commanded you, be strong and courageous. Do not be terrified, do not be discouraged, for the Lord, your God, will be with you wherever you go."

She closed her eyes and prayed. *Please help me, Lord. I know I need to do this.* In the quiet moment following her prayer, she felt her nervousness melt and a thought entered her mind that seemed to be God's answer. *I will help you, Michelle. I will go before you.*

She soaked in the words and rested back into the soft cushions of the couch. *Thank you, Lord.*

Trevor looked particularly handsome as he sauntered into the Coffee Stop. Michelle noticed a couple of the young waitresses whisper to each other, checking him out from a distance.

"Hey there," he said with his disarming smile as he slid into the seat across from her. "You look great."

Michelle could feel the color rushing into her cheeks. *Stop it,* she silently chided herself. "Hi, Trevor. Thanks for coming to meet me."

"My pleasure." He winked at her as one of the waitresses approached their table. "What are you having? It's my treat."

"Just coffee," she replied.

"Coffee sounds great. Me, too." The waitress nodded and took off. "So what's up?" he asked nonchalantly.

"I'm not quite sure how to say this, but..."

"We've got to stop meeting like this," he said jokingly.

"Well, actually, yes."

"Okay...so what does that mean?"

"It means we've got to cool our 'friendship'."

"And why is that? Steve getting a little jealous?" His voice had an edge to it.

"This wasn't Steve's idea. It was mine." She stared down into the steaming coffee in her cup.

"What are you afraid of, Michelle?"

"Who says I'm afraid?" she replied, feeling her defenses rising.

"I think I know fear when I see it," he said, taking a sip of coffee and studying her face.

This just unnerved Michelle more. "Stop staring at me."

"I'm not staring at you. I'm just wondering what's really behind this."

"Trevor, you know that I'm married." She suddenly felt her confidence rising. The verse from Joshua replayed quickly in her mind.

"And, so?"

"And so we've got to take a breather from our relationship. It's too close."

"Too close for who?"

"For me."

"Okay, Michelle. I respect your space. Just let me know when you get over this hurdle and feel more secure about it."

"If that ever happens, I'll let you know."

He nodded, but she noticed he suddenly looked vulnerable, like someone who had fears of his own. "You'll be busy finishing up your master's program and getting your internship completed for your license. You won't miss having me around," she offered.

"You're wrong there, Michelle. I value our friendship and all your input."

She didn't know what to say.

"Well, I guess you said what you wanted to tell me." He rose and picked up the bill.

"I'm sorry if I hurt you, Trevor. I just can't compromise my marriage."

"Don't worry about me. I'll be fine." He gave her a sad, puppy dog smile and walked away.

She stared into her coffee cup, praying she was doing the right thing. What if God wanted her to be friends with him, to help him learn about her new faith?

CHAPTER TWENTY-SEVEN

As Michelle walked back into her house after her meeting with Trevor, her cell phone started ringing. She dug through her purse and flipped it open.

"Hello?"

"Mrs. Baron?"

"Yes."

"This is Rhonda at Dr. Foster's office."

"Oh, hi." She kicked off her shoes and sat down on the edge of the couch.

"I discussed your questions about infertility testing with the doctor, and she'd like to meet with you and your husband to go over the information. When would you be available to come in together?"

Michelle asked the nurse to hold on as she went to the kitchen to get Steve's day-planner. She was able to set up an appointment for the following week.

As soon as the nurse hung up, Michelle dialed Steve's number at work. "The doctor's office just called," she told him excitedly.

"Okay. When are you going in?"

"She wants to see both of us together. I set up an appointment for next week."

"Can we talk about this tonight?"

"I guess. Why?"

"I just think we are rushing all this."

"Oh," she replied, a little disappointed.

"We'll talk tonight, babe. I've gotta run. I've got a

deposition in 15 minutes."

Hanging up the phone, she sunk down into the chair and rested her head in her hands.

That night, Steve opened up to Michelle about all he was feeling. "We're not trusting God with this, babe. We need to just relax and wait on His timing. I'm swamped at work right now; you're just getting going with school again and trying to keep in touch with your mom. We've got time to think about a baby. If it happens, great. But I don't see any reason to start a bunch of expensive medical tests already."

Michelle looked down at her hands on her lap. She could feel tears beginning to fill her eyes. She forced them down into a hidden place in her heart. A place she could only share with God.

Steve squeezed her hand. "Can we just give this a little more time?"

She kept her head down but nodded.

"If nothing's happened by summer, we can talk about it again."

She nodded again, swallowing her frustration and fears.

"You okay?" he asked, turning her face toward his.

"I guess."

"We will have a baby, Michelle. I promise."

"Okay." She kissed him lightly on the cheek and walked out of the room.

Michelle spent the next morning in prayer, pouring her heart out to God and pleading with Him for a baby. She knew Steve was right. They had plenty of time. But she had such a strong yearning. It was more powerful than any desire she'd had in the past. Surely God would answer a fervent prayer like hers.

By 11:00 she was already starting to get hungry. She knew she should just get a quick bite and work on her homework, but she really wanted to hang out with a friend. Picking up the phone, she decided to call Monica.

"Hey, girlfriend," Monica exclaimed when she heard Michelle's voice on the other end. "I was wondering if you lost my number or something."

"I'm sorry. I know I haven't called for a while. It's just been really hectic around here with the holidays and everything." She paused then added, "Hey, thanks again for all the cat sitting."

"No problem. Want to go to yoga with me today?"

Michelle's mind flashed back to a picture of Bev, the instructor, reading the tarot cards for her before her father's suicide attempt. The death card had fallen in the center of the spread. She cringed at the memory. "I'm kind of out of the yoga thing, now."

"Yeah. It's been a long time since you went."

"Anyway," Michelle continued, "I was hoping maybe we could do something together, just the two of us — like have an early lunch."

"That sounds fun. Where do you want to meet?"

"Why don't you come over here? I have some stuff to make tacos."

"Can I bring anything?"

"Just your usual friendly self," she said warmly.

The two of them had a great time catching up on all the news in each other's lives, and Michelle was really glad she had decided to call Monica. Max pranced around as if he enjoyed having both his 'mothers' together in one room.

"He really loves you," Michelle said with a smile.

"That's 'cause I spoil him." Monica scooped the cat into her arms and cradled him like a baby while she scratched under his chin.

"I can see that."

"He's such a cutie," Monica crooned as she gave Max an Eskimo kiss.

"Speaking of babies..."

Monica looked up instantly. "You're pregnant!"

"Well, no. But we're trying."

"That is so exciting, Michelle. I keep talking to Tony about maybe starting a family, too. He always worries about the money since construction work is so unpredictable. Wouldn't it be cool if we both had kids at the same time?"

She wasn't sure if she should tell Monica about the infertility specialist. It seemed so personal. Instead, she told her about her plans for the nursery.

"Noah's ark? How cute is that?" Monica said enthusiastically. "It goes right along with your interest in learning about the Bible and everything." The way she said it sounded as if this was a phase in her life.

"I guess you could say that," Michelle replied. "I really hope my kids will feel the same way – about reading the Bible, I mean."

"Oh, yeah. Me, too. I want my kids to explore everything," Monica said agreeably, completely missing the thrust of Michelle's comment.

Rather than getting into a heavy philosophical discussion, she asked, "Want to go up and see what I've got for the nursery so far?"

Monica eagerly agreed. She loved the little lamp and the rocking chair. Michelle showed her the catalog she got from the store with all the baby furniture and decorations.

"This room is going to be adorable, Michelle. I want to be the first to know when you find out you're pregnant, after Steve, of course."

Michelle smiled but made no promises, knowing she would want to tell her mom and Kristin right after Steve. A little flutter of fear grabbed her heart for a moment. What if she never did get pregnant?

Icy rain fell as Michelle pulled out of the college parking lot a week later. With only three weeks until the end of class, she was afraid it would be impossible to share her faith with Dr. Chambers. It frustrated her because she felt nudged to do so, not only by her grandfather's suggestion, but also whenever she prayed for her professor.

Each class session she hoped for a moment alone with him before leaving. And each time, it seemed like students surrounded him with questions about their term papers or the final.

I wonder if Kelly would have any ideas, she thought as she carefully maneuvered her car through the limited visibility. Maybe I'll drop by and surprise her.

As she pulled up in front of Kelly and Ben's house, she saw the light on in the front room. Kelly often had a fire in the fireplace on days like this, and Michelle was looking forward to visiting with her friend and possibly sharing a hot cup of tea or coffee.

"Michelle. What a great surprise," Kelly exclaimed as she opened the front door and hugged her sweater to repel the cold air. "Come in — quick!"

Michelle shut her umbrella, and shaking the water

out of it, hurried inside.

"Whew! It's freezing out there," Kelly said, helping her out of her dripping raincoat. "I'll hang this out in the garage for a while. Why don't you go sit by the fire?"

"Thanks." Michelle slipped her shoes off and headed for its blazing warmth. She rubbed her cold hands together then stretched them out toward the flames.

"Have a seat," Kelly suggested, and gestured toward the rocking chair flanking the hearth. You can put your feet up and get warm. I'll go heat up the coffee."

She sank into the rocker and extended her legs, resting her stocking feet on the hearth. Soon they took on a toasty warmth. "Need any help out there?" she called toward the kitchen.

"Nope. I'm on my way," Kelly replied as she pushed open the kitchen door with her hip and carried the tray of coffee mugs and creamer out to the front room.

"That smells like heaven," she commented as Kelly placed the tray on the hearth.

"Hawaiian hazelnut. I thought we could use a little slice of the tropics today." She smiled and handed Michelle a mug. "Creamer?"

"Is it that decadent stuff you gave me last time I was here?"

"One and the same – creamy French vanilla parfait."

Michelle poured some into her cup, watching the ivory liquid swirl in the dark coffee. "Now I'm really glad I stopped by."

"Me, too," Kelly replied with a warm smile. "Don't you have class today?"

"Yep. Just left there."

"Oh. For some reason, I thought it was later in the day."

"We're supposed to go till 5:00, but we voted to skip the break in the middle of the two-hour block for the rest of the term and finish early. It was Dr. Chambers' idea."

"So, I'll bet you'll be glad to get out of his class after all you've told me about him."

"Yeah. I sure won't miss his lectures," she agreed. "But there's something I want to do before the end of the semester."

"What?"

"Well, at Christmas time, my grandfather kind of challenged me to pray for Chambers and to look for an opportunity to share what God has done in my life over the past year. But every time I try to talk to him after class, he's always surrounded by other students who have questions to ask about stuff."

"Wow, Michelle. I don't know if I'd have the nerve to talk to someone like him myself. You're pretty brave to even try."

"So, do you think I should just forget it?"

"No. Not at all."

"Every time I pray about him, I feel like I'm supposed to tell him about my dad. He actually kind of reminds me of how my dad was before all this happened to him," Michelle explained.

"That sounds like a good opening. You could probably just start by telling him what you just told me – that he reminds you of your dad. That would probably get his attention and make him curious."

She nodded. "It's so easy for me to think of what I want to say when I'm at home, but when I get to class, I feel so nervous, like what if I say the wrong thing or something."

"How about this?" Kelly began. "You could write him a letter while you're at home and all your thoughts are organized. Then you could give it to him at the end of class one day."

"That's a great idea. I could say something about him reminding me of my dad and then hand him the letter."

"The other good thing about doing it that way is it gives him a chance to read it on his own without having to respond to you. If you talk to him in person, he might try to argue with you or discredit what you're saying. But if it's in a letter, there's no one there for him to argue with. And if you give it to him on the day of the final, he can't try to corner you after the next class and see if he can dissuade you."

"You're brilliant, Kelly," she said excitedly. "I knew you'd have good advice for me."

The two girls sipped their coffee and chatted about Kelly's growing abdomen, their husbands, and the Bible study Ben was hosting for the new fellowship. He'd landed a job as a substitute teacher for the local school district, so he was gone most weekdays teaching a variety of grades and subjects as he worked to support their growing family while trying to launch the new church.

After about an hour, Michelle glanced at her watch. "I'd better get going," she said.

"Thanks for stopping by. It gets kinda lonely around here during the day."

"We'll have to set something up to get together more often. I'm registering for spring quarter at PNU next week. Then I'll know my schedule better."

"Sounds good," Kelly replied with a smile. "Maybe we can do something with the guys one of these weekends, too."

"Yeah. Let's do it." She agreed, picking up the tray to take it back to the kitchen.

"I'll get your raincoat," Kelly said.

As Michelle headed home, she said a little prayer thanking God for her friendship with Kelly and for the idea about how she could share her faith with Dr. Chambers. She'd start to write the letter this week and have it ready to give to him after the final.

Rick Chambers handed out the final and finished his instructions to the class. Then he took his seat and began paging through the term papers he'd just collected. He'd get as much grading done as he could during the two-hour final, and then give the rest of the papers to his T.A. to score.

By the end of the first hour, a few students had turned in their finals and left. That was either a very good sign or a bad sign. He'd seen some students ace the test in an hour. But those were the exception to the rule. Often the ones who finished first were just trying to escape their own realization that they should have studied harder.

He walked around the periphery of the room, stretching his legs and taking a look at the progress of those remaining. Then he sat back down and picked up his red pen.

Ten minutes before the end of class, he made an announcement. "Time's about up. If you are already finished, look over your answers and then you can bring them up to me. I'll be collecting everyone's tests in ten minutes."

A few students shifted in their chairs and took their tests up to his desk. When the time was up, Rick announced, "This concludes the allotted time for the exam. Please pass your tests forward and then you are dismissed." He walked along the rows and collected the remaining tests.

As the students filed past him and out the door, he noticed one young lady lingering behind. Michelle

Baron. He found her very attractive, but she was so quiet in class that he knew little about her. As the last student exited, she approached his desk.

"Dr. Chambers?" she said in a soft voice.

"Yes?"

"I wanted to give you something." Michelle held out an envelope toward him.

Rick reached for it. *Probably another student crush*, he thought to himself as he smiled at her. "Shall I open it now?"

"No. Just open it when you get home."

Yep. Another girl falling for him. "Okay. I'll do that." He winked at her.

Michelle blushed and walked out the door.

Rick sipped his wine, soft jazz music filling his living room. He flipped open his attaché case and was about to look over the students' exams when he spotted the envelope from Michelle. He smiled and shook his head. Too bad the college had a policy against teachers dating students.

He walked over to his favorite chair, set the wine glass on the end table, and peeled open the flap. Unfolding the letter within, he began to read.

Dear Dr. Chambers,

I'm writing you this letter because you remind me of my father, and I wanted to share with you what happened to him and how it changed my beliefs...

This was not at all what he had expected. He reminded her of her father? What did that mean?

Like you, my dad was always a really confident man – a self-sufficient guy who had no need of God or religion. He was a very successful businessman and was proud of all that he had accomplished.

Rick nodded to himself, took another sip of wine and continued reading. As the story unfolded, he learned that Michelle's dad had been involved in some kind of embezzlement charges and had ended up attempting suicide. He rubbed his face with both hands and shook his head. *Poor girl. She's really been through it. Guess her dad wasn't as strong as he thought he was.*

As he read on, Michelle's intimate details about her time in the hospital began to touch a tender spot in his heart. Her description of the little chapel and the time she spent praying and seeking answers brought his own mother to mind. He recalled the final days of her life as she battled the cancer that had ravaged her body. Yet she never gave up hope, even as her organs began failing, one after the other.

"I know God's with me, Rick. I'm not afraid," she'd said as she cradled her well-worn Bible in her arms. He'd tried to understand her faith and had even prayed a prayer of desperation on her behalf, but of course there was no answer. She died still clutching that old book.

As Michelle concluded her letter with a description of the peace God had given her in that chapel and the strength He continued to give her in other areas of her life, Rick suddenly felt a sense of envy coupled with despair. Although he knew logically that God did not exist, he wished he could have the faith and peace his mom and this student had found.

Michelle's postscript invited him to join her and her husband at a Bible study held in Sandy Cove by a friend of theirs. A tug on his heart encouraged him to go. Just to let Michelle know that he appreciated her letter. He carefully folded the paper and tucked it back into the envelope. "I'll think about it, Michelle," he murmured as he walked into the kitchen to refill his glass.

CHAPTER TWENTY-EIGHT

The next four months were busy for Michelle. She enrolled in the university and was taking a full course load. In addition, she made trips to Seal Beach every six to eight weeks to see her parents and brother. Her father was always so happy to see her, and she knew it helped her mom to have another pair of hands around.

They had received word from Clark Christianson that all charges against John had been dropped, and Michelle could see a new peace permeating her father's countenance. Mather's even offered his job back whenever he was able to return, but it seemed doubtful he'd ever have the stamina and drive to return. Just being able to hug her dad meant so much to Michelle, and the mental images from the hospital were gradually being replaced by new memories of him sitting up, standing, and even taking a few steps.

Although the attempt for a baby seemed to have shifted to a back burner in their lives, Michelle still grieved every month when she discovered she still had not conceived. By the end of the spring term, her focus shifted.

The next two weeks were consumed with preparations for Kristin's wedding. Michelle flew down one week early, as planned, and spent time helping Kristin with the final details regarding flowers, photos, and her last minute shopping for her honeymoon.

Sheila threw a shower the second day Michelle

was home, so she had a chance to see old friends and many of Kristin's family members.

Most of the time, she tried not thinking about her desire for a baby. Each night she would crawl into her old childhood bed, pick up her Bible, and dig into the scriptures, underlining or highlighting every verse of encouragement she could find. She fell asleep clutching her teddy bear and clinging to God's promises.

"I can't believe I'm actually getting married tomorrow," Kristin said to Michelle as they hugged after the rehearsal dinner.

"Everything's going to be so beautiful," she said with a smile. "The rehearsal went really well."

"I wish Steve could have been here," Kristin said. "It must be hard to have him working such long hours."

"I'm getting used to it," she replied, hoping Kristin did not detect any animosity in her voice. She didn't want to burden her on the night before the wedding.

"Michelle," Kristin said, "I want to ask you something."

"What?"

"Would you stay with me tonight? I don't think I'll be able to sleep a wink."

Laughing, she hugged her again. "I'd be happy to. We can have a little slumber party."

Mark walked over and asked, "What are you two talking about over here?"

The girls both looked at each other and laughed. "What? Did I say something funny?"

"We're planning a slumber party," Kristin said coyly.

"A slumber party?" His eyebrows shot up questioningly.

"I'm going to keep an eye on your bride tonight," Michelle explained.

"Oh. Okay. Just make sure she makes it to the church on time." He gave Kristin a squeeze and kissed her on the forehead. "See you tomorrow."

"I'll be there."

Three hours, one movie, and two bowls of popcorn later, Michelle and the bride-to-be were stretched out on parallel sofas in the living room sharing memories from the past and dreams for the future.

"I hope Mark and I have as great a marriage as you and Steve," Kristin said with a smile.

Michelle did not know what to say. She just nodded her head and made some comment about being certain Kristin and Mark would be happy.

"Is there something wrong, `Shell? I mean, I know you guys have been going through a lot with everything with your dad and then not being able to get pregnant."

"Yeah. But let's not talk about us. This is your special time. Don't let our stuff be a burden to you."

"Don't be silly. I care about you and Steve. You could never be a burden to me. I'll be praying for you guys about the baby thing especially."

Michelle smiled, but she felt heaviness deep inside. "Thanks, Kristin," she said. "God has been really helping me. It's like He is going through this with me." She thought back to her time at the beach and how Jesus seemed to meet with her there and comfort and encourage her.

"He is going through it with you. With both of you." Kristin reached over and squeezed Michelle's hand.

A sigh escaped her lips like a candle being extinguished. "I don't know if Steve feels that way. We haven't talked much lately. We've been going to church with Ben and Kelly at this little chapel on Main Street, but I'm hoping we'll get more involved when Ben starts his own church meetings next month."

"It'll be great for you guys to be part of that new church from the very beginning. Mark is so excited for Ben. He thinks Sandy Cove will be the perfect location." Kristin said enthusiastically.

She nodded and tried to refocus her thoughts from Steve to the new church. "Do you think you guys might actually consider moving up there like you said?" she asked hopefully.

"We've talked about it, but nothing's definite yet. After the honeymoon, we're going to spend some time considering all the options."

They talked a little longer about Kristin and Mark's plans. Then Kristin asked Michelle if she'd liked to pray with her.

They held hands and prayed for each other, for Kristin's wedding and her new life with Mark, and for Michelle's marriage and her desire for a baby.

"I actually think I could fall asleep now," Kristin said. "Me, too," she replied with a new countenance of peace.

The wedding was breathtakingly beautiful. A small chapel was the perfect size for the intimate group of guests attending. Red roses, ferns, and baby's breath accentuated the gracefully draped tulle at the end of each pew. Kristin was aglow in her flowing gown and fingertip veil.

As they exchanged vows, Michelle flashed back to her own wedding. She glanced at Steve sitting with her mom and Tim. She caught his eye and smiled. He nodded his head slightly and smiled back.

After the ceremony, Steve joined Michelle in the back of the chapel and escorted her to the reception. When the festivities were over, they headed to Michelle's parents' home for the night. Steve had a busy schedule at the firm the next week, so they flew back to Sandy Cove in the morning.

Michelle wanted to talk to Steve again about going back to see Dr. Foster for a follow-up appointment, but his mind was occupied with work. He brought a brief from the office with him, and his attention was focused on the document rather than on her.

Reaching for the travel Bible in her purse, she found the book of Psalms and spent the rest of the flight reading and marking verses.

A week later, Michelle flipped the kitchen calendar to June. Another month had passed. Her classes were out for summer, and she was restless and depressed. Finally Steve agreed to see Dr. Foster again. Michelle made the appointment for the following week.

Kelly's baby came two days later. He was the most adorable little boy Michelle had ever seen. His bright blue eyes sparkled in his chubby cheeks and the little wisp of blond hair on his head formed a tiny curl. "He's so precious, Kelly," Michelle said as she peered at the blue cocoon in Kelly's arms. Steve stood beside her, his arm draped over her shoulder.

"Want to hold him?" Kelly asked, looking at Michelle.

"I'd love to." She held out her arms as Kelly leaned from the hospital bed and placed the newborn babe in the cradle of her embrace. Little Luke's mouth opened in a tiny circle as he yawned. Michelle sighed, a smile lighting up her face. "He's perfect, Kelly. Absolutely perfect."

Steve looked over his wife's shoulder. "He looks just like Ben. Same blue eyes."

"Yep. Ben's strutting around here like a peacock." Kelly looked tired but full of joy. "He'll be back any second. He just went down to buy me a candy bar. I'm sure he'll want to see you guys."

A little quivering cry escaped from Luke. "Here. You'd better take him," Michelle said, placing the baby in his mother's arms.

"Might be hungry," Kelly said, starting to shift in the bed to nurse him.

Steve took that as his cue to step outside. "I'll go find Ben."

As Michelle watched Kelly feeding her baby, she thought about their upcoming appointment with Dr. Foster. *Please help us find out what the problem is, God.*

Dr. Foster welcomed Michelle and Steve into her office and glanced over their file before beginning.

"So you have been using the Clomid for nine months and following the recommended schedule and have not conceived?"

Michelle nodded nervously as she twisted a piece of her hair.

"Let's pursue a battery of simple tests, and we'll

see what we can find out. First, I want to have a sperm count on Steve and check for motility. Then we will follow that with some blood work on you, Michelle, just to ensure you really are ovulating. That will help us evaluate the effectiveness of the Clomid in your treatment."

"Okay," Michelle replied. Steve leaned forward in his chair and nodded.

"I'll send the nurse in to explain the procedure for Steve's test. We should have the results within a day or two. Then I'll call you and we can set up the blood work. I'll give you the lab order today before you leave. Keep taking the Clomid for this month and we'll test you mid-cycle to see what is happening with your ovaries." Dr. Foster stood up, extended her hand and added, "It's been nice meeting you, Mr. Baron."

"Likewise," Steve replied as he rose and shook her hand.

The doctor turned to Michelle. "Don't get discouraged. I know you're eager and it's hard to wait."

Michelle forced a smile in reply.

"If it's any consolation to you, it's very rare for me to sit across my desk from a patient and tell her she will be unable to conceive a child. I'm confident we can work together to accomplish your goal of starting a family."

"Thanks, Dr. Foster. We'll be eager to hear from you later this week."

After she'd left the room, Steve glanced over at Michelle. "Well, I guess you're off the hook for the first test."

"Yeah, but all the tests after that will be mine." She smiled again and squeezed his hand.

Within minutes the nurse came in and explained the information to Steve. He seemed embarrassed to be part of this testing process, but Michelle was proud of the way he willingly agreed to pursue it.

That night they went out to dinner at the Cliffhanger. They arrived at sunset and were able to get a window seat to watch the sky fade from blue to warm shades of pink and orange to purple before darkness swallowed the horizon. Most of their conversation revolved around small talk about Steve's work and Kristin's wedding.

This is really strange, Michelle thought. It's like we're on a first date or something. I hope we get this testing over with quickly so that we can get on with our lives.

Steve was staring out the window. He gave voice to her thoughts. "Let's just hope this testing doesn't take too long. I really hate medical stuff like this."

Michelle sighed and smiled. "Want to go to a movie tonight?" she asked, hoping the change of subject would lighten the air.

"If we can catch an early one. I've got a meeting at 8:15 tomorrow morning."

They decided to stop by the local triplex theater to see what was playing.

Dr. Foster's receptionist called the following Tuesday, and Michelle answered the phone. After identifying herself, the nurse said, "Dr. Foster would like to meet with you and Steve again this Friday afternoon."

"Already?"

"She wants to go over the first test results with you, and she asked me to schedule both of you to come in together."

"Is there something wrong?"

"I really don't know. She just asked me to call and

set up an appointment."

Michelle quickly looked through Steve's home copy of his day-planner. "It looks like anytime after 4:00 would work for my husband."

"Let's make it 4:15. Dr. Foster has her last appointment at 5:00 that afternoon."

"Okay. 4:15. Got it."

"See you Friday."

After Michelle hung up the phone, she got a sinking feeling in her stomach. Why would the doctor want to meet with them so quickly? Michelle's stomach tightened into a knot. Was there something wrong with Steve? She'd never thought of that possibility. How would he handle it if the problem were his?

I need to talk to someone before I call Steve. She thought about Monica but quickly dismissed that idea. She needed someone who could really reassure her. Someone like her grandfather. But she couldn't call her grandfather with something this personal about her marriage. She felt too awkward and embarrassed.

Kristin. I'll call her.

She punched in the number, and Kristin answered on the second ring. "Hi Kris, it's me."

"`Shell — I was just thinking about you."

"Really?"

"Yeah. I'm at my parents' house sorting through stuff in my closet and packing boxes of old memorabilia to take over to our apartment. I found the scrapbook we made in 5th grade. Remember? The one with the ladybugs on the cover?"

Michelle laughed. "I remember. I can't believe you still have that old thing."

"I know. I was really surprised when I found it here. So anyway, what's up with you?"

"Well, actually I need to talk to you about something really personal." Her voice shook slightly as she spoke.

"Are you okay?"

"Yeah. But I'm a little worried about something."

"What is it?" Kristin sounded genuinely concerned.

Michelle explained to her about the doctor appointment earlier in the week and about her husband's test.

"Yeah, I've heard it's pretty common to test the guy first."

"Really? I hadn't even thought about that when we went in for the appointment," she admitted.

"Makes sense to rule it out first, I guess. So anyway, tell me what's happening?"

She took a deep breath. "The nurse just called and said that Dr. Foster wants to meet with me and Steve on Friday."

"So soon?"

"Actually, I knew she'd get the results back quickly. She told us it would only take a day or two and she'd call and set up my blood work after that."

"So now she wants to see you both first."

"Yeah." She could feel her eyes starting to tear up. "There must be something wrong, Kristin, or she wouldn't be asking to see us like that."

"You sound really worried."

She bit her lip and nodded, afraid she'd cry if she said another word.

"Are you still there?"

"Mm hmm," Michelle managed to reply.

"Let me pray for you guys."

"Okay. Thanks."

Kristin prayed for God's will for Michelle and Steve, for His perfect peace, and for wisdom for the doctor.

"Amen," Michelle echoed as she felt the burden

of worry begin to lift from her heart. "Thanks, Kristin."

"Anytime, `Shell. Call Steve. And call me this weekend to let me know how it goes on Friday."

"I will," Michelle promised.

Steve and Michelle sat holding hands as Dr. Foster went over the test results with them. "It appears Steve has a very low sperm count as well as slow motility and slightly abnormal morphology," she explained looking down at the report and back up at them. "This means the reduced number of sperm are not only 'slow swimmers', but have some variations in shape which may limit the sperm's ability to penetrate and fertilize the egg."

Steve felt like he'd been slugged in the gut.

"What are the chances of us conceiving?" Michelle asked tentatively.

"Because of the multiple factors involved here, it is unlikely you will conceive without assistance. This doesn't mean you won't have a baby, Michelle. It just may require more medical intervention than you had planned on."

"Like what?"

"Like artificial insemination. In your case, I would recommend a combination of your husband's sperm and a donor's sperm to increase the likelihood of success."

"A donor's sperm?" Steve seemed concerned about that idea.

"Yes. We have anonymous donors, often from local colleges. We would select a donor who had similar characteristics to yours. That way the baby is likely to have a family resemblance regardless of whether the father's sperm or the donor's sperm actually fertilizes the egg. By using your sperm along with the donors, it would keep the possibility open that you could be the biological father."

"So we wouldn't know who the real father was?" Michelle asked.

"If you mean the biological father, that's correct. You would not know. However, with the advances in DNA testing, it would be easy and relatively inexpensive to find out whether or not it was Steve. But that shouldn't be the goal here." Dr. Foster reached over and picked up a photo of her with two children on her lap. "These are my kids. They are both donor sperm babies. But their real father is my husband, not the donor."

Steve tried to absorb this information, but all he could think of was getting out of this office and sorting through this thing with Michelle. How badly did she really want this baby? Maybe it wasn't God's will for them, at least not right now.

The doctor kept talking. She explained in-vitro fertilization and handed Michelle brochures describing both procedures in detail. "In-vitro is a very expensive process and there are no guarantees. I really think your best bet would be the insemination."

"We'll read through it over the weekend. Thanks, Dr. Foster," Michelle said quietly as the three of them stood up.

Michelle knew Steve was in no mood to discuss the doctor's findings on their way home. He kept his eyes firmly on the road and drove in silence while the radio droned on about the weather and traffic reports. As soon as they arrived, he grabbed his briefcase out of the back seat of the car and headed to his desk in the family room.

Michelle called home to talk to her mom and get

the day's report. Then she wandered upstairs. She discovered Max curled up on the rocking chair in the baby's room. Picking him up gently, she sat down in the warm seat cushion and began to rock. She thought about all the doctor had said, as tears slid silently down her cheeks and landed on the kitten's soft fur.

CHAPTER TWENTY-NINE

"Talk to me," Michelle said as they sat down to eat their breakfast the next morning.

"What do you want me to say? That I'm sorry?"

"Don't be ridiculous, Steve. This isn't your fault."

"Oh really? Then whose fault is it?"

"It's nobody's fault. It's just the way things are."

"Listen, Michelle, I know you really want to have a baby, but we weren't even planning on doing that right now until what happened with your dad."

"So what are you saying? That you don't want to try anymore?" Her eyes were swimming.

"I'm just saying, maybe this isn't the time. Maybe God has a different plan."

"Like what? Like us never having a baby?"

"Maybe. Or maybe He wants us to adopt a kid or something."

"Steve, you said it's practically impossible to just go and adopt a baby. And it's expensive." Michelle could feel her heart twisting into knots along with her stomach.

"Why does it have to be a baby? You should see some of the pictures of kids in the orphanages of Ukraine that Ben showed me the other day. He and Kelly went there on a short-term mission trip a couple of summers ago, and he was telling me there are tons of abandoned kids living in those orphanages."

"I really want a baby, Steve. I want to start out at the very beginning."

"Well, maybe there are babies in those orphanages, too," he suggested.

"It wouldn't be the same."

"The same as what?"

"The same as having a baby of my own. I want to be pregnant like Kelly and feel a baby moving inside me. I want to buy maternity clothes and go to childbirth classes and be able to nurse my own newborn."

"I know you do, babe. But let's just make sure we're open to whatever God might have for us."

"What's that supposed to mean? That I don't pray enough or don't care what God wants?"

Steve stood up and started to carry his empty plate to the sink. "I just think we should slow down a little with this."

"Whatever," she replied after he had left the room. She trudged over to the sink to rinse the dishes. Helping herself to another cup of coffee, she sat down with her Bible, and flipped it to the page she had marked.

"Delight yourself in the Lord, and He will give you the desires of your heart." *Okay, Lord. You know the desires of my heart.* She sipped on her coffee while she reread the verse over and over. *I really want to do this*, she thought as she picked up the brochure for the artificial insemination.

That night, Michelle prepared Steve's favorite dinner. She wanted everything to be perfect. Her stomach was coiled in a knot when he came in the door after work.

"Hi, handsome," she said nervously, wrapping her arms around him and searching his eyes to read his mood.

Steve smiled a sad, tired smile and gave her a kiss. "Something smells good," he commented, tipping his head in gesture toward the stove. He released her from their embrace and went to stir the simmering pot of homemade spaghetti sauce.

"It'll be ready in a few minutes. Why don't you sit

down by the fire and relax with Max while I finish up in here."

"I guess we're getting kicked out of the kitchen, pal," Steve said as he scooped Max into his arms and went to the family room. Michelle could hear him turn on the news and pictured him sitting by the fire rubbing Max's belly while the cat happily purred.

This is it. Oh, God. Please help Steve listen. She carried the plates, heaped with spaghetti and garlic bread, into the family room.

"Thanks, babe," Steve said, perking up when his plate was placed on the coffee table before him. He said a quick prayer and turned his attention back to the television as the sportscaster described the latest basketball games of the NBA.

"Could we maybe turn that off?" she asked.

"Just a sec. Let me see the score." A moment later, Steve flipped off the TV.

They sat in silence, eating their dinner. "This is really good," he said with a smile. "Thanks." He tipped his head to look into her eyes. "So how was your day?"

Michelle glanced away. "Fine. How about yours?"

"Busy. As usual."

Silence.

"Steve?"

"Yeah?"

Michelle put her fork down and turned toward him. "Can we talk?"

"I thought that was what we were doing."

"About what Dr. Foster said."

"Oh. That again," he replied, turning his attention back to his food.

She could feel her heart starting to ache in her chest. It was clear from her husband's tone of voice that he really didn't want to talk about it.

"Go ahead." He looked back at her with a

guarded expression. "Say whatever you want to say."

"I really want to do this thing, honey. I don't want to wait or think about adoption. Can't you just accept that this may be the only way we can have a baby?"

"What? To have some other man's kid?"

"It wouldn't be another man's kid. It would be our baby."

He shook his head and frowned.

"You're not being logical. Why would it be okay to adopt a kid, but not do the insemination? At least with this, we would know I'm the biological mother, and it would be possible you could be the biological father. Doesn't that make more sense to you than just finding some kid in Ukraine and bringing him here?"

He sat silently staring at the fire. When he looked back up at her, both their eyes were filling with tears. "I love you, Michelle. I know this means a lot to you."

She nodded, a lone tear seeping out of the corner of one eye, slipping down her cheek. "For some reason, it seems like now is the time I'm supposed to have a baby. I can't really explain it to you. It's just something I feel in my heart."

Sighing, he pulled her into his chest holding her close. "I'll tell you what. Let's look into the adoption thing and if it doesn't work out, we'll try insemination."

"I want a baby, Steve. Not an older child."

"I know. Let me just see what I can find out about private adoption. Maybe we can try both options and trust God to bring us a baby in His time and way."

She nodded. "Okay."

Steve could not get to sleep. He kept thinking about their appointment with Dr. Foster and the insemination process. While he wanted to make his wife happy, he still didn't feel right about all this. Something about the donor thing didn't seem like a good idea. What if the guy had some serious health problem their kid would inherit? Or what if he decided he wanted to have some kind of right to see the kid or play a part in its life? He punched his pillow and tried to settle into a different position hoping he could fall asleep.

After fifteen minutes of staring at the clock, he got up and went downstairs. Pulling a legal pad out of his briefcase, he started making a list of pros and cons for the insemination. At the bottom of the page, he wrote some questions for Dr. Foster. Tearing that piece from the list, he left the questions on the kitchen table. He'd have Michelle ask Dr. Foster about his concerns.

Satisfied he'd be able to sleep, he headed upstairs, climbing into bed beside Michelle. She stirred slightly. He moved close to her, draped his arm over her body and drifted off.

"What's this?" Michelle asked the next morning as she was buttering Steve's toast. She held up the paper by the phone with the questions on it.

"Those are some questions I want you to ask Dr. Foster."

"Oh. Okay. When did you write these?" she asked.

"Last night. I couldn't sleep."

"But you're okay with everything, right? We're still going to go ahead with this."

He took the plate of toast from her and kissed her cheek. "Just get the answers to those questions for me, alright?"

"Alright." Michelle studied his face for signs of a change of mind. He looked fine. Calm and confident – so handsome in his slacks, shirt and tie.

"I might have to work late tonight," he said as he quickly polished off his breakfast. Picking up his briefcase, he leaned over and kissed her good-bye.

Michelle adjusted his tie slightly. "Have a great day. I'll call you after I talk to the doctor."

"Okay, babe. Love you," he added as he left for work.

"Love you, too," Michelle added quickly, before the door could cut off her words.

She felt excited and energized as she bolted up the stairs to get ready for her day. *I just know this is going to work.* She'd call the clinic as soon as they opened at 9:00, then she'd call Kristin.

She wanted to look through the catalog and start selecting her next purchases for the nursery. After pouring over the pictures of cribs and dressers and folding down the corners of pages she wanted to show Steve, she checked the time: 9:05. She could call now.

Picking up the brochure about artificial insemination from the table, she dialed the number stamped on the back. Then she remembered Steve's questions, and retrieved them from the kitchen.

Max seemed to sense her excitement and started to follow her every move.

"Sandy Cove Fertility Clinic," the receptionist's voice said in a cheerful tone.

"Hi. My name is Michelle Baron. My husband and I were in to see Dr. Foster."

"Oh hi, Michelle. I remember you."

"My husband had a few questions he wanted me to ask Dr. Foster, and then I think we want to go ahead with what we discussed with her at our appointment."

"You're in luck. Dr. Foster is right here. Her first

patient is due in ten minutes." Michelle could hear the transfer of the phone from the receptionist to the doctor.

"Hello?" the doctor's voice sounded brisk, professional.

"Hi, Dr. Foster. This is Michelle Baron. My husband, Steve and I were in to see you this week."

"I remember. Have you had time to discuss what we talked about?"

"Yes. I think we're going to go ahead with the artificial insemination the way you recommended."

"With the donor addition," the doctor stated for clarification.

"Yeah."

"Okay. We can get that rolling right away. I'll put you back on with the receptionist, and she can get you the next available appointment. Are you still on the Clomid?"

"Yes. I'm on my second pill for this month."

"Good. That'll give us a little time to pull everything together."

"Dr. Foster?"

"Yes?"

"Steve had a couple of questions he wanted me to ask you."

"Fire away."

"He wanted to know if it might be possible the donor could have some kind of health issue that could be passed on to our baby."

"That's a valid question. Actually, Michelle, we are very thorough about screening our donors. We only accept healthy individuals with no known family history of hereditary diseases or conditions."

"I figured that was probably the case," she replied, her excitement mounting.

"Anything else?"

"Yeah, but I don't know if you can answer this one. He was wondering if the donor ever tries to contact the child or become involved in his or her life."

"Tell your husband we maintain strict confidentiality in all these matters. Our rules are written to protect the recipient couple from any kind of invasion by the donor. There is no way your donor will ever be able to find out who you are or whether or not he has fathered a child."

"Okay. Thanks, doctor."

"You're welcome, Michelle. I know this is a big decision, but I believe you are making the right one. I have never once regretted my two inseminations and the wonderful kids that were products of those choices."

Her reassurances drifted through the phone and calmed Michelle's racing heart. "I really appreciate you sharing that personal part of your life with us."

"That's why I'm in this field, Michelle. I know how it feels to want a baby and not get pregnant the usual way. Trust me. You won't regret this."

"Okay. I believe you."

"Well, I'm off to see my first patient. Here's Andrea. She can set up an appointment for you."

She could hear Dr. Foster instructing the receptionist to book an appointment within the next few days. Her heart was thumping loudly when Andrea came back on the line and gave them an appointment for that Friday.

After hanging up, Michelle picked up Max, stroking his soft fur. "Okay," she said aloud, gently placing him back at her feet, "I've got to call Steve." She dialed his office, but the secretary told her he was in court and would be back around 3:30.

Somewhat disappointed, she decided to call Kristin. Kristin picked up after the third ring. "You sound out of breath," Michelle said.

"'Shell? Oh, I'm glad I answered this. I was just about to run out on some errands."

"I can call back." She tried not to sound disappointed.

"It's okay. I can talk for a few minutes. How's everything?"

Launching right in, she explained about their appointment with Dr. Foster.

"How's Steve handling all this?"

"He's doing okay. Neither of us expected there to be any problem with him. It kind of threw us both for a loop."

"So what do you do now?" Kristin asked.

"Steve's going to look into private adoption as a back-up option, but I'm hoping I can convince him to go for the artificial insemination. The doctor will mix donor sperm with Steve's. That way the baby might end up being his biological child anyway."

"Sounds like a big decision."

"Yeah. But whenever I pray about it, I feel like God is telling me to try every door. I guess that's another good reason to look into the adoption thing. But I told Steve I really don't want to adopt an older kid. If we can get a baby, that would be fine." She could detect defensiveness in her own tone of voice. She silently chided herself for feeling that way.

After a short pause, Kristin replied, "God will guide you guys, 'Shell. The adoption idea sounds like it could be a good one too. I know you've really felt a burden for unwanted babies ever since you spent time at the crisis pregnancy center."

"Like I said, I'm fine with adoption, as long as it's a baby. But Steve thinks it's really expensive, and I'm sure it's hard to find a baby with so many girls opting for abortion."

"Yeah. I know. It's sad," Kristin commented, adding, "You know I'll support you in whatever decision you two make. When do you think you'll know about this insemination thing?"

"I don't know. It's up to Steve."

"I'll be praying for you guys. Keep me posted," Kristin said.

"I will. And thanks for your prayers."

As soon as she hung up the phone, the doorbell rang. It was Kelly. She looked really cute with baby Luke asleep in the color- coordinated sling against her chest.

"Kelly. What a surprise! Come on in." Michelle hugged her and brought her into the warmth of the kitchen.

"I came over to talk about something important." She sounded excited and yet nervous. "Ben and I could use your help."

"What? What's up?"

"We found a building for the church. It's only about a quarter of a mile from here. We can rent it once a week to start with and then go from there."

As they sat together at the kitchen table, Kelly explained that it was a local middle school, willing to rent out their auditorium during off-school hours. She described the old, Spanish style architecture with its arches and ornate tile work. "You're gonna love this place, Michelle."

"So how can we help?" she asked, eager to learn more.

"First, you can pray we get the best possible deal."

"Got it."

"And then, you can join us for our first meeting to organize the plans for the services and outreaches to the community to invite people to come."

"Sounds like fun. We'll be happy to help."

"Thanks, Michelle. We just don't have many friends around here yet. I was hoping I could count on you."

"You can," Michelle reassured her. She watched Kelly sparkle while she talked about the new church. She looked so happy as she discussed the details, while little Luke slept peacefully in his cocoon.

Steve called that afternoon and Michelle told him about her conversation with the doctor and their upcoming appointment. He sounded distant, but did not put up any protest.

"So are you working late?"

"Yeah. It might be ten or eleven by the time I get home."

After they hung up, Michelle looked around the empty room and sighed. Maybe Monica would like to have dinner with her. She called to ask her, but Monica was sick with a bad cold. "Guess it's just you and me, Max," she said to the cat.

CHAPTER THIRTY

The next few weeks were a rollercoaster of emotions for Michelle. Steve seemed much more interested in the adoption idea than he was with the insemination option. He was able to get a recommendation from his uncle for a family law attorney in Portland. After contacting her and explaining his uncle's referral, Veronica Blake offered her services at a significantly reduced rate. Steve was thrilled to report the news to Michelle.

"Seriously?" her voice asked excitedly over the phone.

"Seriously," Steve replied.

Immediately, the same thought played on the recorder in her mind. *Try every door.* Maybe this was God's answer for them.

"She's faxing me the forms today and we can start filling them out tonight," Steve continued.

"Great. I've got class until 7:30, but I'll come straight home afterward."

"Okay, babe. Have a good class."

"Thanks," Michelle replied before hanging up. Her heart was racing with excitement. It looked like the adoption idea might be the answer. Wanting to tell someone, she dialed Kristin's number but got voicemail. This was something she couldn't leave on recording.

Grabbing her purse and keys, she headed out the door to Ben and Kelly's house.

Steve and Michelle filled out all the forms and faxed them back to Veronica Blake. Three more months passed and they heard nothing. Michelle started back to school, this time at the university. She spent some time volunteering on a crisis pregnancy hotline, hoping to save the lives of other women's babies.

But sometimes she would come home and collapse on the bed in a fetal position and weep. So many women had unwanted babies, and it seemed as if the baby she so desperately wanted would never be hers.

The call came, as Michelle was about to rush off to class late one afternoon in October. "Mrs. Baron?" a friendly voice asked.

"Yes?"

"My name is Beth Woods. I'm calling from Veronica Blake's office."

Michelle let her purse slip off her arm and onto the table as she sat down.

"I have some wonderful news for you," Ms. Woods stated enthusiastically.

"You do?" Michelle asked, trying to hold her hopes in check and ignoring Max's pleas as he rubbed against her leg.

"Yes. A young woman, who has decided to relinquish her baby for adoption, came into our office yesterday. She looked through our file of potential adoptive couples and selected you and your husband."

"She did?" Michelle was stunned. Her heart began to hammer in her chest.

"Yes. She was very impressed that your husband is an attorney and you are studying to become a teacher. She believes you'll be able to provide her baby with a great future."

"Oh, my gosh. I can't believe it. When is she due?" Michelle asked.

"You have a little time. She's twenty-six weeks along. The baby is due in fourteen weeks — January 20th. It's a boy."

"Fourteen weeks. That should give me enough time to finish the nursery." Michelle said to herself as well as Ms. Woods. Then she quickly added, "What do we do from here?"

"I'm preparing the documents you and your husband will need to sign," Beth explained. "Should I fax them to Mr. Baron's office?"

"Yeah. That would be great. I'll call him to let him know."

"Okay. Sounds good. And congratulations, Michelle. You are about to become a mom."

As soon as they hung up, she punched speed dial for Steve's cell phone.

"Hi, babe," he answered. "On your way to class?"

"No. I think I'm skipping it today."

"What's up? Are you sick?" He sounded concerned.

"No, but I've got to talk to you about something. When will you be home?" she asked. "Well, I was planning to work late because of your class. I've got some briefs to prepare for later this week. Is it something that can wait?"

"It's really important, honey. Could you just come home? You can bring the briefs and work on them here after we talk." She could hardly contain her excitement, but somehow it didn't feel right to tell him over the phone.

"Okay. I guess that would be fine. Let me get some paperwork together, and I'll be home in about half an hour."

Hanging up the phone, she headed upstairs to the room that would soon become their nursery. She looked over the purchases she'd made already and began compiling a list of the items she'd need to buy before the baby arrived. Max continued to try to get her attention with his plaintive wails.

"Okay, okay. Let's go get your dinner," she said as she scooped up the cat and started toward the kitchen. After feeding Max, she surveyed the refrigerator for possible dinners. She and Steve usually ate takeout on their own the nights she had class. But tonight was special – a time for a real celebration!

After sharing the excitement of the news and a surprise dinner out, Michelle and Steve climbed into bed, his paperwork untouched. "I love you, honey," she sighed softly as they snuggled together.

"Love you, too, 'Mom'," he replied with a grin.

They held each other tightly as Steve said a prayer, thanking God for the wonderful opportunity that lay before them.

As they said their "Amen," the recurring thought inched its way into Michelle's consciousness. *Try every door.* What did it mean? Hadn't they done that? Wasn't this the door God had for them?

Michelle called home the next morning. Before her mom could even ask how she was, she dove right into her news.

"You're what?" Sheila asked.

"We're adopting a baby," she repeated. "It's a boy."

"Michelle, that is so exciting! I'm really happy for you. What made you guys decide to adopt?"

"We've been trying to get pregnant for a while, now. Remember, I talked to you about it last Christmas?"

"That's right. You did say something about it. You said you were taking fertility drugs. But I don't think we talked about you two adopting."

"It sort of happened quickly. We put in the paperwork a few months ago, but I thought it would take a lot longer time than this, so I haven't been telling people. Then we got a call yesterday that a girl has picked us for her baby."

"Picked you? I thought they didn't ever get to know who got the baby."

"It's different with private adoption, Mom. Girls go through albums of applications. They get to know lots of stuff about the adopting couples, like their jobs, hobbies, interests, how long they've been married – all that kind of stuff. Then they get to pick who they think would be the best parents for their baby."

"Well this girl certainly knew what she was doing picking you two. You and Steve will make wonderful parents, Mimi. I'm so happy for you. I can't wait to tell your dad."

"Is he there? Can I tell him?"

"He's at physical therapy. Do you want him to call you when he gets back?"

"Sure. That would be great."

As Michelle hung up the phone, she breathed a prayer. *Thank you, God. I'm so very happy! You truly have answered my prayers.*

Michelle worked feverishly on the nursery over the next couple of months. Everything had to be just right. After much searching through name books and discussing lots of options, they'd settled on Caleb because it meant faithful. God had been faithful to bring their desire to fruition, so it seemed natural to give their baby boy this name.

When Michelle told her grandparents, they relayed to her the story of Caleb and Joshua spying out the Promised Land and how they had been the only men with the courage God required to face the giants they saw. *Perfect,* Michelle thought to herself.

She found some wooden block letters at the local craft store and bought the five she would need to spell the baby's name over his crib. The soft blue walls combined with the brown and cream-colored Noah's Ark décor was the perfect room for a baby boy. She could hardly wait to bring little Caleb into this room for the first time.

Sitting in the rocking chair taking in the results of her hard work, she reminisced about the babies she'd seen at the hospital and the certainty in her heart that she could easily love any one of them as her own. Surely this was a gift from God – the ability to take someone else's child into her home and heart.

Just a few more weeks. Then she'd finally be a mom!

It was hard to believe another year had passed. This Christmas was a joyous celebration for Michelle and Steve as they eagerly awaited Caleb's soon arrival. They traveled down to Seal Beach and Michelle's mom threw a baby shower for them. A cute decorative little Noah's Ark set, crafted of wood, was the gift from her grandpa. "Did you make this?" Michelle asked.

"You bet, pumpkin," he replied with a grin.

Her mom and grandmother made a quilt that went along with the theme. She could barely contain her excitement and gratitude.

More than a year had passed since her dad started rehab. It seemed like he had reached his final potential. Although he wrestled with headaches and had issues with short-term memory, he'd been able to advance to the point of walking haltingly with the assistance of a cane, and his speech was coherent and more fluently connected. He still groped for words at times, but overall, the initial frustration and travail to communicate had been replaced by a quiet, slow and methodical manner of speaking that revealed the humble and gentler man who had replaced the old John Ackerman.

Sometimes Michelle missed the strong, self-confident father she'd grown up with. She also worried about the toll this new version of her father took on her mom, who had to dedicate the majority of her time to caring for a semi-invalid. Tim tried to help out on a regular basis, and it made Michelle proud to see her younger brother maturing into a responsible, caring man.

Best of all, she was so thankful her dad had survived to become a grandpa himself.

All too soon, it was time to head home for the final stretch before little Caleb would be welcomed into their family.

The last two weeks dragged on endlessly. A nervous anticipation mixed with an unexplainable uneasiness made it difficult for Michelle to sleep at night. By the grace of God, she had managed to pass her final exams before the holidays, but she was having difficulty focusing on the night class she had agreed to take this semester.

She was just switching over a load of laundry in the garage one morning when Steve showed up unexpectedly. "Hey, honey. What are you doing home?"

she asked.

Then she noticed his face. Something was very wrong.

"Steve? Are you okay?" she asked, putting down the clothes in her hand and walking over to him.

"Let's go inside," Steve replied. He draped his arm around her shoulders and guided her into the kitchen.

"You're scaring me, Steve. What is it? Is it my dad?" she asked, her mind racing with anxious thoughts.

Steve sat her down at the table, reached over and took both of her hands in his and looked into her eyes. Tears were pooling in his own eyes as he began to speak. "It's the baby, Michelle."

"What? What's wrong with Caleb? Did something happen to him?" Michelle was desperate for answers and fighting the urge to flee to somewhere else – a place where bad news couldn't find her.

He took a deep breath. "He's fine. He was born late last night. But..." he paused and took another breath.

"But what?"

"But the birth mom has changed her mind, honey. She's decided to keep him."

She pulled her hands away from his. How could this be happening? They'd done everything they were supposed to. "Can she do that?" she asked incredulously.

He nodded. "Yeah. She can."

"But I thought all the documents were signed." Michelle pulled on a strand of hair at the nape of her neck, trying to maintain her composure while they sorted this thing out. It had to be some kind of misunderstanding. They had rights. Surely they had rights to Caleb.

"We signed all the documents on our side, but the birth mother doesn't have to sign her part until after the baby is born. There's always a chance she might change

281

her mind. Remember? Veronica explained that to us when we first applied."

"So there's nothing we can do? We have to forget about Caleb just like that?" Michelle stood up and stormed out of the room. Her heart took her upstairs to the nursery and she slumped down into the rocking chair in tears.

A moment later, Steve walked in. "I wish I could fix this for you."

He was clearly in as much pain as she was, but Michelle was unable to respond to his distress, except to nod.

That night, Michelle cried herself to sleep, haunted by the persistent words, *Try every door.* After what had just happened, she wasn't willing to try any door.

Michelle buried herself in grief for the next six weeks. She continued attending classes, but she refused to seek out family or friends. Her mother tried to get her to come back down for a week or two, but the thought of facing everyone's sympathy was more than she could bear.

As she went through the motions of life, she was careful to avoid the nursery, the doors now remaining firmly shut. She attended church services with Steve, but her heart was not in it. When one of the young moms offered her a baby to hold, she politely declined.

All Michelle wanted now was to silence the warring voices within that had left her weary and confused.

The voice of reason spoke to her mind, telling her that all the advice from family and friends to wait and be patient was the logical answer, a common sense approach.

There was still hope if she just gave it time. A deeper voice of yearning from her heart continued to ache and plead for fulfillment now, in spite of the pain she wanted to bury and forget. And a still small voice in her spirit gently reminded her once again to try every door.

One Sunday, something in the message caught her attention. Ben was going over a passage in the New Testament where Jesus challenged His followers to pick up their crosses and follow Him. Ben explained that Jesus was asking them to surrender their lives and all they held dear and trust Him with their future.

Surrender. The thought pierced Michelle's heart. She knew she'd never surrendered her life fully to God. Yes, she'd asked for His help. And she'd tried to learn what the Bible said about how to live her life.

But she could not remember a single moment of actual surrender.

Focusing her attention back on Ben, he asked them to turn to Psalm 37:4. "Delight yourself in the Lord, and He will give you the desires of your heart." It was a promise she'd clung to in her struggles to have a baby.

"There are two ways to look at this," Ben explained. "You can believe that God will give you whatever you desire as long as you enjoy a relationship with Him. Or, and I believe this is the actual meaning, as you surrender your life to God and learn to get your joy in life from that relationship, He will begin to plant His desires for your life into your heart. Those desires will bear fruit.

"So instead of wondering why God isn't giving us what we desire, maybe we need to allow Him to give us the desires He knows will bless us in the long run."

He closed with another Old Testament verse: Jeremiah 29:11. "We are not surrendering to a God who doesn't care about us. Quite to the contrary, we read here that He already knows the plans He has for us, and they are plans for good, not evil. Plans to give us hope and a future."

Hope. She felt her heart racing as the concept of surrender began to take root. It was as if God was directly talking to her through Ben, and she knew she had an important decision to make.

That night after Steve was asleep, she crept out of bed and into Caleb's nursery. Turning on the little Noah's ark lamp, she sat down in the rocking chair. As she rocked, she poured her heart out to God. She let him into the most tender places, as she grieved for the loss of a baby she would never know; a baby who would never sleep in the nursery prepared so lovingly just for him; a baby who would never hear her whisper his name as she rocked him to sleep.

Then she prayed for little Caleb, asking God to watch over him, to help his mom take good care of him, and to draw him close to Jesus. She prayed he would grow up to be a strong and wise man, and God would give him a wonderful purpose for his life. Her tears mingled with her prayers, but now these were tears of surrender, not frustration and grief.

Finally, she laid her life out to God. *Help me to trust you, Lord. Help me to surrender everything to you. Show me what you desire for my life, and give me the strength to accept whatever that may be.*

A feeling of complete peace engulfed Michelle. She sat rocking, and allowed the sweet love of her heavenly Father to wash over her in waves, cleansing the wounds and healing her broken heart. *I'm all yours, God. If the life you've planned for me doesn't include having a baby, then help me know where to go from here.*

A few days later, Steve came home with a dozen roses, surprising her with a dinner date at the Cliffhanger. As they dined by candlelight, Steve broached a subject that had been shelved for quite a while. "I'm ready to try the insemination procedure," he said.

She looked at him. Hope for a baby, a thing that had died with the loss of Caleb, tried to push it's way through the sealed soil of her heart. She'd made her peace with God and hesitated to let it break the surface, but a familiar voice in her mind allowed it to peek through.

Try every door, Michelle.

Was God telling her something? Something she'd ignored ever since the idea of adoption had become an active pursuit?

"Are you sure, Steve?" She asked as she studied his face.

"I've given this a lot of thought, Michelle. It was definitely not something on my radar when I first considered becoming a parent. But Ben's message about surrender really made me think. After all we've been through – the waiting, the attempt to adopt, watching you grieve over Caleb — I believe we should try every door."

Try every door. Michelle's heart sang as she again surrendered, this time to tears of joy. She wrapped her arms around him and whispered, "I love you, babe."

It was time. Time to try every door.

Later that month

It was a dreary day at the beach. Michelle huddled in her beach chair with a blanket tightly wrapped around her. Lord, please let this work.

She watched the gulls circle overhead and listened to their mournful cries. Her heart was as turbulent as the sea. She was relieved the insemination was over, but her emotions vacillated between a nervous excitement over the possibility of conceiving and unexpected feelings of frustration and loneliness.

Although it was his idea to go through with it, Steve had seemed somewhat withdrawn, since their decision to try the insemination. He worked late almost every day, often coming home after she had drifted off to sleep. He still hugged and kissed her goodbye in the mornings and told her he loved her, but it seemed mechanical and routine, rather than heartfelt or passionate. Clearly, surrendering to this was more difficult for him than he had anticipated.

Michelle stared out over the crashing waves, thinking back to the last encounter she had with Trevor at this very spot. He had always made her feel so special. But she'd cut off their friendship for the sake of her marriage. Now Steve was miles away in his own struggles and fears.

As she felt her loneliness begin to engulf her, she cried out to God. *Help me, Lord. Give me the strength to weather this.*

A still small voice spoke to her spirit. *I will never leave you nor forsake you.*

Replaying the words in her mind, she felt almost as if Jesus' arms were wrapped around her holding her close. She closed her eyes and soaked in the feeling – a feeling of being special, like Trevor had made her feel, and yet very different — a sense of deep inner peace, unlike the nervousness that accompanied all her encounters with him.

She sat there for a long time, praying for Steve, for their marriage, and for God's will regarding a baby. As she stood to leave, she breathed a final silent prayer. *Thank you, Lord. I love you.*

CHAPTER THIRTY-ONE

Dr. Foster sat down at her desk and grinned at Michelle. "Well, Mrs. Baron, it looks like you're going to have a baby."

Michelle could feel goose bumps on her arms. "Are you sure?"

"Positive. A December baby."

"I can't believe it worked the first time," Michelle said smiling and shaking her head in amazement.

"You lucked out. Must be in the stars for you."

"I've been praying so hard for this to work," Michelle replied.

"Well, I'm really glad for you. Now we just need to go over your schedule of OB appointments. We should be able to get a heartbeat on the ultrasound at the next appointment. Why don't you bring your husband along? It usually blows their minds to see a baby's heartbeat so early."

"I'll try," Michelle replied, her smile fading somewhat.

"Give him time, Michelle. He'll come around. It's a huge blow to most men's egos to discover they are infertile. At least he was willing to go along with the insemination. He'll work through the rest."

Michelle nodded, silently hoping she was right.

"Anybody home?" Steve called out as he entered the house that evening.

No answer.

"Hello?" he called again as he walked toward the stairs.

"Hello," Michelle called back from the baby's room. "Be right down."

I wish she wouldn't spend so much time in that room. What if this whole insemination thing doesn't pan out? He went to the kitchen and picked up the mail. As he was opening the first bill, Michelle came in grinning from ear to ear.

"I went to see Dr. Foster today."

"Really? For what?"

"To find out if I'm pregnant."

"So soon? I thought it took awhile before you could find out."

"I guess you weren't listening at our last appointment," she said tentatively.

"Sorry, babe. I've had a lot on my mind. So tell me what she said."

"A December baby!" She looked so excited.

He tried to respond positively, hugging her with as much enthusiasm as he could muster. Then he pulled back and looked into her eyes. "I'm really happy for you, honey."

"For me? What about for us?" she asked, her voice taking on an edge.

"I mean us." *Can't she see I'm doing the best I can here?* "I just know this has been such a big thing for you."

Michelle's smile dissolved. "Yeah." She turned away to avoid his eyes.

Steve sighed. He didn't have any other words to offer her. He ached for his relationship with his wife, which seemed to be going downhill fast. And he ached for the son or daughter that might very well be fathered by another man. His wife and another man creating a baby. He wanted her to be happy, but it was hard for him to be excited about this.

Michelle busied herself with cooking dinner, and Steve went to turn on the news, sinking lifelessly into the couch. He tipped his head back and closed his eyes, massaging his scalp with both hands as if to free himself from the torment in his mind.

They ate dinner in front of the television, and soon afterward Michelle said she was tired and was going to bed. As she went upstairs, he punched the off button on the remote control and pulled a file out of his briefcase. Work would help him get his mind off the uneasiness he couldn't seem to shake.

Michelle took her Bible from the nightstand, needing God's presence in her loneliness. Words were mingled with tears as she once again poured her heart into His strong and loving hands.

I will give you peace, a still small voice promised.

Michelle nodded and took a tissue to wipe her eyes and blow her nose. Everything was quiet downstairs. She listened for Steve's footsteps coming up to their room, but all she heard was silence.

She placed her hand on her abdomen. A little baby is starting to grow inside of me. Thank you, Lord, for giving me this chance to be a mom. Help me be a good mom, no matter how Steve reacts to all this.

As she finished praying, Max jumped up on the bed, startling her. "Come here, little guy," she said, taking him in her arms. "Guess what, Max? I'm going to have a baby."

Max just purred, then wiggled from her arms and

jumped into the rocking chair to curl up for the night.

When Michelle woke up the next morning, Steve's side of the bed was still untouched. The alarm clock said 5:47, so she knew he hadn't left for work yet. Wrapping a robe around herself and stepping into her slippers, she headed downstairs. As she entered the family room, she could see Steve asleep in the recliner with a file from work on his lap.

She quietly walked over and turned off the lamp beside the chair.

Steve shifted and made a sound, and she reached out and took his hand. "Steve?" she said in a voice just above a whisper.

"Hmm?" he replied, as he wrestled to sit up and open his eyes.

"You fell asleep down here last night. It's almost 6:00 AM. Do you want me to start a shower for you?"

He raked his fingers through his hair and stared at her. "Sorry, babe. Guess I lost track of time."

"It's okay. Here, let me help you." Taking the file off his lap, she helped him out of the recliner.

"I'm alright." He got his bearings and pulled away from her.

"Do you want me to get the water running?"

"I can do it. Just throw some bread in the toaster for me in a few minutes, if you don't mind."

If I don't mind? What's that about? I fix him breakfast every morning. She just nodded in reply and watched him stagger up the stairs.

Within a half hour, he was eating his toast and heading out thedoor.

"Will you be home for dinner tonight?" Michelle askedhopefully.

"Not sure. I'll call and let you know." He gave her a perfunctorykiss on the cheek and then grabbed his briefcase and left.

She sank down into the chair at the kitchen counter. *What is happening to us? This should be the happiest time of our lives.*

The rain began to fall outside, and she felt her last remnant of joy drain away as the drops ran down the kitchen window. Then an idea came to her. No one except Steve knew about their baby. Today would be the day to call her mom, her grandparents, Kristin, Kelly and Monica. They would all help her celebrate the good news.

Michelle felt a renewed energy as she set a goal to get her house in order and herself bathed and dressed before she began calling her family and friends. She put some of her favorite music on the CD player and danced her way through her housework. By 10:00 she was dressed and ready to make her calls.

Her mother was very excited to hear the news. "Wait until I tell your father! He will be thrilled," she promised enthusiastically. "Should I tell Tim?"

"Yeah. Tell him he's going to be an uncle." Michelle's heart felt light as she shared her joy with her mom. "But let me tell Grandma and Grandpa."

"Okay, dear. Have your grandmother call me after you two talk."

"I will. Promise."

She got similar reactions from her grandparents and Kristin. Everyone was excited and filled with congratulations. Next she called Kelly. As soon as she told her the news, Kelly insisted on coming right over. "I want to pray for you and the new baby. I'll be right over."

Guess Monica will have to wait, Michelle thought as she started a pot of coffee and took some muffins out of the refrigerator to heat up.

"Michelle — this is the best news I've had all week," Kelly exclaimed as she bounced Luke on her hip.

"Let me see that little guy," Michelle said happily, reaching for the baby. She nuzzled his neck and inhaled the fragrance of baby lotion. Her eyes sparkled, and smiling at Kelly she said, "I can hardly wait to feel my baby move."

"It's the most exciting thing in the world, Michelle."

They shared coffee and muffins, talked about baby names, and looked at Michelle's catalog from the baby store.

"It's all right for me to tell Ben about this, right?" Kelly asked.

"Sure. But don't expect a lot of excitement from Steve when he talks to him about it." Michelle's dark cloud began to settle back over the kitchen.

"Why? You guys decided all this together, right?"

"Yeah." She wanted to tell Kelly the whole story about the infertility tests and the insemination, but she was certain Steve would not want her to know. "I guess he's just having a hard time adjusting to the actual reality of it."

"Maybe he's not sure he's ready to share you with a baby."

"Maybe."

They decided to head to the store to buy some of the items Michelle had circled in the baby catalog.

"This will be so much fun," Kelly said. "I'll look for a new changing table while we're there. We can take Ben's truck. He's got the camper shell on so we can fit a lot of stuff into the back and not worry about it getting wet," she added.

Thankful to have someone who really understood her excitement, Michelle silently prayed, *Thank you, Lord, for bringing Kelly and Ben up to Sandy Cove.*

The shopping trip was just what she needed, and she came home with a musical mobile, as well as some wall decorations. Looking around the nursery again, Michelle tried to imagine a tiny baby asleep in this room.

CHAPTER THIRTY-TWO

The next eight weeks were exciting times for Michelle. She tried not to let Steve's reservations affect her bliss as she feverishly worked to decorate the baby's room. She and Monica sponge painted one of the walls with puffy clouds and then added a sun and rainbow to enhance the Noah's ark theme.

Today was a big day – their first ultrasound. She stood in the nursery soaking in the ambiance and praying for everything to go well at the doctor's appointment. Steve had agreed to accompany her and would be arriving momentarily.

Max strutted into the room and began rubbing against her legs, begging to be held. "Oh, okay," Michelle replied as she picked him up. "Needing some more attention?" she asked, scratching him behind the ears. He purred contentedly, angling his head for further strokes.

"Honey?" Steve's voice lifted from below. "Are you ready?"

"Uh, oh," Michelle said to Max as she put him down. "Coming. Just a sec."

She hurried into her bathroom, ran a brush through her hair and applied some lipstick, then grabbed a sweater and headed downstairs. "Sorry. Didn't mean to keep you waiting." She gave him a quick kiss.

"I'm not the one in a rush," he replied as they walked out to the car.

She tried to ignore his comment. Sometimes it

seemed like he was starting to get excited about the baby, but other times she could tell he was struggling to keep up a front.

Soon they were in the ultrasound room. Steve sat in a chair beside the examining table from which he would be able to observe the monitor where the images would be displayed.

"I'm nervous, Steve," Michelle said as the technician applied a clear gel to her abdomen.

Squeezing her hand, he tried to reassure her.

"I take it you've never done this before?" the red-haired, freckled young tech asked. Her clear green eyes sparkled as she smiled at them. "You'll be amazed. It is so cool to see the baby's heart beating."

Michelle smiled. "It's hard to believe she already has a beating heart."

"She?"

"Or he," Michelle added.

Moments later the tech located the tiny new baby and an image appeared on the screen. The heartbeat was clear and steady, faster than Michelle had expected. "Does everything look okay?" she asked apprehensively.

"Looks great to me. Here's the head and the little legs. Over here you can see an arm."

Both Michelle and Steve were engrossed in the image on the monitor. "Wow..." Steve said.

The awe in his voice surprised Michelle. She looked over at him and saw an expression she hadn't seen before. His eyes were riveted to the image on the screen. She thought she saw tears.

"Are you okay?" she asked softly.

"Look at that, Michelle. It already looks like a baby," he said.

"I know, honey. Isn't it amazing?" Together they studied every feature on the screen, holding tight to each other's hand.

"Well, that's about it for today," the tech said, invading their little world. "You can pick up a copy of the video and some still shots on your way out. Then you can start showing your family and friends your new baby." She winked at Michelle as she rubbed the gel off with a paper towel. "Need to use the restroom?"

"Yep," Michelle scooted off the table.

"Right this way."

When she got back, Steve said, "Let's go somewhere and talk."

He seemed so different, so much gentler, like the Steve who had romanced her in college.

"Okay. Where do you want to go?"

"How about the Cliffhanger for lunch."

"Wow, are you sure? That place is so expensive."

"Yeah. Let me just call Roger and let him know I'll be late getting back."

As they pulled into the parking lot of the restaurant, Steve was still trying to process the emotions that had overtaken him at the doctor's office. How could he have such strong feelings for a little, tiny creature he'd only seen on a computer monitor? Was this what Michelle had been feeling the past couple of months as she thought about the baby and prepared its nursery?

"I love you, Michelle," he said as he looked over at her sitting in the passenger seat.

"Love you, too."

"No. I mean really," he replied, his voice shaking slightly.

She looked into his eyes and saw tears. "What? What is it Steve?"

"I feel like I've really let you down lately. You

know, with all the baby stuff."

"It's okay. I know it's been hard for you." She reached across and put her hand on his leg.

"Something about that ultrasound. I don't know how to explain it, but suddenly I realized that might actually be my kid in there." He took a deep breath. "I guess ever since the insemination, I've just felt like it's not my baby. Like I let another man have a part of you that I can never have." He paused and swallowed. "Can you understand that?"

A tear slipped down her cheek. "Oh, Steve. I'm sorry. I've been so consumed with my own perspective on all this... I guess I sort of lost track of yours."

He gazed out the windshield and said, "Anyway, I'm sorry I haven't helped much with the nursery."

She patted his leg. "Not to worry. There's still plenty left to do," she added, winking.

Looking back into her eyes, he promised, "I'll try to help from here on out."

"Thanks, honey. Thanks for going today. I'm glad you were there."

"Me, too." He cupped her face in his hands, gently kissing her lips. "Hungry?"

"Famished!"

CHAPTER THIRTY-THREE

Steve was determined to make up to Michelle for the time he had neglected her during the first few weeks of her pregnancy. He began surprising her with flowers, buying little knick-knacks for the nursery, and even brought home an outfit for the baby.

"A football uniform? In size 0-3 months?" She laughed, hanging it up on a little blue hanger in the baby's room.

Ben and Kelly were the first to see the ultrasound video. "Look at that kid! What a kick he's got," Ben commented as the baby on the screen moved.

"Would everyone please knock off the 'he' stuff?" Michelle asked with an exaggerated sigh. "What if this is our precious baby girl?"

"Then I'd say she'll make a great soccer player," Ben added with a wink.

Kelly swatted him in the arm. "Quit it, Ben."

"Okay, okay. Just calling it as I see it." He grinned at Steve, who held up his hands as if to say, 'Don't involve me in your mess.'

"Have you guys started picking out names?" Kelly asked.

"Yeah. I think Madison if it's a girl and maybe Jake if it's a boy. Steve isn't sure about Jake yet, but we both agree on Madison."

"It sure is a pain having to consult the guys on this name thing, isn't it?" Kelly asked with grin.

"Sure is," Michelle replied, but her eyes glowed with love as she glanced over at Steve.

Steve and Michelle took a long weekend and flew down to Orange County to share their ultrasound video and pictures with her family and Kristin and Mark. Sheila insisted on having a huge buffet spread, and they had a great time catching up with everyone and showing off the images of the baby.

Michelle's dad was getting stronger and was now home full- time. Tim remained there for the transitional period, but John was getting to the point where he could move around independently and was getting proficient with his cane. The wheelchair was nowhere to be seen.

"You're looking great, Dad," Michelle exclaimed the minute she saw him.

"Thanks...Mimi. You, too." John smiled warmly.

"You're father's got me quite busy these days," Sheila remarked. "Every day we head over for physical therapy, then out to lunch and down to the beach."

"The beach?" Steve asked.

"He likes to sit on a bench at the park by the pier and feed the birds."

"Oh. Good for you, Dad." Michelle put her hand on his shoulder. She thought back to the time when her father was always so driven by work. Although he'd lost that compulsive drive, he seemed to have gained a new peace.

"I look at things... different...ly now," John replied haltingly, as if reading her thoughts.

"I know. Me too," Michelle said, bending over and kissing the top of his head. She couldn't help but think of all the blessings God had given them. How would they have fared without Him?

Michelle savored every moment of her brief visit with Kristin. It was still hard for her to be so far away from her lifetime friend. Kristin and Mark seemed to have settled into married life well, with both of them working at the church and Mark praying about the possibility of coming up to Oregon to help out in Ben's new church. "I sure hope that works out," Michelle said.

"Yeah. Especially now that I'm going to be an 'auntie'," Kristin added with a grin.

While the guys settled in to watch sports on television, the girls took off to shop for baby things. They ended up at a cute shop on Main Street. It was clear from the way Kristin oohed and aahhed at all the tiny clothes, that she was destined to have her own children someday. She insisted on buying Michelle's baby an adorable pink gingham sundress with matching bonnet and socks. "I just know it's going to be a girl," she told Michelle.

"Hooray! Someone who thinks 'girl' for a change."

"Just ignore the guys. They don't know what they're talking about. That ultrasound has Madison written all over it," Kristin added with a grin.

Michelle hugged her. "Thanks, Kristin." Just then she felt her baby move. "Oh my gosh."

"What?"

"I think I just felt her move."

"Oh, 'Shell — I'm so excited for you," Kristin exclaimed.

"Me, too. I can't believe this. I never imagined it would feel like this. Hey, maybe she moved because you called her by name," she added. "Let's go. I want to tell Steve."

Kristin paid for the little outfit, and they headed back to Michelle's parents' house.

When they walked in the door, the men were

engrossed in the game, calling out directions to the players and coaches and reacting to the refs. Even John seemed to be sitting slightly forward, his arms resting on his thighs.

"Steve?"

"Yeah, babe?" he replied without taking his eyes off the television. "No way — that ball was out of bounds!"

"Steve."

"What?" he looked up momentarily.

"The baby moved," Michelle smiled.

"What?"

"The baby. She moved."

Tim reached over and hit the mute button on the remote, and all eyes moved to Michelle.

"I just felt her move when we were in the baby store."

Steve shook his head as if shaking off the game. He stood up and walked over to Michelle, a huge grin on his face. "How did it feel?"

"Weird. Like a butterfly fluttering around inside of me."

He held his arms open as she walked into his embrace.

"Well, I'd say this calls for a celebration," said Sheila, who had been standing in the doorway of the kitchen. "Tim, get the sparkling cider from the refrigerator and turn off that game."

Within moments, everyone had a glass of sparkling cider, and John was proposing a toast. "To my... precious... prin... cess... and... her baby."

"And to Steve, the new papa," added Sheila as she raised her glass.

A warm feeling of peace and joy embraced Michelle. Everything was going to be fine. More than fine.

CHAPTER THIRTY-FOUR

Eight weeks later

It was 10:18 and Steve still wasn't home to take Michelle to her 10:30 ultrasound appointment. At eighteen weeks, they were hoping to learn the gender of the baby. Although Michelle was convinced it was a girl, Steve wanted verification.

As she picked up the phone to call him, she heard his car pull into the driveway. "Bye, Max," she called over her shoulder as she raced out the door.

"Sorry I'm late, babe," he offered. "My meeting went longer than expected."

"I'm just glad you made it. But we'd better hurry."

"Right." He quickly maneuvered the car out of the driveway and headed for the clinic. Thankfully the lights were in their favor, and they arrived at 10:30 on the dot.

After they checked in at the front desk, the nurse escorted them to the ultrasound room. Soon they were watching their baby appear on the screen. Michelle noticed the intensity in Steve's countenance. He asked several questions about the baby's size, its heart rate, and finally about the gender.

"Looks like a girl to me," the nurse replied with a smile.

"Madison," Michelle whispered in awe.

"A girl." Steve's face showed his amazement that

this tiny creature was actually their daughter.

As soon as the ultrasound was over, Michelle raced to the restroom while Steve waited for her in the lobby. When she came out to meet him, he had a funny look on his face. "What is it, Steve?"

"You won't believe who I just saw." Steve's forehead was furrowed and his fists clenched by his side.

"Who?"

"Your friend. That Trevor guy."

"Trevor? He was here?"

"It sure looked like him to me."

"I wonder what he'd be doing at an obstetrics clinic," she said, her brows raised.

"Just what I was wondering. Do you think he might be following you? I mean the guy's weird, Michelle. I wouldn't put it past him."

"Honey, listen. I haven't seen or talked to Trevor since before I got pregnant. Why would he start following me around now? I think you're getting paranoid."

"I'm telling you, I don't trust that guy."

"Okay. I know. But let's forget about him. Maybe it wasn't really Trevor anyway. Maybe it was someone who just looked like him. Besides, you don't have anything to worry about. You're my husband, Steve. I'm in love with you, not him." She took his hand in hers, interlocking their fingers and giving a little squeeze. "And we're having a baby. Can you believe it's a girl? Little Madison. I can hardly wait to hold her."

Steve's expression relaxed some. "Yeah. I guess your right. It's pretty amazing to see her swimming around in there," he added as he patted Michelle's swollen abdomen. "Time to go home, little one, so Daddy can go back to work."

Michelle's heart skipped a beat as she heard him call himself Daddy. She squeezed his hand again. "I love you."

"Love you, too." He opened the car door for her and helped her inside.

After he dropped her off at home, she decided to do some more work in the nursery. She was stenciling a little footstool when she heard the doorbell. "Who could that be, Max?" she asked the cat as she pushed herself up off the floor and headed downstairs.

"Monica!" she exclaimed as she opened the door. "Hey, pal, I've missed you."

"Me, too." Monica stepped in to hug Michelle. "I decided it was time to come and check on you and see how the baby's room is coming along."

"I was just working on it," she said as she brushed a stray hair off of her forehead with the back of her hand. "Come on up. I'll show you."

Before Monica could even get to the bottom of the stairs, Max was right in front of her, meowing and rubbing against her legs. "Thought I forgot about you, didn't you?" She reached down and scooped him into her arms. "You should know better than that." As she scratched his chin, he purred with delight. "Let's go up and see the baby's room," she cooed into his ear. Smiling at Michelle, they started climbing the stairs, with the cat slung over Monica's shoulder.

"You will not believe what I found out today," Michelle blurted out with excitement.

"What?"

"It's a girl. I'm having a girl!"

"That's great! Oh, we'll have so much fun with a little girl. The frilly dresses, the lace socks, the little bows for her hair. Listen to me — I'm starting to sound like it's my baby, too." Monica's grin spread from ear to ear as her eyes sparkled with excitement.

"Well, you will be little Madison's unofficial 'auntie' you know," Michelle said, tossing a smile over her shoulder at Monica who was a couple of stairs below her.

"Did you hear that, Max? I get to be an auntie."

The cat seemed to have had enough of the girl talk and gently pushed himself out of her arms, bouncing back down the stairs to find another adventure.

Monica spent the afternoon with Michelle in the nursery. After the step stool was finished, they stenciled the child's rocking chair Michelle had found at a yard sale and worked on assembling a bouncer Jim and LouEllen had brought to church for them.

"It sure was nice of them to give you a baby gift," Monica remarked.

"I think they're adopting us," Michelle replied. "They are the sweetest people. I'm so glad they make the trip out here every Sunday. It means a lot to Ben and Kelly, too. Speaking of Sunday, have you thought anymore about going to church with us some time? I really think you'd like it, Monica. It's not like a traditional church with organ music and rituals."

"Maybe some time. Right now I'm still trying to learn all the spiritual stuff Trevor is teaching us in our class. I miss you there. I've made a few friends and Trevor always makes me feel welcome, but it's not the same without you."

Michelle shot up a prayer for wisdom then replied, "I don't think I could ever go back to something like that. It's hard to explain, Monica, but I'm getting to know God like a friend right now. It's so much more..." she searched for the word she wanted. "... so much more personal. More real."

Monica studied her face. "Trevor asks about you a lot. I told him you were pregnant. He said to tell you congratulations, and he wishes you the best of everything."

Michelle could feel her heart do a little somersault. She could see Trevor's face in her mind and could feel his kiss from their weekend at the conference.

Would she ever be free of these feelings?

"What is it?" Monica asked.

"Nothing. Just remembering something about Trevor." Michelle started busying herself putting cardboard pieces back in the bouncer box. She remembered what Steve had said about seeing Trevor at the clinic.

"Monica?"

"Yeah?"

"Something weird happened today at the clinic."

"What?" Michelle turned to look at her friend.

"Steve said he saw Trevor in the lobby while I was in the bathroom."

"That's weird. I wonder what he was doing there?"

"That's just what we were wondering." She hesitated, choosing her words carefully. "You don't think he could be...um...following me, or anything, do you?"

"Following you? Why would he do that?"

"I don't know. It just seems strange that he would be at an obstetrics clinic. I mean if it was a regular doctor's office, that would be different."

"Yeah. Well, he does seem to really care about you a lot, Michelle. I mean he asks about you every class. It's hard to imagine him as... you know... like a stalker or something. I mean, this is crazy. There must be some logical explanation."

"You're right. And hey, maybe it wasn't really him. Steve might have been wrong."

"That's probably it. It was probably someone who just looked like him. That happens to me all the time. People are always telling me I look like someone they went to school with or something like that."

Michelle nodded, her face relaxing somewhat but her finger nervously twirling the hair at the nape of her neck.

CHAPTER THIRTY-FIVE

Monica loved a mystery. Although she could tell Michelle wanted to drop the subject of seeing Trevor at the clinic, she decided she would find out exactly what he was up to. *After all*, she rationalized, *I don't want anyone stalking my friend. Besides, it'll give me a good excuse to talk to Trevor alone.* Trevor's magnetism was not limited to Michelle. Like her friend, Monica was also a married woman, but she couldn't help daydreaming about what might have happened if she'd met Trevor before Tony.

Her hands were shaking as she arrived at the New World Bookstore, where she hoped to see Trevor before the rest of the students arrived for his class. After greeting Starla, she asked if anyone was upstairs yet.

"Trevor went up a few minutes ago. He likes to meditate before the group arrives," Starla replied.

"Okay. Thanks. I think I'll go on up."

As she entered the small attic room, Trevor's back was to her. He was sitting in a lotus position in the very center of the wood floor on a black cushion with gold tassels. The floor creaked under Monica's foot as she stepped inside. Her heart started to race and she felt her face flushing.

"Come in, Monica," he said in a soothing voice without even turning to look her way.

How does he know it's me? she wondered, taking another step in his direction.

Trevor gently lifted himself to a standing position

and turned to face her. His face was very serene and his eyes sparkled as he smiled at her. "You're early today."

Monica cleared her throat, willing her voice to speak. "Uh, yeah. Sorry. I didn't mean to interrupt you."

"Not to worry. I was just centering myself and clearing out any bad vibes from the room." His hand reached out and rested on her shoulder. "Are you alright? You look a little uneasy."

Oh brother. Now he thinks I'm a nervous schoolgirl or something.

"I guess I was just a little surprised you knew it was me at the door without even turning around."

He chuckled and gave her shoulder a little squeeze. "It was your fragrance. Love's Breeze, I believe."

"Oh. You're right. It is Love's Breeze," she stammered, her cheeks turning to crimson.

"So what brings you here early?" He released his hold on her shoulder and gestured to one of the floor cushions as he sat back down.

"I saw Michelle yesterday. She said to tell you hi." Why did I say that? Michelle will kill me.

Trevor's eyebrows lifted into gentle arches over his eyes. "Really? And how is she doing these days? You said she's pregnant."

"Yes, actually she's expecting in early December. She and Steve are really excited. I was helping her decorate the nursery when I was there yesterday."

Trevor nodded, a thoughtful smile caressing his face. "Speaking of Steve," he said, "I think I saw him the other day at a clinic."

"Really?" Monica was stunned that he actually brought it up.

"Yeah. It's a small infertility clinic not too far from here. Maybe you've seen it. It's called Sandy Cove Women's Fertility Clinic."

"Oh yeah. I know the one. That's where

Michelle's doctor is."

"Well then Steve must have been there with her for one of her appointments."

"Probably," she replied. "So do you ever talk to Michelle anymore?"

"You know, I haven't seen or talked to her for quite a while. Maybe I should swing by and congratulate her."

She was just about to ask him what he was doing at the clinic when another member of the class walked in. Trevor's attention immediately shifted to the other student, who wanted to know if it was too late to enroll her friend in the next session.

Well, at least I found out it really was him at the clinic. I'll have to warn Michelle he might be dropping by. She tried to refocus herself on the class that would begin soon, but she was dying to find out what Trevor had been doing at a fertility clinic.

Trevor was sitting in his living room, a new age flute CD playing in the background. He was looking at a picture of Michelle he had taken at one of their classes. As he sipped his wine, he savored her beauty. *Oh, Michelle. If only you could see the bigger reality, the inevitable destiny of our souls.* He sighed, dropping her photo on the coffee table and blew out the large, multi-wick candle he lit every night.

"If my plan works, maybe you'll see we were really meant to be together," he said to her picture. He got up to go to his bedroom, still holding the glass of wine in his hand. Sitting down on the edge of his bed, he picked up the phone and dialed. "Ginger?" he asked. "It's Trevor Wind. Got a minute?"

Ginger Stiles was a student from a previous class he'd taught on meditation. She worked at the clinic as one of Dr. Foster's nurses.

"Hey, Trevor. It's good to hear your voice," she purred.

"Want to go for a little bike ride?"

"Sure! I can be ready in ten minutes."

"I'll be there." Trevor hung up the phone, smiling to himself.

Steve seemed to be in a particularly good mood when he got home that evening. "Hi, beautiful," he said to his wife as he embraced her in the kitchen. "What's cooking? It smells great."

"I put a roast in about an hour ago. It's almost ready." She gave him a kiss and handed him the photos from the latest ultrasound. "More pictures of little Madison," she said with a grin.

"Let me see that gorgeous kid." He took the pictures and started flipping through them. "Yep. Looks just like her mom," he observed with a wink.

"Steve?"

"Yeah?"

"You seem so different lately."

"Like how?"

"Like you're really excited about the baby."

Setting the pictures down on the counter, he and looked up into her eyes. "And?"

"And I just wondered what changed your mind?" She felt like she was stumbling over her words, not saying exactly what she meant. "I mean, other than the ultrasound, was there something else that changed the way you feel about all this?

Steve put his hands on her shoulders and cocked his head to one side. "You know I was never opposed to us having children, right?"

"Right."

"It was just the insemination thing that threw me for a loop."

"I know. That's what I'm talking about. How did you get past that?"

"I had a talk with Jim and LouEllen after church awhile back."

"Was that the time when you guys were standing under that big tree over by the parking lot? I thought maybe you were talking about the bake sale."

"No. We were talking about you."

"What were you saying?" she asked, as she sunk down into one of the chairs at the kitchen table.

Steve sat down across from her, reaching out and taking her hand in his. "LouEllen was talking about how you were 'glowing' since you found out about the baby. Jim winked and told me what a lucky guy I was to have such a beautiful wife who wanted to be a wife and mom more than a career woman." He paused and squeezed her hand. "It made me realize how I was losing touch with all the dreams we had been trying to build since the day we met – our life as a couple and someday as a family."

Michelle smiled, her eyes tearing up. "Jim and LouEllen are the best, aren't they? It's almost like having Grandpa and Grandma nearby."

"Yeah. They really got me thinking that day. Then, when we went for the first ultrasound and I saw the baby and how excited you were, it suddenly became exciting for me, too. It's like God opened my eyes to the miracle of that new little life and told me He was entrusting her to my care."

A tear slipped down Michelle's check and she brushed it off with her free hand, a nervous laugh

310

escaping as she said, "Why do pregnant women have to cry about everything?"

He stood up and pulled her gently to her feet. As she rested her head against his chest, he held her close. "I love you, Mrs. Baron," he murmured into her hair.

"You too, Mr. Baron."

Ginger was waiting out in front of her apartment when Trevor pulled up on his motorcycle. She hopped on the back, and they took off for a ride along the coast. The sky was clear and a full moon danced on the surf.

When they got to his favorite beach, he pulled the bike to a stop and climbed off, helping Ginger dismount as well. They walked to the rocks overlooking the water and sat down.

"So, how's work?" he asked, his voice thick with meaning.

"Great. Everything's going along perfectly. You heard she's pregnant, right?"

"Yeah."

"And you're the donor."

"Well, I was hoping I was, but I just wanted to confirm it with you."

She feigned dismay. "Since when have I ever let you down?"

"Never." He gave her a quick kiss. "Thanks, Ginger."

"Sure. No problem." She smiled at him like a star-struck schoolgirl. "So tell me, why was this so important to you?"

"Her husband's an old friend of mine. They've wanted to have a kid for a while now. I just thought maybe I could help, without them ever finding out. You know, sort of storing up some good karma for the future."

"Well you were the perfect candidate since you and her husband have such similar characteristics."

"That's what I was hoping. Anyway, I'm just glad I could help. Maybe someday, in another life, they'll thank me."

"It'll have to be in another life, Trevor. No one can ever know about this. You understand that, right? That was part of the deal. This stuff is strictly confidential. I could lose my job and my license if it ever got out that I arranged this for you."

"Not to worry, sweet Ginger," he replied, drawing her into an embrace. He could feel her melt in his arms. She looked up at him and they kissed, gently first and then more passionately, Trevor's hands beginning to explore the curves of her body as his mind imagined Michelle in his arms.

Michelle and Steve made love that night tenderly, expressing feelings that had been suppressed for months under the stress of all the infertility testing and the insemination process. It was almost like they were newlyweds again, rediscovering each other and the perfect bond God had created for their marriage.

Steve slept soundly. In the early morning hours, he awakened to the sound of Michelle's muffled voice.

"No, Trevor. Give her to me. No. She's mine."

He reached over and gently shook her shoulder. "Michelle? Hey, babe — wake up."

She made a groaning sound and turned toward him. She slowly opened her eyes, looking a little disoriented. "Wow. I was having a really weird dream," she said.

"I know. You were saying something about Trevor and about giving something back to you."

"It was the baby."

"The baby?" Steve sat up against the headboard.

"Yeah. Trevor had the baby. He wouldn't give her back to me." Her eyes started to fill again.

"Hey, don't cry. It was just a dream." He wrapped his arms around her, and she nestled against his chest. He could hear her sniffling and feel her trembling slightly. "Shh. It's okay," he soothed. Gradually she relaxed in his arms. As he stroked her arms, cuddling her close, he couldn't help wondering if a connection existed between seeing Trevor at the clinic and this dream about the baby. *Is it possible Trevor could be the donor?* "No," Steve said aloud to himself.

"No, what?" she asked, pushing away from him to look at his face.

"Nothing."

"Tell me. Tell me what you were just thinking." Her expression was serious.

"It just kind of freaked me out that you were dreaming about Trevor."

"It wasn't a romantic-type dream, if that's what you were thinking."

"I wasn't thinking that. I guess it just bothers me that I saw him at the clinic, and now you had this dream about him taking the baby."

"It is weird isn't it?"

"You don't think Trevor could be the donor, do you?" he asked.

"Oh, my God. I hope not." She looked really troubled. "It can't be. That would just be too much of a coincidence."

"But he does have similar features to me. Remember how the doctor said they try to pick a donor who is about the same height and build of the father with similar coloring." He studied her face for a reaction.

"This is crazy. It was just a dream. Trevor couldn't be the donor. He'd never do anything like that, anyway. He's way too caught up in all his New Age stuff."

"I hope you're right. I don't know if I could deal with him being the biological father of our baby," he replied, feeling his old feelings of hostility and jealously toward Trevor surfacing. He didn't trust the guy for a minute. He'd seen the way Trevor looked at Michelle, and he could guess what he'd been thinking.

"We don't ever have to worry about that. Remember, Dr. Foster said it's confidential who the donor is."

"Yeah. Right." Steve forced a smile and kissed her on the forehead. Just then his alarm clock started to ring. "Guess it's time for me to get up." He gently lifted her off his chest and got out of bed.

As Michelle was folding laundry in the family room, she heard what sounded like a motorcycle come up the driveway. She peered out the window through the shades. Trevor was getting off his bike and placing his helmet on the seat.

Oh my gosh. What is he doing here? She checked herself in the mirror and hurried to the door.

"Trevor. What a surprise." Michelle stood in the doorway, her heart pounding.

"Hi, Michelle. I was in the area and decided to swing by."

Michelle just nodded. "I see."

"Can I come in?" Trevor gestured to the living room behind her.

"Uh, yeah, I guess so." Michelle moved to the side, and Trevor walked past her as Max trotted over to see who it was.

"This must be Max. Monica mentioned him to me." Trevor squatted down and scratched the top of Max's head.

Michelle wasn't sure what to do. She didn't really want Trevor in the house, and she was mentally kicking herself for letting him in. "So how've you been?" she asked.

"Fine. Great. How about you?"

"I'm fine. Busy."

"How's your dad doing?"

"He's better. He's home now. It's really a miracle."

"Sounds like it. That's great."

An awkward pause hung in the air. Then Michelle said, "Would you like to sit down?" She gestured toward the sofa, and Trevor took a seat, peeling off his leather gloves and setting them down at his side on the cushion. Max jumped up and climbed into his lap, while Michelle sat in a nearby chair, her heart pounding.

"So you're having a baby," he observed, glancing at her swollen abdomen.

She smiled. "Yeah. We are. She's due in December."

"She?"

"Uh huh. We're having a girl. Madison."

"Madison. Nice name." He leaned forward and put his hand on her knee. "Congratulations, kitten," he added, using the pet name he'd given her during her class with him.

Her stomach did a flip. She stood up. "Thanks, Trevor. Thanks for coming by. I wish I could visit more, but I'm really kind of busy today."

"No problem. I just wanted to check on you. It's

315

been a long time." He rose to face her. "I'm really happy for you. You deserve this baby. Really."

Michelle nodded. "Thanks." She turned and walked over to the door.

"Guess I'm getting the boot, Max," Trevor said as he followed her. "I hope you'll stay in touch, Michelle. I'd love to see Madison after she's born."

"Maybe. You know Steve's not very fond of us being friends." She was feeling even more uneasy.

"Hey, speaking of Steve, I saw him awhile back. He was at the clinic. It must have been for your doctor's appointment or something."

"Yeah." Michelle hesitated and then decided to just ask. "What were you doing there?"

"Actually, it's kind of embarrassing."

"What?"

"Well, ever since my sister went through her bout with infertility, I've been trying to do my part to help others out. I'm a donor at the clinic. It's supposed to be confidential, so don't tell anyone, okay?"

Michelle could feel the blood draining from her head. She felt sick, like she might faint.

"Are you okay? You don't look so good," he asked as he placed a hand on her shoulder.

"I'm fine." She threw open the door, hoping the fresh air would clear her head.

"Well then, I guess I'll go." With both hands on her shoulders, he brushed his lips over her cheek. "I miss you, Michelle. Bye."

She pulled back. "Bye, Trevor. Don't come over here again."

He seemed to ignore her remark, climbing on his bike and starting it up. Michelle closed the door, leaning her back against it and slipping to the floor, hugging her bent knees to her chest. Max paced back and forth in front of her mewing and rubbing against her shins.

CHAPTER THIRTY-SIX

Michelle heard Steve come in through the kitchen door. It had taken her most of the day to recover from Trevor's visit and decide if she should or shouldn't tell Steve. She knew he'd be upset about Trevor being here, and she could only guess how he'd feel if he found out Trevor really was a donor at the clinic. Most of all, she didn't want to lose the closeness she and Steve had in their marriage now. She decided not to mention the visit at all.

"Hi, honey," she said as she gave him a hug and kiss.

"Hi, babe. How was your day?"

She turned away. "It was fine, how about yours?"

"Hectic. Lots of meetings." He walked over and grabbed a bottle of water from the refrigerator. "When's dinner?"

"I thought we'd call for pizza." Michelle had neglected to fix dinner, so consumed with her thoughts from earlier that day.

"Sounds good. Want me to call?"

"No. I can do it. Why don't you go in the family room and relax?"

"I think I'll go up and change first." He put his hands on her shoulders just like Trevor had that morning.

Michelle shuddered.

"What was that? Are you okay?" he asked.

"Yeah. I'm fine. Just got a chill for a second."

"Well, maybe you should sit down and relax, and let me take care of ordering the pizza."

"No, really — I'm fine. Just go get changed." She pushed away from him.

"Okay. If you say so." A puzzled look on his face pierced her.

She could hear him talking to Max as he went into the living room. She rummaged through the junk drawer looking for pizza coupons. Then scanning the sheet for the phone number, she called and ordered their dinner. Her stomach was in knots and the last thing she felt like doing was eating, but she knew Steve must be starved.

A few moments later he came back into the kitchen with something black in his hands. "What are these?" he asked, handing Trevor's gloves to her.

Michelle stared down at the gloves. Then she started shaking her head back and forth.

"Michelle, what's wrong?" He lifted her chin with his finger and looked into her eyes, his face knit into an expression of concern mingled with fear.

"I wasn't going to tell you," she began, her voice catching in her throat.

"Tell me what?" Now he looked more upset than ever.

"Trevor came by."

"Here?"

"Yeah."

"When?"

"This morning." She sank down into the kitchen chair, bracing herself for his response.

"What happened?"

She just shook her head and looked away, not wanting him to see the tears beginning to fill her eyes.

"Hey, did he hurt you?" Steve asked, putting the gloves down and draping an arm over her shoulder.

She shook her head no.

"Talk to me. Tell me what happened."

Like a dam breaking, she poured out the whole story, feeling horrible and yet somehow relieved to have it out in the open. When she looked up at him, she was stunned. He was looking away, tears about to spill out of his eyes. Other than his emotions during the ultrasound, she couldn't remember ever seeing him cry before. It scared her.

"Steve, are you okay?"

"Great. Just great." He walked over to the sink and gazed out the window.

She put her hand on his back, but he shrugged her off, his voice shaking as he said, "Not now."

She let her hand drop to her side. "Steve, don't pull away from me."

He turned around, shook his head, and walked out of the room.

CHAPTER THIRTY-SEVEN

December 5th

Michelle and Steve managed to somehow make it through the ensuing months. Neither of them could shake the fear that Trevor might be Madison's biological father. Steve's enthusiasm for the baby had waned considerably although he'd faithfully attended all the childbirth classes and feigned excitement whenever they were with family or friends. No one knew about the concern they both shared. They'd agreed it was better to keep it between the two of them.

Trevor kept his distance but periodically asked Monica to tell Michelle hi or that he was eager to see the baby after she was born. Michelle would just nod at Monica's messages, trying not to show how deeply they disturbed her.

As the leaves turned colors and then fell to the ground, her swelling abdomen made it more and more difficult to do the normal tasks of life. They spent a quiet Thanksgiving at home since she was not up to traveling. Now only a couple of weeks remained until Madison would be born.

Gazing out the kitchen window, she saw the chilling wind and dark clouds overhead. Steve had just left for work an hour earlier, and Michelle suddenly felt the strangest sensation she had ever experienced. A gush of warm water rushed down her leg. "Oh my God," she whispered. It wouldn't stop coming. She quickly shuffled into the bathroom, grabbing her cell phone off the table. Easing herself down onto toilet, she hit the auto-dial button for Steve's phone.

"Hello?"

"Steve?"

"Yeah. What's up? Are you okay?"

"Actually, I think my water just broke."

"What? Are you in pain?" His voice sounded genuinely concerned.

"No, but I think you'd better get home," she replied, her voice shaking.

"I'm on my way. I'll be there in a few minutes."

"Okay. Bye." She hung up and sat nervously waiting for Steve's arrival, tears beginning to blur her vision. A short time later, she heard his voice.

"Michelle? Where are you?"

"I'm in here. In the bathroom," she called back at him.

He burst into the room. "Is this it? Should I take you to the hospital?"

Michelle nodded, brushing her hands across her eyes. "Call the doctor. Tell her we're on the way."

"Okay. Do you need anything?"

"Maybe something else to wear. This is such a mess." She looked up at him and felt like a fool. Suddenly she felt overwhelmed. Who did she think she was having a baby? She wasn't ready to be someone's mother. She could barely take care of her husband and her cat.

"I'll be right back."

He left the bathroom, and she could hear him taking the stairs in large leaps. He was back in a minute with a terry cloth robe and clean nightgown. "How's this?"

Michelle didn't know what to say or do. She just took the robe and gown, trying to figure out how she was going to stop the water from running down her legs when she stood up. "Did you call the doctor?"

"I'll do that right now." He hurriedly dialed the clinic. "Is Dr. Foster there? This is Steve Baron. I think my wife Michelle's in labor. Her water broke."

She watched him listen to the receptionist.

"Yeah. Okay. I'll take her right over. We go in the emergency entrance, right?"

Another pause.

"Okay. Thanks." He turned and looked at her. "It's time. Let's go." He helped her stand up, as she wrapped the robe around herself like a coat. A small amount of water continued to trickled down her leg.

"We'd better take a towel for me to sit on in the car."

Steve grabbed one off the rack. "Are you ready?"

Starting to tear up again, she said, "Yeah I guess. Did you get my bag?"

"Got it."

"Okay. Let's go."

Dr. Foster finished her exam. "Looks like you're having a baby today, Michelle," she said with a smile.

Steve squeezed her hand, and Michelle tried to look happy, but her insides were in a knot. Suddenly the whole thing seemed so scary, so final.

The anesthesiologist came in a few minutes later and set up her epidural. By this time the contractions were strong, and she was thankful to know that relief was imminent. Within twenty minutes, she was feeling much better. Steve took a short break to grab a candy bar out of the machine in the hall and change into the scrubs the nurse gave him.

When he came back, he looked more like a doctor than a lawyer. "Ever thought of changing your profession?" Michelle asked, trying to distract herself from her own fears.

"Dr. Baron. What do you think?" He asked with a wink. He looked nervous too.

"How about 'Dad'?" the nurse asked with a smile as she studied the monitor.

During the next few hours, Steve contacted Michelle's parents, tried to keep her comfortable, and prayed for everything to go well. Around dinnertime, the nurse came in and checked her again. "It looks like you'll be ready to push soon." She left the room, promising to bring Dr. Foster back with her. They were both quiet when the doctor came in a few minutes later.

After examining Michelle, she said, "It's time. Let's have a baby."

The room became a flurry of activity as the nurse got Michelle ready and notified the pediatric department they would soon be needed to examine the infant. Before she knew it, Michelle was pushing with Steve by her side coaching her along. He breathed with her when the doctor said to breathe, and he helped her sit up and grab her knees when it was time for each push.

A half hour later, Dr. Foster placed little Madison on Michelle's abdomen. Overwhelmed with love, she reached down and held onto the baby's warm, sticky body.

"She's perfect. An absolute ten," the doctor said with a smile.

"Oh, Steve," Michelle looked up into his eyes and could see the tears forming there again.

"She's beautiful, honey." He bent down to kiss her forehead.

The nurse took Madison to clean her, and the doctor finished up with Michelle. "I know you two will want some time alone. We'll get you settled in your room with your new daughter. Congratulations to you both."

"Thanks, Dr. Foster. Thanks for everything," Michelle said with a teary smile.

As soon as they were alone, Michelle called her mom. Sheila squealed with delight, telling her how much she wished she were there, and promising to get on the first flight possible.

"That'll be great, Mom. They said I can probably go home tomorrow afternoon."

Next Steve called his uncle and then Roger at the office, who promptly gave him the rest of the week off, encouraging him to take as much time as he needed. After calling Michelle's grandparents, they began phoning and texting friends.

Kristin was the first friend Michelle called. "Michelle — I'm so thrilled for you and Steve! What does she look like? Tell me everything."

Michelle gazed down at Madison who was sleeping in the basinet beside her bed. "She has blond hair and blue eyes."

"Sounds like she looks a lot like Steve."

She smiled and glanced over at her husband. "Yeah, she really does." Resting her head back against the pillow, she silently prayed that her husband would love Madison as much as she already did.

CHAPTER THIRTY-EIGHT

The next few weeks were exhausting for Michelle. Although her mom came up and spent a week helping her, it seemed like she was on a non-stop treadmill of feeding Madison, changing diapers, and sleeping whenever she could. She tried to savor little moments with her newborn, cradling her tiny body close and inhaling the sweet baby smells as she thanked God for the chance to be a mom.

Although Steve seemed upbeat and tried to help her out as much as possible, she noticed he spent little time holding Madison or bonding with her. Whenever she tried talking with him about it, he pulled into a shell, claiming he just couldn't relate to babies. But she knew that wasn't the real issue.

Steve was afraid. Afraid Madison wasn't really his. All Michelle could do was pray that somehow he'd forget about biology and let himself love their beautiful daughter. Sometimes her heart ached as she looked down at her baby's sweet face. Would Maddie miss out on the father she deserved?

It was less than two weeks before Christmas, and the house showed no signs of an approaching holiday. Michelle tried to rally her energy to decorate at least a little. Her whole family would be coming up for a few days, and she wanted everything to look nice.

"Steve?" she said quietly into the phone, hoping not to wake Madison who was sleeping in her cradle.

"Michelle? Is everything okay?"

"Yeah. I just wanted to ask a favor."

His voice was muffled as she heard him say something to someone in his office.

"Steve? Are you there?"

"Sorry, babe. I'm back. What do you need?"

"I was hoping you could pick up a Christmas tree on your way home tonight." Michelle noticed the baby beginning to stir.

"Sure. No problem. It might be a little late though. I've got a brief to finish."

"Okay. I'll keep your dinner warm," she offered.

"That's all right. Don't worry about dinner. I'll send out for something. Just take care of yourself, and I'll be home as soon as I can."

He had been working late a lot lately. That seemed to be his pattern whenever he was uncomfortable or upset about something at home.

"Steve?"

"Yeah?"

"Is everything okay?" She tried to hold her voice steady.

"Everything's fine. I just have to finish this brief." His muffled voice told her he was talking to someone else in the office again, a hand covering the mouthpiece. "Listen, Michelle, I'm kind of busy. Is there anything else you wanted?"

"No. I guess that's it."

"Okay, then I'll see you when I get home. I'll bring the tree."

"Thanks, honey." As she hung up, Madison began to whimper. "I'm coming, Maddie," she said, swallowing her hurt.

326

"Want to decorate the tree tonight?" Michelle asked the next morning, as Steve was getting ready for work.

"If I get home in time. I'll call you." He gave her a peck on the cheek and headed downstairs. "Did you make me a sandwich?" he asked over his shoulders on the way down.

"I'm sorry, babe. I forgot." She mentally kicked herself. "I'll be right down to make one."

"Don't bother. I've gotta run."

She heard him leave through the garage as Maddie started to cry. She pushed herself out of bed and went to her daughter. "I know, sweetie. You're hungry, too." Would she ever be able to pull herself together to meet the needs of her baby and husband at the same time?

As she was nursing Madison, she thought about Steve and the struggles he was having bonding with their baby. A lonely feeling engulfed her. She needed someone to talk to – someone older – but she didn't want to worry her mother with all she was going through taking care of her dad.

Help me, Lord. I need someone to tell me what to do.

As she sat and prayed, her grandmother's face came to mind. *Perfect.* She valued and trusted her grandparents' wisdom. Surely Grandma Joan would have an answer.

She waited until after breakfast to call. Even though she knew her grandparents were early risers, she also knew her grandmother usually spent at least an hour pouring through her devotionals and her Bible each morning while she sipped her coffee.

On the second ring, Grandpa Phil picked up. "Hello?" His voice always warmed Michelle's heart. It was a gentle voice. A voice of compassion.

"Grandpa?"

"Michelle? Is that you?" She could hear a spark of excitement in his tone, and it made her smile.

"It's me, Gramps. How've you been?"

"Just fine, pumpkin. Getting these old bones going for another day," he added with a chuckle. "How's my favorite granddaughter?"

"I'm good. Busy with the baby and trying to keep up with life." She hoped her voice sounded upbeat.

"I remember those days. You're poor grandmother was such a trooper, up several times a night and then up at dawn with your mother." He hesitated and sighed. "Those were the days..." A fondness crept into his voice.

"Sounds like you really cherished them," she replied.

"It was different when we had our babies. Dads weren't really that involved, but I'll tell you a secret, sweetie. I just couldn't keep my hands off your mother. She was the most precious, the most beautiful baby God ever created..." His voice trailed off as if deep in thought. "Well, anyway," he continued, coming back to the conversation, "I'm sure Steve feels the same way."

"I guess," she replied.

"Mimi, your grandmother is chomping at the bit to talk to you. She's standing here with her hand out, so I'd better give her the phone. You take care, now. We're eager to see that darling baby of yours in a couple of weeks."

"Okay, Gramps. Love you."

"Love you, too, Michelle. Here's your grandmother."

Michelle and Joan exchanged greetings and caught up on surface things. Then Michelle began to reveal the real reason for her call. "Grandma, I'm worried about Steve," she began.

"Steve? Why? Is there something wrong with him? Your mother hasn't said anything about him being sick or anything."

"It's nothing like that. He's just so busy. So distant." Michelle was groping for words to explain their situation.

"Well, he's got a demanding job. Maybe that's it. Maybe this is just a particularly busy time at work, dear."

"It's more than that, Grandma. It's like he's pulling away from us." Her voice began to quiver.

"Oh, honey. It's a big adjustment becoming parents. Maybe he feels overwhelmed by the responsibility. I can only imagine how hard it must be for men, having the burden on their shoulders to support and provide for their families."

"That might be part of it, but there's something else. Something I haven't told anyone," she sniffed, reaching for a tissue to wipe her eyes and nose.

"What is it? Tell me, baby."

The floodgates opened in Michelle's heart. As she wept, she explained to her grandmother about the infertility tests, the insemination, and Steve's insecurities, telling all but her fears about Trevor being the biological father.

"Oh, sweetheart. You've been keeping in a big secret for a long time. There, there," she said softly to calm her. "I know this is hard for you, but it is not too big for God. Do you hear me, baby?"

"Mm hmm."

"I'm going to pray now, okay? And then we're going to see what God shows you. He'll know what's best for you two."

"Okay, Grandma."

"Lord, my sweet Michelle needs you. She doesn't know what to do. Father, You have created this precious new baby. We know you are going to take care of her and of Michelle and Steve. Help Steve, Lord. Give him the wisdom he needs to press through his insecurities and to be a father to baby Madison. Bolster his confidence, show him his role here, and help Michelle to love him and be patient with him as he works through this. Thank you, God, for this family. Bless them, protect them, guide and direct them. We pray this in Jesus' precious name, amen."

"Amen," Michelle echoed, a new peace flooding her heart and mind. "Thanks, Grandma. You're the best."

"It'll work out, Mimi. I mean it. Give Steve time. We'll be praying down here."

"Grandma?"

"Yes?"

"Don't tell Mom, okay? She has enough to worry about with Dad."

"Okay, baby. My lips are sealed."

"Oh, Grandma, I love you." Michelle sighed as she pictured her grandmother's weathered face in her mind's eye.

"I love you, too, honey. We'll see you soon."

After she got off the phone, Michelle peeked at Madison, who was fast asleep in the cradle. "It's going to be okay, Maddie. Everything's going to be okay."

Steve was on his lunch break, eating a sandwich from the local deli as he conducted a word search on his computer. DNA testing he typed into the search engine and instantly a list of websites appeared. He scrolled down until he found one entitled, "Fairfield Laboratories, DNA and Paternity Testing." He clicked on the title and began to explore the sight. Within five minutes he had his answer.

It was only 5:20 when Steve walked in the door that night carrying a bag in one hand and his briefcase in the other. "Michelle?" he called, as Max trotted over to him. "Hey, boy, where's your mom?" Max purred momentarily as he let Steve scratch his chin, then he darted over to the cupboard and began pacing back and forth demanding dinner.

"Okay, okay. I'll feed you," he said, joining him at the other end of the kitchen.

Just then Michelle walked into the room, Madison in her arms. "Steve — I thought I heard something in here. What a great surprise!"

"Hey, babe," he replied, pouring the dry food into Max's bowl. "I brought us Chinese," he added and gestured toward the bag on the table.

"Yum. I'm starving." Michelle said, opening the bag with her free hand. "Smells heavenly."

"I thought it would speed up the process of getting the tree decorated before it gets too late." Steve was smiling and looked happier than Michelle had seen him in quite a while.

Thank you, Lord. Whatever you're doing, it must be working.

"Here. Hold Madison while I serve it up," Michelle said, handing the baby to him. She noticed how awkward he seemed as he reached out to take her. "She won't break, Steve. Just hold her up against your shoulder," she added, draping a burp cloth there.

Madison bobbed her head for a moment and then rested it down against him. Steve slowly sat down at the kitchen table, a nervous look on his face.

"Relax," Michelle said. "I'll have this served up in no time."

She moved around the kitchen getting plates, glasses and silverware and setting them on the table. Then she opened the cartons of food and served it up.

"What do you want to drink?" she asked.

"Whatever you're having is fine," Steve replied, still frozen in the same position.

Michelle poured them both some milk and peeked at Madison's face. "She's asleep," she said quietly. "Here. I'll take her and lay her down in the cradle."

Steve seemed relieved as she gently lifted Madison off his shoulder. The baby stirred slightly in her arms and then was still again. She left the kitchen and was back in a minute.

"Okay, let's eat." She reached out her hand to Steve as they bowed their heads in prayer.

After dinner, Steve brought the tree in and set it up in the corner of the living room. It was full and fragrant.

"It looks great!" Michelle exclaimed. "This is our first Christmas as a family."

He agreed, studying the tree to see if it should be turned or adjusted in any way.

By now, Madison was awake and watching from her swing as they put the lights, garland, and decorations on the tree. "Next year, we'll need a fence around this to keep you away," Michelle said to her daughter, picturing her toddling around by then.

"Your mom's right," Steve added. "Hey, maybe we need one this year, too." Max had snuck in from the other room and was eyeing a shiny ornament on a lower bough.

"Uh, oh. Forgot about him," Michelle said.

As they stood admiring the glittering tree, Steve draped his arm over her shoulder.

She felt a warmth rush through her and a desire for her husband that she hadn't felt since the baby was born. "It feels good having your arm around me."

He smiled, then lifted her face with his hands and kissed her slowly, deeply. "I love you, Michelle."

"I love you, too, honey." She looked up into his eyes and could see pain. "What? What is it?"

"Nothing," he replied, pulling her close as she relaxed into his arms.

Although the house was sparsely decorated and Michelle was physically exhausted, this Christmas held a special glow for her. Holding tiny Maddie in her arms as she rocked beside their Christmas tree filled her heart with joy.

Sharing this holiday with her parents was really special, too. Her dad looked so proud as Michelle's mom helped him hold Madison. And her brother was having a blast in his new role as Uncle Tim. He'd bought Madison a tiny newborn onesie with a surfboard on the front and "Seal Beach Baby" on the back. "I know she's not technically from Seal Beach," he explained. "But I want her to know her roots."

Steve was attentive to Michelle although unusually quiet around her family. He continued to be hesitant to hold Madison. Although he never refused when Michelle handed her to him, he didn't initiate contact. Michelle and her mom did most of the care giving, which seemed pretty normal to her. But it surprised and hurt her a little when she noticed that even Tim acted more interested in holding Madison than Steve did.

CHAPTER THIRTY-NINE

The day after everyone left, Steve came home from work with Chinese food again. As they finished their dinner he said, "We need to talk, babe. I've got something to tell you." He took her by the hand and led her to the couch where they sat down side by side.

Michelle's heart was pounding in her chest. She searched his face for a clue — anything that would tell her that everything was okay. He looked nervous.

"I've been doing a lot of thinking lately," he began.

"About?"

"About us. You and me and Madison." He paused, looking into her eyes. "I need to know, Michelle."

"Know what?" She began twisting a piece of hair at the nape of her neck, her heart pounding in her chest.

"If I'm Madison's father." Steve's eyes pleaded with hers for understanding. He reached over and gently guided her hand away from her hair as he'd done so many times when she was upset or afraid.

She stiffened, and even though his touch was gentle, it caused her skin to crawl. *How could he do this? Why couldn't he just accept Madison as their daughter?* She sat there staring at him, anger welling up inside. "Why does this have to be such a big deal to you? Can't you just love her and trust God about the rest?" Her voice was laced with fear.

Steve cocked his head to one side and squinted

his eyes, examining her face. Then he shook his head, as if he could not believe what he saw. He stood up and went to the window, gazing out to the street. "I should have known you'd never understand. It's a whole different ball game for you. You know you're her mom."

"Look, Steve," she said as she stood up, preparing to leave the room, "you knew from the start this was how it would be. We decided together to do the insemination. You were okay with it then. Now that we have our beautiful baby daughter, it's suddenly not enough for you." Her voice shook as she started toward the stairs.

"Michelle, don't walk out of here. We need to finish this." He reached out to her, putting his hand on her shoulder. "I'm trying. I want to love Madison like she was my own. I can't explain why this is so important to me, but it is."

Michelle could feel her heart racing. "What is it that you want?"

"I want to do a DNA test. I downloaded all the information from the internet today."

"And what if the test says someone else is Madison's biological father? Then are you going to leave us?"

"No. Nothing like that. You know I love you. I'd never leave you." He pulled her into an embrace. "This is just something I have to do. If it turns out Maddie isn't my child, I'll figure out how I can come to terms with that. But I've got to do this test. Try to understand."

Michelle pushed away from him. "I think you're a fool to do this. You're asking for trouble."

"Maybe. But I need to know."

Madison, who had dozed off in the swing, started to cry. Michelle went over to her and lifted her out, cuddling her to her chest. "Mommy's here," she said gently.

The DNA kit arrived in the mail on Saturday. The timing couldn't have been better. Michelle was at the grocery store, and Madison was asleep in the cradle. Steve immediately opened the package and set about collecting the sample cells by rubbing a swab inside his own mouth and another one in Madison's, careful to follow the directions for transferring them onto the enclosed slides.

Madison started to fuss, so he picked her up and put her into the swing, counting on its gentle motion to lull her back to sleep. Then he packaged the slides in the return mailer and put it into his briefcase. As soon as his wife got home, he'd take it to the post office and mail it.

An incredible sense of relief washed over him. He sat watching Madison swing back and forth, her eyes beginning to shut as she slipped off to sleep. A weight lifted from his shoulders, and he felt energized. He decided to straighten up the kitchen and do the dishes to surprise Michelle.

As he worked, Max played with a toy mouse under the kitchen table, flipping it in the air and then pouncing on it. "You go, killer," Steve teased.

By the time Michelle got home, the kitchen was spotless. He opened the door for her and took the bags out of her arms.

"Wow — the kitchen looks great. How's Madison?" she asked, heading for the family room to check on her daughter.

"She woke up once, and I put her in the swing," Steve replied, placing the groceries on the table.

As he began putting the food away, Michelle came back into the room. "She's still asleep. Guess I'll get the rest of the groceries."

Steve grabbed her hand. "I'll get them, babe. You

can finish putting this stuff up." A few minutes later, he left again, this time with the package for the lab in his hand. Michelle was about to nurse Madison, so he figured it was a good time to go to the post office.

While driving, he prayed. *Lord, please guard this package. I need to know the truth.* At the post office, he handed the mailer to the clerk and watched it drop into the big canvas bag behind her.

Joan sat on the porch swing, gazing out over the front lawn, deep in thought. Her heart was heavy for her granddaughter. Although she'd promised Michelle not to talk to Sheila about what was going on, she hadn't said she wouldn't discuss it with Phil.

"What's got you so pensive today?" her husband asked as he joined her on the swing.

She took his hand in hers. How she loved this man. "It's Michelle, Phil."

"You seemed a little troubled after she called. Anything I can help with?"

She squeezed his hand. "I think I need to tell you so we can pray about it together."

"Okay, sweetheart, I'm all ears."

She began slowly; trying to give him all the details Michelle had shared with her. When she was finished, she slumped back into the swing and sighed.

Phil sat thoughtfully for a few moments. "The Lord has a plan in this, Jo. Let's pray."

She agreed, and they bowed their heads together, committing their granddaughter's situation into the hands of their sovereign God.

While Michelle and Steve were lying in bed that night, he reached over and took her hand, bringing it up to his mouth and gently kissing it. "I did the DNA test today. We should get the results in a couple of weeks."

"Okay." Michelle felt like he had stabbed a knife in her heart.

"I love you," Steve added softly.

"Yeah."

CHAPTER FORTY

The next two weeks were filled with tension in the Baron household. Madison got a cold, and Michelle focused all of her energy on trying to keep little Maddie as comfortable as possible. Her relationship with Steve had deteriorated to a polite but distant aloofness. Although he tried to reach out to her with flowers, little treats from the local bakery, and the suggestion of a date night, she had erected a protective wall around her heart.

The envelope from the lab arrived on Friday.

She was sitting on the edge of the couch, her heart beating loudly as she looked down at it in her trembling hand. The return address looked harmless enough. Fairfield Lab, Portland, Oregon. But this envelope contained information that could change her life forever.

Madison whimpered from her cradle in the corner. "It's okay, Maddie," Michelle cooed as she gently stroked her daughter's back.

Oh Lord, she sighed, once again gazing down at the unopened envelope. Help me. Help us accept whatever this says. Help Steve to learn to love Madison, no matter what.

The presence of God wrapped around her like a warm blanket.

I know the plans I have for you, plans for good and not for evil. Plans to give you hope and a future.

Taking a deep breath, she responded aloud,

"Thank you, Lord." Her quivering hands began to pull open the envelope. Then she stopped herself. *I can't do this on my own. I've got to call Steve first.*

She set the envelope down and dialed Steve's office. His secretary told her he was on another line and didn't want to be interrupted. "Just tell him I called," she said before hanging up.

She began pacing the floor, twisting her hair as she waited. Ten minutes later the phone rang. It was Steve. "Hi, babe."

"Hi," Michelle replied.

"It came."

"What?"

"From the lab. I've got the letter here." Her stomach was twisting into knots. She picked up the envelope, her hand trembling.

"Did you open it?" he asked.

"Not yet."

"Don't. I need to talk to you first. I'm coming home."

"Okay," she replied.

After they hung up, she fingered the envelope, then set it down in her lap. She was sitting there praying when Steve arrived. He took it from her and placed it, unopened, on the table.

"Michelle," he began, "your grandfather called me today."

"What did he say? Is it about Dad? Is everyone okay?" Her mind raced with worry.

"Everyone's fine."

"Then what is it?" Michelle relaxed a little. "Why did he call?"

"He called because your grandmother told him what was going on with us."

Feeling her defenses rising, she said, "I'm sorry, Steve, but I had to talk to someone."

"It's alright. I was upset at first, but then he started talking to me about everything." Steve paused then continued, "Your grandfather has a lot of wisdom."

"Yeah, he does. What did he say?" She sat back down on the rocking chair, and he sat nearby on the couch.

"He told me he'd been praying for me … for us … and that God gave him an illustration from scripture to share with me." Looking at her earnestly, he continued. "Then he started talking to me about Jesus, and he reminded me that Joseph wasn't Jesus biological father."

"That's right. I never really thought about that," she replied.

"It made me realize that God wants me to be Madison's father — that it doesn't matter whether or not we are related by blood. God made this family. He gave me you as my wife and Madison as my daughter."

Michelle studied his face. "Are you sure, Steve? This really changes how you feel about Madison?"

"It's never been about Madison, honey. She's a sweet baby. Who wouldn't love her?"

"Then what is it? Were you afraid about Trevor? That he might be her biological father?"

"I'm sure that was a big part of it," he said, looking at her squarely in the eyes. "I don't like that guy, and I don't like the way he's tried to make himself such a close friend and confidante to you."

"Steve, you've got to know I would never give up what we have – our life together—for any friendship with anyone. Including Trevor. As far as I'm concerned, he's out of the picture. I told him that, myself." Michelle hesitated, then continued, "So should we open it?" she asked as she handed him the envelope from the lab.

He took it from her and worked his thumb under the flap, peeling the envelope open. Sliding the paperwork out, his eyes skimmed for the results.

Michelle watched her husband's face dissolve into tears of relief. "What? What does it say?"

He handed her the document.

"DNA from the two parties submitted match. Paternity is confirmed."

As she read the results, she grinned broadly. "Steve — this is amazing! God truly gave us a miracle with little Maddie."

He wrapped his arms around her crushing her to his chest, tears of joy mingling with their embrace.

The peace the Lord had given Michelle earlier that day washed over her again. God had performed two more miracles. Steve's heart had softened. And the concerns about Trevor had been erased.

"Michelle — this means I'm Madison's real father. I mean she's really mine! In every way. Wait until your grandfather hears about this!"

She beamed at him as she retrieved their baby from her cradle. "Want to hold your daughter?"

He reached out and took Madison into his arms. She nestled her tiny head into the base of his neck. "Come here," Steve said to Michelle.

As she moved closer, he wrapped his free arm around her, and she encircled his waist in an embrace.

Max, who had been patiently waiting for someone to notice the toy mouse he had dropped at their feet, began to prance back and forth, rubbing up against their legs and crying for attention.

"Not now, Max," Michelle said. She wanted to remember this moment forever. Resting against her husband's chest, she could hear his heartbeat and the soft cooing of their baby girl.

Finally, they were a family. God had faithfully guided them through the tears and into a wonderful new chapter of their lives.

NOTE FROM THE AUTHOR

Dear Readers,

When I began writing Through the Tears, it was to share the heartache many couples experience when their attempts to conceive a child fail. Many, if not most, married couples intend to eventually become parents. Sometimes that dream is threatened by infertility. I have experienced the disappointments and fears that accompany that process.

Conversely, there have always been women, single and married, who find themselves suddenly confronted by an unwanted pregnancy. They are often faced with decisions that reflect a desperation many of us will never experience.

Prior to Roe V. Wade, the needs of these two groups were often met by each other, and adoption was a blessed option for both. Since that landmark legal case was decided, the scales have tipped. Unwanted pregnancies, more often than not, are resolved in a doctor's office or clinic rather than through an adoption agency or service.

As I researched the number of abortions performed annually, I came upon the following website:

http://www.numberofabortions.com

It has an abortion counter that functions much like the national debt clock we've seen on the news and talk shows during these difficult financial times. I was astounded to see the numbers increase every second, as I sat and gazed at the counter. Literally every second, a baby somewhere in the world was losing his or her life to abortion. Meanwhile, as a woman who has experienced her own struggle with infertility, I knew that as many or more women were simultaneously discovering that they had once again failed to conceive the child they so desperately wanted. It pierced my heart and brought tears to my eyes.

I can still remember the struggle my husband and I experienced as we found ourselves wrestling with infertility. The tests and eventually my surgery and fertility drugs were a journey that gave us such an appreciation for the miracles of conception and birth. Of all the earthly events in our lives, I can say with confidence that becoming parents ranked highest. Our children are the joy of the past, our friends in the present, and the bright hope of the future.

Though many of you may already know this, I also learned that Norma McCorvey – aka. Jane Roe of Roe V. Wade — never did have the abortion that was so vigorously pursued in that landmark court case. She subsequently became a pro-life advocate, expressing grave regrets for the legal precedence her case established. Recently, she participated in a film production called *Bloodmoney* to expose the financial greed of the abortion industry, and the deceit this industry has perpetrated upon women for the sake of the almighty dollar.

Culture has programmed us over the past 40 years to see abortion as a legitimate reproductive right for women. Having never been confronted with an unwanted pregnancy, I can only begin to imagine the fear and desperation many teens and adult women have experienced who have walked through this difficult and very personal decision. Michelle's story in Through the Tears is not meant to cast dispersion on any of the women who have wrestled with this experience.

Rather, it is to illuminate the other side of this

issue – the many women whose hearts are breaking because they cannot conceive, and who would welcome into their lives and homes the babies that other women feel unable to raise themselves. I also wanted to present an option that many young mothers do not even realize they have – the option of safe surrender, which most states offer to those who have chosen to have their babies and then end up overwhelmed and desperate to get out from under the monumental responsibilities that go along with parenting. Perhaps the knowledge of this option will encourage more women who are wrestling with their decision to give parenting a chance.

A second topic for the story arose as Michelle returned to college, where I knew she would be likely to encounter professors who would challenge and attempt to destroy her new Christian faith. As a teacher myself, I am deeply disturbed by this trend in higher education. Many of the colleges which were formed for the express purpose of educating men and women to serve in the ministry of Jesus Christ (including most ivy league schools) have recently taken the contrary role of dissuading students from the most precious of all possessions – a faith that gives their lives meaning, not only today but for all of eternity. This trend is a shameful indictment on "higher learning." It exposes intolerance toward the Christian faith by many pseudo-intellectuals who are in positions of influence.

I hope Michelle's journey in Through the Tears will spark discussion and possibly even action on the part of some readers. If you have a burden for unwanted, unborn children, I urge you to consider reaching out to volunteer at a crisis pregnancy center where women are presented with the developmental facts of their unborn baby and the pro-life options of adoption and safe surrender.

If you are currently a student at a college or

university or are an alumnus of such an institution, don't be afraid to let your voice be heard regarding professors like Dr. Chambers. Write letters to the school's publications as well as to the dean or president of the school, blog about your experiences, become active in organizations like Campus Crusade for Christ, and ask God to show you how you can personally share your testimony. Other Christian students, who may not have the confidence to speak out, will be blessed by your courage.

I'll be eager to hear your stories and experiences as you step out in faith! Don't miss the third book in the *Sandy Cove* series, *Into Magnolia*, about Michelle's ministry as she begins her teaching career at Magnolia Middle School. A preview of *Into Magnolia* follows this note.

May God strengthen and equip you for every good work.

With love,

Rosemary Hines

P.S. I would love to hear from you! Please feel free to email me at **Rosemary.W.Hines@gmail.com**. If you'd just like to be added to my email notification list for future releases or special offers, all you need to say in your email is "Add me!" and I'll be sure you are added to my contacts. You'll be the first to know when I'm about to run a special on one of the books or when a new book is in the works. ☺

You can also visit me on the web at **www.RosemaryHines.com** and keep up with my blogs and news on my Facebook author page: **https://www.facebook.com/RosemaryHinesAuthor Page**

And don't forget to visit my Amazon author page, where

you'll find all the titles in the Sandy Cove Series: Rosemary Hines Amazon Author

ACKNOWLEDGMENTS

I am so very thankful for those who have come alongside me in Michelle's journey. If it weren't for the support and encouragement of these family members and friends, I would not have completed this project.

Among those who willingly extended their help, I am most appreciative of my editors and readers whose input made this story into the novel it has become. From content editing and suggestions, to technical advice and corrections, I want to thank my daughter, Kristin, my sister, Julie, and my friends, Nancy, Catherine, and Bonnie. Their priceless input refined Through the Tears, making it a more compelling tale.

Big thanks also go to my son and photographer, Benjamin, for the photo displayed on the cover of this book. His eye for capturing an image that communicates the longing in Michelle's heart is truly a gift from God.

A sweet blessing to me along this journey has been the rekindling of an acquaintance with Kathy Gilbert, the "Book Lady" for Calvary Chapel ministries. I was touched and humbled that she would choose the first book in this series, *Out of a Dream*, as one of the fiction selections to review and recommend at the Calvary Chapel West Coast Pastors' Wives Conference, hosting over 800 pastors' wives from Calvary Chapels across the United States and abroad. Her endorsement, based on the ministry potential of that story, profoundly influenced several of the scenes in *Through the Tears*, which she later recommended at another conference.

Finally, I am thankful for my husband, Randy, who walked with me through our own journey of infertility and into the blessed role of parenting. Special thankful memories to Dr. William Bazler (aka, "the Baz"), who helped us on that path but did not live to see the story it would eventually inspire.

BOOKS BY ROSEMARY HINES

Sandy Cove Series Book 1

Out of a Dream

Sandy Cove Series Book 2

Through the Tears

Sandy Cove Series Book 3

Into Magnolia

Sandy Cove Series Book 4

Around the Bend

Sandy Cove Series Book 5

From the Heart

Sandy Cove Series Book 6

Behind Her Smile

Sandy Cove Series Book 7

Above All Else

CPSIA information can be obtained
at www.ICGtesting.com
Printed in the USA
LVOW08s1546190317
527723LV00003B/305/P